The Filey
Connection

A Sanford 3rd Age Club Mystery (#1)

David W Robinson

www.darkstroke.com

Discover us online:
www.darkstroke.com

Find us on instagram:
www.instagram.com/darkstrokebooks

Include **#darkstroke** in a photo of yourself
holding his book on Instagram and
something nice will happen.

To my wife, Carol, whom I met in
Filey, and whose love of this
Yorkshire seaside town has taken us
back there many times
over the last three decades.

About the Author

David Robinson is a Yorkshireman living in Manchester. Driven by a huge, cynical sense of humour, he's been a writer for over thirty years having begun with magazine articles before moving on to novels and TV scripts.

He has little to do with his life other than write, as a consequence of which his output is prodigious. Thankfully most of it is never seen by the great reading public of the world.

He has worked closely with Crooked Cat Books and darkstroke since 2012, when The Filey Connection, the very first Sanford 3rd Age Club Mystery, was published.

Describing himself as the Doyen of Domestic Disasters he can be found blogging at **www.dwrob.com.**

The STAC Mystery series:

#1 The Filey Connection
#2 The I-Spy Murders
#3 A Halloween Homicide
#4 A Murder for Christmas
#5 Murder at the Murder Mystery Weekend
#6 My Deadly Valentine
#7 The Chocolate Egg Murders
#8 The Summer Wedding Murder
#9 Costa del Murder
#10 Christmas Crackers
#11 Death in Distribution
#12 A Killing in the Family
#13 A Theatrical Murder
#14 Trial by Fire
#15 Peril in Palmanova
#16 The Squire's Lodge Murders
#17 Murder at the Treasure Hunt
#18 A Cornish Killing
#19 Merry Murders Everyone

The Filey Connection

A Sanford 3rd Age Club Mystery (#1)

Prologue

"G'night, Mave. See you Friday." With a wave to her best friend, Nicola Leach staggered off towards the Sanford Park Hotel.

Drunken thoughts reeled through her mind. Should she have reminded Mavis not to be late on Friday morning? Should she have had that last Bacardi and coke? Should she have offered to ring to make sure Mavis wasn't late on Friday morning?

She paused outside the hotel. The heat of a summer night, mixed with an excess of alcohol and cigarettes, sapped her energy to the point where even breathing was hard work. She looked back towards the Foundry Inn, but she couldn't see the pub for all those leafy trees overhanging the pavement, and there was no sign of Mavis. No sign of anyone. The road disappeared into infinity and she could not see even a pair of headlights.

With a grunt, she moved on.

It had been a good night. Plenty of drink, plenty of screeching on the karaoke, one or two men willing to spend money in the hope of a promise, and it hadn't cost her much. Good thing, too. She needed every penny for Filey on Friday.

She stopped again at the far corner of the hotel, trying to remember how many drinks she had paid for out of her own pocket. Couldn't have been more than one or two. The rest of her night had come out of the wallets of the men. And for once she hadn't given them anything in return. She cackled at the night. "That'll teach 'em to call me Knickers-off."

Setting off again, she glanced onto the hotel car park. Liberally planted with trees to protect the privacy of the hotel guests, it was a known haunt for lovers. How many times had she had bit of fun on the back seat of a car parked under shade of those trees? She could see only one vehicle tonight. One of those 4x4 things, its exhaust fumes chugging into the night air.

Handy a car like that, Nicola thought. Plenty of room in the back for hanky-panky. Not like some of the cramped sheds she had been in.

The vehicle began to move and she called out, "You don't have to stop for me. I don't care what you're up to."

She staggered along the pavement, dimly aware of the 4x4 turning from the car park onto the road in her direction, crawling along twenty yards behind her.

"Wonder if he's after giving me a lift." She chuckled at the thought of a kerb crawler mistaking her for a brass. She'd never charged for it in her life.

The branches of a sprawling yew spread above her and bowed towards the pavement; Nicola stepped wide to avoid them. Headlights blazed and the engine roared. She whirled. The awful reality of what was about to happen seeped through the drunken haze. Her mouth fell open and she tried to scream.

***

Hands shaking, he rooted through his pockets and pulled out his mobile. Calling up the menu, he dialled.

A few seconds later, the connection was made. "It's me," he cried. "It's all gone wrong. She's dead."

Chapter One

A hot July sun beat down on the West Yorkshire town of Sanford, softening the tarmac of Doncaster Road and inflaming the tempers of drivers trapped in the daily crawl to work.

The lucky ones would reach the traffic lights which caused the problem, and then turn into Sanford Retail Park. The less fortunate would skip across the junction, travel on a few more yards and promptly run into the next jam, caused, this time, by the lights controlling traffic entering and leaving Doncaster Road Industrial Estate.

Between the two sets of lights, those travelling towards the town centre who looked to their right, across the four lanes of the dual carriageway, could see Britannia Parade, a ramshackle line of shops, all that remained of the area's former glory. Those fortunate drivers travelling out of Sanford would have to look to their left, but they had the advantage that they could turn off into the lane behind the parade, park and visit the shops if they so wished.

Dennis' Hardware & DIY stood on one corner, Toni Stylist at the other end. Sandwiched between them, Doncaster Road Laundrette's doors were open from nine in the morning until nine in the evening, Patel's Newsagency and minimarket kept even longer hours, opening at six and closing at ten in the evening. And in the centre of the parade, its double front reflecting the fierce glare of the sun, stood the Lazy Luncheonette.

Middle-aged Sanfordians remembered the place when it was Joe's Café, more elderly residents, those whose memories stretched back into the 1950s and early 60s, remembered when it was run by Joe's father as Alf's Café.

It had been a permanent fixture since the end of World War Two, and it had flowered during that golden era when Sanford was known for the pit and foundry, and the money in the workers' pockets fed a vibrant, thriving economy.

Everyone knew Joe Murray, the present proprietor. Short and rakish, wire haired and bad-tempered, his reputation transcended the generation gap.

There was neither rhyme nor reason to Joe's irritability. He was the same in the oppressive heat of high summer as he was in the biting cold of January. He lived in the flat above the café, and therefore did not commute, so the slow-moving crawl to work along Doncaster Road did not affect him. He had no bosses to chew him out when things went wrong. He was the boss. He had no wife demanding parity with the Joneses, or whining to be taken on holiday to foreign climes. His wife had left him over a decade previously, departing to a better life abroad. Yet still he was grumpy, snappy, permanently irritable. He was simply built that way.

Circumstances often exacerbated his exasperation. A busy Wednesday morning and the dray men of Sanford Brewery turning up late for breakfast would do the trick. Add to them, Damon Allbright a spirited apprentice from Broadbent's Auto Repair Centre, and the atmosphere in the Lazy Luncheonette became almost explosive.

With a cheeky gleam in his eye, Damon urged, "Come on, Joe. The guys'll be doing their heads in."

Joe bagged up the sandwiches, his financially astute brain adding up the total as he did so. He scowled across the counter, his glower reducing the apprentice mechanic to a grinning idiot. "Don't start with me, young Allbright, or you get my boot up your backside. If those idiots at Broadbent's rang the order through, you could come and collect it when it was ready instead of standing there, cluttering up the place."

"Yeah, but who'd pay for the phone call?" Damon grinned again. "They're all like you. Tight gits."

Joe passed his eye over the queue behind the young lad:

several brewery drivers and their mates, all with lorries full of beer and soft drinks to be delivered, waited impatiently for breakfast. Honing his attention on Damon, he demanded, "Thirty-one pounds sixty."

"Not cheap either," chuckled Damon, sorting out the cash.

"Just gimme the money and clear off," Joe snapped. "And tell your boss, if he and his crew hassle me much more, I'll take my car to Hathershaw's for servicing."

"That heap of yours?" Damon handed over the money, took his change and grinned again. "It's a hunk of junk and I don't think we'd miss it."

He hurried out before Joe could give him another earful.

The Lazy Luncheonette was at its busiest between seven and nine in the morning. Joe opened up anytime after 6 a.m. but rarely saw a soul except for the occasional passing trucker, until the dray men from Sanford Breweries, a mile or two along Doncaster Road, turned out in their lorries. Things picked up when other factories, most notably Broadbent's, started work at 7:30. It was during this period that he needed the assistance of his staff, Sheila Riley, Brenda Jump and his nephew, Lee. The café could not run smoothly without them. What he didn't need on a hot and busy Wednesday morning was a long queue of draymen already behind schedule.

"Coupla forklift drivers turned in late this morning, Joe," the next customer told him.

"I'll bet they were out on the beer last night," Joe complained.

Sheila danced through from the kitchen carrying orders. "Oh to be young and full of beer," she said, weaving her way through the crowded cafeteria to deliver the meals.

Joe took orders for three more full English breakfasts from the brewery drivers, rang up the cash and passed the orders through to Brenda in the kitchen. "Either that or their wives were nagging them."

"Oh to be young and in love," Sheila said, delivering two slices of toast to a middle-aged, stout man by the door.

"It ain't love, it's lust," Joe grumbled.

"Oh to be young and in lust," Brenda called through the hatch.

"And you'd know about that," Joe said. "The lust bit, anyway." He passed a beaker of tea across the counter to the brewery man waiting for service. "And what the hell are you grinning at?"

"You, Joe," said the driver. "You're such a miserable old bugger."

Joe held out his hand. "Six fifty for cash." He took the money and gave change. "I pay my taxes and that gives me the right to be miserable if I want."

The driver laughed, took his tea and moved to the table where his mates sat.

"I'll just check with Joe," he heard Sheila say.

The café door chimed as it opened and four more customers, a gang of council employees repairing the road 100 yards away, walked in as Joe took the next order.

"Joe," Sheila said coming back to the counter. "Eddie Dobson is here asking about places on the trip to Filey, and he wants to know if we can spare ten minutes right now."

Joe glowered. "Now?" he demanded. "I'm up to my eyes in muck, bullets and bacon sandwiches? We need to be here, working, not chit-chatting. Leave it and tell him to come back later."

"You heard the man," Sheila's voice reached him.

"I'll do that," the customer responded to her.

Sheila wove her way through the crowded cafeteria back to the counter. "It was just a question," she grumbled at Joe

"I don't want questions at this hour," Joe griped. "I don't have time to work out the answers."

As if commenting on his demand, there came a loud crash from the kitchen as a couple of plates hit the tiled floor. It was followed by a cry of "Oh, Lee," from Brenda, and Joe's temper racked up several points.

Abandoning the counter, he marched into the kitchen, where his giant nephew, a former prop for the Sanford Bulls Rugby League team, was clearing up the mess of broken crockery and spoiled food.

"You great clumsy idiot, I swear you'll bankrupt me one of these days."

Lee's red face glowed even redder. "Sorry Uncle Joe."

"Just get it cleaned up and get a bloody move on," Joe fumed and stormed back to the counter where he glowered at his next customer. "What are you having?"

"Full monty, Joe," ordered the driver. "Any danger of extra sausage with that, Lee?" the driver shouted to the kitchen.

"No worries," Lee called back as he shovelled up the remains of the damage food and crockery.

"You talk to me, not the underlings," Joe snapped at the driver, and then grumbled through the hatch, "And you, boy, speak as your father taught you to speak."

"It was me dad who taught me to say that, Uncle Joe. When I was in Australia."

Joe concentrated on the first of the council workmen. "What do you want?"

"Not lessons in speech, that's for sure," retorted the workman. "I'll have a bacon on toast, Joe, and a mug of tea."

Joe scribbled the order out and poured the tea. "Diction," he said. "Not speech, diction."

"Aye, well tell Dick's son to make the bacon crispy."

***

The Lazy Luncheonette had seating for up to eighty people, with four-seater tables along each wall, and eight-seaters down the middle. The laminate tops and faux leather, fixed seats were easy to keep clean, as were the walls decorated with pine slats. The floor's off-white, marble-effect, non-slip tiles could be problematic in the wet winter months, but Joe was a stickler for cleanliness and at those times, he or one of his staff could be seen manning the mop at times during opening hours.

"Cooking and cleaning," he often said. "It's the hallmark

of the Lazy Luncheonette."

With the time just after 10a.m. the rush was well and truly over, the schoolchildren were all in their classrooms, and the shoppers making for Sanford Retail Park had had their cups of tea and set about the morning's retail therapy.

The heaviest washing up was out of the way and Brenda was out delivering a sandwich order to a small engineering company a mile or so along Doncaster Road. Sheila joined him, leaving Lee to prepare lunches. He would take his break at eleven. The café was all but empty; one middle-aged woman with striking black hair and a pale complexion, who had been there for an hour, sat by the door reading a magazine. "Reminds me of Morticia Addams," Joe had muttered when she first entered and sat down. The traffic on the road outside was gone, and Joe was almost at peace with the world. It was the time when he took his first break, and commandeered the table closest to the counter to take on the cryptic crossword in the *Daily Express*.

Puzzles and mysteries were one of the mainstays of his life. Spread on various shelves along each side wall of the café were Joe's booklets, his 'casebooks' as he liked to call them, detailing the various crimes, mysteries and puzzles he had solved over the years. A renowned amateur detective, every time he, Sheila and Brenda cracked a crime or provided answers to a mystery, he would type up an account on his computer, and put it together as a booklet which he kept in the café for his customers to read while they ate.

"What happened to the bloke asking about Filey?" he asked as Sheila joined him.

Joe was Chair of the Sanford 3rd Age Club, Sheila the Secretary and Brenda, the treasurer. For Joe, it provided a welcome break from the ups and downs of running the Lazy Luncheonette, and for all of them, it provided a social life.

"He said he'd be back later," Sheila told him. "It's Eddie Dobson. You know him. Joined a month or two back. He's been trying to get on the Filey trip ever since."

"I've never met him," Joe retorted.

The club ran a number of outings and holidays for the

10

members. Joe used his negotiating skills, honed to a fine art through many years of arguing with suppliers for the café, to extract the best possible prices. The next outing was just two days away; at ten o'clock on Friday morning, the coach would depart the Miner's Arms carrying 71 passengers to the Beachside Hotel in Filey, where they would spend the weekend, which included an Abba tribute show in Scarborough on Saturday evening, before returning to Sanford on Monday morning.

But the trip had been a sell out since it was first announced early in April, and Joe said as much to Sheila.

"The Filey coach is full. I'm not booking a second coach for one body."

"It's not as if it comes out of your pocket Joe. Club funds pay for it," Sheila said.

"And how closely would the club question me if I wasted their money?"

She frowned. "Anyway, Eddie said he'd call back later. Or not at all considering your temper."

"Blame the dray men, not me," Joe replied penning the word 'barrow' into 1 across. "They were late getting out of the brewery and late getting here. They threw everybody's schedule out, including mine."

"Yes, but there's no need to be so rude, Joe," Sheila argued.

"I wasn't rude, just honest. You were giving me earache over the Filey trip when we were knee deep in it."

From behind them came the sound of Brenda entering through the back door and muttering something to Lee, who laughed in response. Brenda came through to the café and dropped Joe's car keys on the table.

He looked up into her dissatisfied face. "What's up with you?"

"Your car is what's up with me," she replied, moving back behind the counter and pouring herself a cup of tea. "When did you last have it cleaned?"

"I don't," Joe replied. "It goes just as fast with the muck on it."

"Joe, we're carrying food in that four-wheeled shed," Brenda grumbled and helped herself to a chocolate bar.

"Yes, but the sandwiches are all wrapped up," Joe countered.

Brenda joined them, tucking herself into the seat alongside Sheila. "Your car has got things living in it," she said. "I'm sure it has. Look at the state of my overall." She gestured at her pale blue and white-checked tabard. "Covered in hair." She pointed at Sheila. "Yours is the same."

Sheila hooked her neck down and plucked a black strand from her white sleeve. "It can't have come from Joe's car. I haven't been anywhere near it this morning."

"Well mine did," Brenda declared. "I don't know whether it's Joe's or his dog's." She picked a grey strand from her shoulder.

"I don't have a dog," Joe reminded her.

"You should get the thing valeted," Brenda moaned.

"Whoever heard of anyone valeting a dog?" Joe retorted.

"The bloody car, not your dog."

"I told you, I don't have a dog," Joe reminded her. "And have you seen how much valeting costs?"

Joe glowered, Brenda maintained her defiance and he backed down.

"All right, all right. I'll get the Dyson out this afternoon and run it over the interior. Happy?"

"Take it down the car wash after, and I'll maybe shut up."

Joe was about to tackle her again, but the bell chimed and the cafe door opened. He looked past Sheila and a mixture of emotions crossed his craggy features; pleasure, suspicion and more irritation.

"Gemma? What do you want?"

She laughed. "Nice way to greet your favourite niece, Uncle Joe."

"My favourite niece the policewoman," Joe retorted and stood up. "Let me get you some tea." He moved behind the counter.

Sheila stood up. "Well, it's lovely to see you again, Gemma, but you want to see Joe, and Brenda and I have work to do. Never a minute's peace when you work for the slavemaster."

"Not so enthusiastic, Sheila," Brenda said. "I haven't had my break yet."

Detective Sergeant Gemma Craddock's steel blue eyes took them all in with a solemn gaze. "Don't go, Mrs Riley. It's not just Uncle Joe I need to speak to. It's all three of you."

Pouring tea for her and another cup for Brenda, Joe's eyes darted back and forth from the cups to the table where both his staff appeared just as intrigued as he.

Gemma, he guessed, would be in her mid-thirties now. Her father had married Joe's sister-in-law by marriage, making Gemma his niece by marriage, and Joe, who had enjoyed a close friendship with her policeman father, remained secretly proud of Gemma's progress on the Sanford force.

He emerged from the counter and placed a cup of tea in front of his niece. Sitting opposite, he invited, "All right. What do you want?"

Gemma took out her pocket book. "Do you know a woman named Nicola Leach?"

Joe laughed. "Knickers-off Nicola? Yeah we know her."

Gemma's eyebrows rose, and Brenda explained, "She had a bit of a reputation with men, which is why we called her Knickers-off."

"A bit of a reputation?" Joe's eyes were popping. "She was like a bloody piranha. She could strip a man to the bone and screw him to the mattress in a matter of minutes."

Sheila frowned. "Are you speaking from experience, Joe?"

"Hearsay," he replied, and grinned at his niece. "She's pushing sixty, too, the randy old sod."

Gemma was not smiling. She swallowed a shot of tea, and then took a deep breath. "I'm sorry to say she was knocked down and killed last night."

In the stunned silence that followed, the dark haired woman by the door stood up and left, and the only sound that could be heard was Lee pottering in the kitchen.

Sheila broke the silence. "Dear God."

"It was a hit and run," Gemma told them. "Happened about eleven thirty last night, as she came out of the Foundry Inn."

Joe shook himself out of his stupor. "Witnesses?"

"Only one," Gemma admitted. She checked her pocketbook again. "A woman named Cora Harrison. She was waiting for a taxi on the Foundry Inn car park and saw it all. Rang us immediately. One of the uniformed lads took the call. She said she'd seen a Land Rover come out of nowhere, hit Mrs Leach and then just drove off."

"Too much to hope that this Cora whatshername, got the registration number?" Brenda asked.

Gemma shook her head. "Too dark, she told us. And if you think about it, it is pretty gloomy round that area when the pubs are shut."

Joe stared despondently at his newspaper. "This is sad, but what brings you here?"

"When our boys got there, they checked her personal effects. Usual stuff in her purse; bank cards, bus pass, and a diary which gave her home address as Oakland Street, Wakefield Road Estate. We also found a membership card for the Sanford 3rd Age Club. When I heard that, I thought I'd come and see you this morning, see what you could tell us about her."

Taking out his tobacco tin and cigarette papers, Joe nodded at Sheila and Brenda. "They knew her better than me."

"Merry widow," Sheila declared. "Well, merry divorcee. I'm not sure that her ex-husband is actually dead."

"Alfie Leach is still alive and he still lives in Sanford," Brenda asserted. "Somewhere over the west side, I think. Leeds Road Estate."

Gemma scribbled a note in her book. "And his name is Alfred? Have they been divorced long?"

Brenda chewed her lip. "Must be about three or four years now, eh Sheila?"

Sheila nodded. "I think it's longer. Peter, my husband, died six years ago, and I remember seeing Nicola at the cemetery on the first anniversary of Peter's death. She told me then that she and Alf were separated."

"You surely don't think Alfie ran her down, do you?" Joe asked.

"We don't think anything at the moment, Uncle Joe," Gemma replied. "Chances are it was someone who had one or two over the odds, didn't see her, ran her down, and then legged it to avoid the breathalyser. No one's saying it was deliberate." She wagged a scolding finger at him. "Don't you go poking your nose into this. I know what you're like."

"If one of my members has been killed by a hit and run driver, it's my duty to turn up whatever information I can," Joe protested.

"Yes, but it's not murder, and we don't need amateur sleuths like you sticking your oar in."

"Amateur?" Joe sneered. "The only amateurs round here are you and your lot."

"I'm warning you, Uncle Joe, if we get any complaints about you, we'll have to act." Gemma drank more tea. "We spoke to Eric Wilkinson at the Foundry Inn, and he tells us Nicola was quite tanked up when she left. Does she have a habit of getting drunk?"

Joe snorted and Brenda laughed.

"She hangs around a lot with Mavis Barker," Sheila explained, frowning at her companions' levity.

"Mavis has hollow legs," Joe said. "Drinks like a fish."

"And Nicola had crab's legs," Brenda said. "They had a habit of clamping themselves round men. It's the reason Alfie and her were divorced."

Gemma suppressed a smile. "Mrs Riley?"

"I'm sorry to say that behind their disgraceful humour, Joe and Brenda are right. Both Mavis and Nicola are known for their drinking and, shall we say, one night stands."

Sheila gave Brenda a withering stare. "But Mavis and Nicola are not the only ones growing old disgracefully in this town."

Unfazed by the insinuation, Brenda laughed. "I have my share of adventures, Gemma, but I'm not a patch on Mavis or Nicola. They were going through the men over forty in this town like it was an Olympic sport."

"You think there may be a motive there?" Joe asked.

Gemma chuckled. "You're doing it again. No I don't. I'm simply trying to ascertain just how responsible Nicola Leach may have been for the accident. If she was drunk she may have been careless stepping into the road. There's a tree that overhangs the pavement close to where she was hit. She steps round it, another drunk comes along and wham! They meet in the middle."

"So who's this woman?" Joe asked. "The witness?"

Gulping down the last of her tea, Gemma put her pocketbook away and frowned. "Funny thing, that. When we went to the address she gave us, it turned out to be a scrap yard on Beamish Road, and they'd never heard of her."

Joe's eyebrows rose. "And you don't find that odd?"

Gemma laughed. "No, we don't. It happens all the time, Uncle Joe. People witness an accident, they call it in but they don't want to be involved so they give us a false name or a false address." She got to her feet, leaned over and pecked Joe on the cheek. "I'll tell Mum I was here, and I'll see you all later."

Chapter Two

With Gemma gone, Joe glanced at his watch, and swallowed his tea. "Listen, I have to go to the Foundry. Reckon you two can cope? I'll be back before the factories break for lunch."

Sheila and Brenda agreed. "No problem, Joe," Brenda said, "but remember, when it comes to favours, it's one you owe us." Her eye carried that naughty twinkle again. "I'll collect for both of us."

"May I remind you, Joe, that Gemma asked you to mind your own business?" Sheila said.

"And may I remind you just how far my reputation has travelled?"

"Further than his meat pies," Brenda agreed with mock-solemnity.

"Exactly…" Joe frowned. "There's nothing wrong with my meat pies."

"Just get on with it, Joe," Sheila sighed.

"How many times have I actually solved a crime before Gemma and her pals?" Joe allowed his arrogance to pour out. "People know about my powers of observation." He waved at his casebooks. "Why else have they called me in to crack their little puzzles and mysteries? And it's not just here in Sanford, is it?"

"No," Brenda said. "You've travelled as far afield as Wakefield and Bradford."

With a dismissive wave, Joe threw off his white smock. "I'll be back in time for the rush."

He hurried out through the kitchen and rear door to his car. Notwithstanding the temperature in the kitchen, the heavy July air still hit him like a hammer when he stepped outside. Opening the car door, and climbing in, a wall of heat enveloped him. He wound back the sun roof, and opened windows on both his and the passenger side before firing the engine.

The ageing Vauxhall estate complained as he reversed it gently from the Lazy Luncheonette's rear yard onto the cobbled back lane which ran the length of the parade. Slotting the automatic transmission into 'Drive' he chugged forward, turned sharp right at the end, and waited for a gap in the Doncaster Road traffic. Familiar, innocuous actions which he carried out almost on automatic pilot, while his agile mind sifted the information he had at his disposal.

Putting aside his conceit, what he had said to the two women was the truth. He had been called upon to crack many a puzzle and minor crime. He never charged for his services. When asked to investigate anything, from theft to murder, his only stipulation was that he be permitted to change the names of the parties involved and write it up as one of his 'casebooks'. No one refused. Everyone recognised him as a sharp and intuitive detective.

"The only way you can pull the wool over my eyes is to buy me a jumper two sizes too big," he would often say.

And yet he had the feeling that someone was pulling the wool over Gemma's eyes right now, and by default, his. It was something small, something insignificant, something already lodged in his encyclopaedic brain, but for the moment it evaded him.

Turning left into the main road, then left again at the lights, into the retail park, he doubled back at a small roundabout, returned to the lights and when they changed in his favour, he turned right along Doncaster Road, heading east: a convoluted route, but it was the only way to turn right from Coronation Parade onto Doncaster Road.

It reminded Joe of the convolutions of his problem. One of his members was dead, run down in an apparent road traffic accident, but the only witness had given a false address, and for all he and the police knew, a false name. To Joe's logical mind, it spoke of a deliberate act and a

18

conspiracy to cover it up; as if someone had turned left in order to turn right. He knew where the left turn had taken them (running down Knickers-off Nicola) but he did not yet know where the right turn led.

The Foundry Inn stood a mile and a half along Doncaster Road on the way into Sanford. An old, redbrick building built sometime before the Second World War, it was, as its name suggested, close to the site where an iron foundry had stood.

Joe remembered that foundry from his childhood. A couple of miles from Sanford Main Colliery which kept the furnaces supplied, it had turned out motor components. He would watch the workers come off shift at two in the afternoon, their faces covered in factory grime, and the air zinging with the tang of molten iron and coal fumes.

He also recalled his teens, when he would be out drinking with pals, and many of the men on the 2-10 shift would come out of the foundry and straight into the Foundry Inn to quench their thirst with a couple of pints before going home, and the bar would ring to their constant shop talk.

Such scenes were anathema to most people these days, but Joe and many of the town's elders recalled those days with great fondness. It was a time when Sanford had been alive with industry. Now the town was stultified, running an economy based on services; an economy that was failing the people it was meant to serve.

Fifty yards on from the pub stood the Sanford Park Hotel. A five-storey block, forming an almost perfect cube, it was the only three-star hotel in town, designed to cater for the few visitors who came to Sanford; mostly race goers when there was a meeting at Pontefract, 10 miles down the road. The place had changed hands four times since its construction in the 1970s, and rumour had it that it passed most days devoid of clientele. In the early days of the 3rd Age Club, he had approached the management with a view to renting a function room for the weekly disco, but their prices were nothing short of outrageous. In the end, they had opted for the top room of the Miner's Arms where the landlord, Mick Chadwick not only kept better beer, but knew how to keep his prices down to attract custom.

As Joe drove towards the Foundry Inn, he could see a police van parked outside the hotel. Two officers had coned off a section of road and were taking measurements by the left kerb. A satisfied smile crossed Joe's brow and he forgot all about Sanford's failing economy and the problems of the Sanford Park Hotel as he realised the tiny doubt which had been nagging him when he left the Lazy Luncheonette.

A line of birch, larch and elm fronted the pub car park, but pride amongst the arboreal display was a huge oak whose upper branches spread close to the pub walls and windows. Climbing out of his car, Joe strolled across to the walls of the Sanford Park Hotel, turned and looked back towards the pub. The lower part of the building, its frosted windows carrying inlaid advertisements for beers and spirits, was almost invisible. Cora Harrison would have waited there for her taxi and if he could not see her position from here... He walked back to the pub and then turned to look along the road. This time, he could not see the police... well, he could, but it was only a part of their van. He could not see the officers carrying out their work.

The beginnings of a theory forming in his mind, he stepped into the bar and found landlord Eric Wilkinson polishing glasses, presiding over a near empty room.

"Quiet yet, Joe," Wilkinson said after Joe asked for a half of lager. "Dinner time crowd'll be in by twelve and I'll ring up a bob or two before three o'clock."

Joe cast his eye over three men, the room's only patrons, playing darts. "Still looking after the sick, lame and lazy, Eric?"

Wilkinson replied with the same fatalism that had overtaken many of the town's small businessmen. "It's nowt to do with me what a man does for a living, or what he doesn't do. As long as he pays for his beer. What are you doing here, anyway? Skiving? I'll bet Sheila Riley and Brenda Jump won't be too happy with you."

"They work for me. They do as they're told." Joe rolled a cigarette. "It's this business with Knickers-off last night. Our Gemma told me some woman saw it all from your car park."

Wilkinson let out an aggrieved sigh. "You're poking your nose into that now, are you? Always summat with you, Joe. I had that niece of yours here first thing asking about it, and I'll tell you what I told her. I didn't see anything, I didn't hear anything. I don't know this woman who rang them and she wasn't drinking in here last night. I could reel off a list of people who were, but I know them all and I've never heard of anyone called Clara Harrison."

"Cora Harrison," Joe corrected him and took out his tobacco tin. "Gemma told me this woman claims to have seen it, but I just stood on your car park and she can't have seen it. Not if the cops are working where Nicola was hit."

"I don't know." The landlord tunnelled his gaze on Joe's cigarette. "But I do know you can't smoke that in here."

"I'm saving it for when I get outside," Joe said and sipped his half of bitter. "Nicola was boozing in here last night?"

Wilkinson nodded. "She was with that mate of hers, rabid Mavis."

"Mavis Barker?"

"The very woman," Wilkinson agreed. "They were well oiled when they left, the pair of 'em. Prattling all night about some do they're going on with that club of yours."

"Weekend in Filey," Joe told him. "This Friday. We come back Monday."

The landlord shook his head sadly. "How do you cope with two old ravers like that for a dull weekend?"

"I don't," Joe admitted as he finished his drink. "I leave it up to Sheila and Brenda. I'll catch you later, Eric."

Joe stepped out of the Foundry Inn and looked towards the police officers once more. They had cordoned off only the left hand side of the road, and he guessed that they would have done most of their work during the night or in the early hours.

21

Moving to the front of the pub, on the pavement, Joe looked at them again. This time, he could see the whole road, and if this was where Cora Harrison had stood, then she could possibly have seen the collision. But the sidewalk was narrow and, at closing time, busy, so most people didn't wait there for taxis; they waited on the car park.

Across the road was a run-down parade of shops and small businesses intermingled with poorly maintained, Edwardian terraced houses. Joe could imagine them in the dark of eleven twenty last night. A few lights on behind closed curtains, but many of the places in darkness. No witnesses.

He walked along the pavement to the front of the hotel where the police were packing up their equipment.

"Find anything?" he asked.

"Just mind your own business..." Constable Vincent Gillespie trailed off as he looked up from stacking up cones for loading into the van. Like most of Sanford's police officers, he recognised Joe as their sergeant's uncle. "Oh, sorry, Mr Murray. Didn't realise it was you."

"No problem, Vinny. Gemma was round my place earlier, and told me what happened. Nicola was one of my members." Joe dug into his pockets, pulled out his brass Zippo lighter and relit his cigarette. Puffing on it, he repeated, "So, did you find anything?"

Gillespie shook his head. "Scientific Support did most of the work just after sun up. About five this morning. All we've found is this." He held up a seal-easy evidence bag in which was a small piece of 1" diameter black tubing bent into a right angle. "Not sure, but I think it might be a corner piece off the vehicle's bull bars."

Joe visualised the front grid of a Land Rover and the familiar bull bars. "But you don't know if it's off the vehicle that hit Nicola?"

"No, sir. The dreaded SS will tell us that. If this connected with Mrs Leach, there'll be evidence on it. If you'll excuse us, Mr Murray. We'd better get going."

"Sure. Just one thing, Vinny. Do you know where the

Land Rover came from?"

Gillespie frowned. "Funny thing, that. According to the forensic bods, it came outta there." He pointed to the hotel car park. He grinned. "Maybe the driver and his woman had been up to what comes natural, eh?"

"Yeah. Maybe."

"The feeling is that Mrs Leach would have stepped round that tree." Vinny pointed at the spreading yew, its branches reaching across and down to the pavement. "I think your Gemma's been onto the hotel loadsa times to get it cropped. It's a bloody nuisance."

Again Joe could visualise the scene. Nicola staggering along the pavement and batting the branches out of her way while stepping round it. It was a course that would bring her close to the kerb edge and make her an easy target.

"Right. Well, thanks, Vinny. I'll see y'around." Joe turned into the Sanford Park Hotel.

After the searing heat and light of the outside, the interior came as a welcome relief, but one tainted with some sadness. If the hotel's exterior gave the impression of a moribund office block dumped out of place in an industrial area, the inside merely added to the gloom. The off-white walls looked dirty, the Formica fascia of the front desk was chipped and scratched and Joe was certain that if he rapped the backs or cushions of the dowdy Dralon-covered seating, a cloud of dust would burst into the air.

In the hotel's favour, however, the air felt fresher inside. The interior of the pub had been cool; the hotel was cooler. Air-conditioning, Joe thought as he approached a middle-aged brunette on reception.

"Good morning, sir. Can I help you?"

"I'm hoping so. Joe Murray. You had a bit of a schimozzle out here last night. Woman got knocked down and killed."

The woman's chubby features changed in an instant. The welcoming smile was gone, replaced by a scowl of deep distrust. "If you're a reporter…"

"Do I look like a reporter?" Joe cut in with a sweeping

23

gesture over his T-shirt and jeans. "I own the Lazy Luncheonette a coupla miles down the road. The woman was a member of the Sanford 3rd Age Club and I run it."

"Then you'd better speak to the police."

"I did and they're not asking the right questions."

"So what do you expect me to do?"

A combination of the morning's frustration, the gloomy hotel interior and the receptionist's surly attitude got to Joe. "You know the day your bosses covered customer service? Was that your day off?"

"Now listen –"

Joe cut her off again more rudely this time. "No, you listen. All I want is some information. Did you have any strangers staying here yesterday?"

"The people who stay here are always strangers," she told him. "We don't get many locals booking in."

"And were there many yesterday?"

"There was no one here yesterday." The receptionist gestured upwards. "Fifty rooms, fifty vacancies. Are you happy now?"

"So there would have been no cars on your car park last night?" Joe demanded.

"There might have been, but I wouldn't know because I was at home. And if you want to know who the cars belonged to or how much the tarts charge for doing it in the back of a car on our parking area, I still wouldn't know. And I'll tell you something else. I don't bloody care. Now if there's nothing else, you'll have to excuse me. Some of us have work to do."

Joe looked around the empty lobby. "Where?"

Without waiting for an answer, he turned and marched back out into the blazing sunshine.

Keeping a wary eye on the time, and the need to be back at the Lazy Luncheonette to help with the midday rush, he drove into Sanford, parked in the multi-storey behind the shopping mall, and made his way through the backstreets to the police station, a distinguished, redbrick building, constructed during Queen Victoria's reign, which was now

24

buried in the backwaters, hidden behind the 21st century façade the town preferred to put out.

Gemma, up to her eyes in paperwork, agreed to see him and took him through the public reception area, into her Inspector's office, where she listened patiently to what he had to say, then reproved him.

"I asked you not to interfere, Uncle Joe, and the first thing you've done is interfere."

"No. I've been out to the scene of the crime," he said, "and learned things that you may not have been aware of."

Gemma tutted. "We were aware of them. We know the Harrison woman wasn't in the Foundry Inn, but she never said she was. We know she wasn't staying at the Sanford Park Hotel, too, because we asked. We also knew the Land Rover came out of the hotel car park and if what you say is true, Vinny may have a piece of the vehicle with him when he gets back here, but it still doesn't add up to a deliberate act of murder."

"As opposed to an accidental act of murder?" Joe demanded. Seeking inspiration, he looked up at the room's only window. Small, high up, all he could see were the blackened bricks of some exterior wall less than a foot beyond the glass. So much for inspiration. "Did you know she probably gave you a false name?" he asked.

"We're aware of the possibility." Gemma shifted uncomfortably in her seat. "At this moment in time, we haven't been able to trace anyone named Cora Harrison in Sanford."

"It was false," Joe declared.

"She could have come from Leeds or Wakefield."

"The name was false and you know it." Joe pressed home his advantage. "The car came out of the hotel car park. She rang you to report the accident, gave you a false name and address, and yet she was stood in a position where she couldn't have seen what happened. Even if she was on the pavement in front of the Foundry Inn, which is unlikely, she couldn't have made out a Land Rover from that distance in the dark. If you want my opinion, this was a deliberate act, and she was in the damned Land Rover when it hit Knickers-off."

"That's going too far."

"Is it?" Joe demanded. "I just checked it out. Like you said earlier, Nicola would have skirted the yew tree blocking the pavement. And right at the very moment, a truck sneaking out of the Sanford Park Hotel's lover's retreat runs straight into her? Sorry, Gemma, but I don't believe it."

Gemma's frustration manifested itself with a hand run roughly though her dark hair. "There are other explanations."

"Gimme one," Joe challenged.

Gemma paused a moment, her eyes flickering around the compact office. "All right. Let's say this woman is out with a man who's not her husband. She's in her lover's car. A lot of people use the Sanford Park Hotel car park for, er, shenanigans, as you've just pointed out. We're always getting complaints about it. We've asked the hotel to cut the trees down so the place is more open, but they say they can't afford it. And we're forever asking them to cut down that damned yew. Anyway, she and her lover have just finished… you know. They see what happens and she knows she has to report it. So she gives us a false handle and address, and they scram. She doesn't wanna hang around to talk to us because her husband may find out what she was up to."

"That doesn't explain how the Land Rover happened to be in just the right place at the right time."

"Uncle Joe, it happens. All the time. People are killed on the roads every day, usually due to carelessness. And in every case, it happens because they were in the right place at the right time. Or the wrong place at the wrong time, whichever way you want to look at it."

Joe thought about it and with a grunt, said, "This Cora Harrison must have used a mobile, then. Have you traced it?"

"Unregistered." Gemma held up her hand as Joe opened

his mouth to protest. "All right, all right. I know all mobiles are supposed to be registered, but do you know how many SIM cards I can buy from local newsagents? And if you think about it, any couple in an illicit affair would use unregistered phones to keep in touch, wouldn't they?"

"So she's using an unregistered phone, and you still don't believe she was up to something." Joe rolled a cigarette.

"You can't smoke that in here," Gemma warned him.

"I know, I know."

His niece huffed out her breath. "I do believe she was up to something, yes, and I just told you what. We have no evidence that the hit and run was deliberate, and unless something turns up, my governor's not going to listen to me or you. Now do me a favour, Uncle Joe, and let it be. Get your club to pay their last respects to Nicola, and leave the criminal investigation to us."

"The phone call? Was it a 999?" Joe asked.

"Of course."

"Recorded?"

"They all are," Gemma replied.

"Then listen to it," he advised her.

Gemma sighed. "Why?"

Joe got to his feet. "Because if she was in the Land Rover, you'll hear the engine running in the background. Listen to it, Gemma. Better yet, get me a recording of it. I know people who'll tell you not only what kind of engine it is, but probably who built it."

Chapter Three

Every Wednesday evening, the top room of the Miner's Arms was given over to the Sanford 3rd Age Club weekly disco.

The club had been the brainchild of Joe and his friends, Sheila and Brenda.

Both women were widowed. Brenda had been a bank clerk before her late husband's failing health forced her to give up work. When Colin died, he left her financially comfortable, and she worked for Joe to give her something to fill the hours rather than any monetary considerations. The same could be said of Sheila. A former school secretary, when her police inspector husband, Peter, succumbed to a heart attack, she was not found wanting, but she needed fresh, more invigorating company than she had with the staff and pupils of Sanford Park Comprehensive. So she took early retirement and came to work for Joe. The two women were the best of friends, which irked Joe only at those times when he wondered whether he should date one or other of them.

Known in the local community as Joe's Harem, Joe had known them both from childhood, when they had all attended the same school, and they had worked for him for over five years. Although he would never admit to it anyone, he considered them indispensable. They could run the Lazy Luncheonette just as efficiently as he, they were unflappable, and they were so indefatigably cheerful that they provided the perfect foil to his sullenness.

Like Joe, Sheila was razor thin and short of stature. An attractive woman in her younger days, the ravages of time and the stress of widowhood had taken their toll. The shower of blonde hair showed streaks of grey, the corners of the eyes were creased, and her figure had lost some of its curves. Not that she was unattractive even now. At the age of 55 she could still turn heads on grab-a-granny nights, but they usually turned slower because most of their owners were in the deeper throes of arthritis.

Brenda was the antithesis of Sheila. A buxom woman, she had no qualms about showing off her finest asset, but aside from her large bust, she showed no sign of being overweight, despite her predilection for sweets. Where Sheila employed a degree of tact and discretion in her daily life, both words had obviously been left out of Brenda's lexicon. Her dress sense was not the only thing about her that was loud. In contrast to Sheila, who maintained an air of formal grace and demure discretion, Brenda dealt with widowhood by enjoying herself quite openly with a number of men. Not that she was as loose-legged or easy as Mavis Barker and Nicola Leach, but she was freer with her favours than Sheila.

Joe, too, was single, but his was a result of a divorce, not death. He and his ex-wife Alison had been married for ten years when she decided she wanted more than life above a workman's café in Sanford. That was ten years in the past, and the last he had heard of Alison she had left the UK for good and was living in Tenerife. Whatever relationships Joe had enjoyed since, he kept to himself with employing a level of secrecy that would have turned MI6 green with envy. Even his family, nephew Lee and niece Gemma, knew nothing about his private life.

The 3rd Age Club was born of the realisation that even in a small town like Sanford, with its population of about 40,000, there would probably be many people in the same position as them.

"There must be hundreds, maybe thousands of middle-aged and elderly people who are single, divorced or widowed, and they have nowhere where they can get together," Sheila had enthused when she first mooted the idea.

Although he felt her numbers were hopelessly overstated, Joe had to agree with her. His life at the time consisted of the Lazy Luncheonette and the local pub.

With him as chairman, Sheila as secretary and Brenda as treasurer, the club launched four years previously and now enjoyed a membership of over 300. They were a motley assortment. Some were widowed, some were divorced, others were still locked in happy or otherwise marriages. Some were still working, others had given it up through retirement, failing health, or simple unemployment. They represented a range of working types; professional, skilled, unskilled, clerical, practical, managerial. But the one thing they had in common was their age: every member was over fifty. Many were at that time of life when every day the grim reaper did not come to call was seen as a bonus, and most had come to the conclusion that if life was a game of two halves, they were well into the second period. All had decided that now was the time to start enjoying themselves, and without exception they would fight tooth and nail to secure whatever pleasure they could.

When not working at the Lazy Luncheonette or unravelling a mystery, Joe threw himself into the 3rd Age Club with gusto. He was the prime mover, the ideas man, the negotiator, and he was also the club's DJ. Mick Chadwick, landlord of the Miner's Arms, provided the room and the sound system, Joe provided the laptop filled with music from the 50s, 60s and 70s, and the karaoke microphones, and ran the show every Wednesday.

By quarter to eight, the room was beginning to fill. Joe picked out a Herb Alpert track, and left it playing as background music. The early arrivals always crowded the bar, not the dance floor, and while they sorted themselves out he and his two companions sat behind the disco set up on the small stage by the windows.

"I notice Mavis isn't here," Sheila commented as the room began to fill with new arrivals.

"Were she and Knickers-off close friends?" Joe asked.

"About the only friend Mavis has, I think," Sheila

replied. "Well, about the only friend who would indulge Mavis's, er, foibles."

"You mean getting drunk and dropping her trolleys?" Brenda said.

"Pot calling the kettle," Joe said, his gaze directed at Brenda.

She returned a sarcastic grin. "I don't get drunk."

Tittering at Brenda's cynical retort, Sheila took a sip of lemonade and more seriously, said, "You'll have to make an announcement, Joe."

"You think they won't all know?" he asked. "They'll have read it in the papers, surely."

"Perhaps, but she was member for a long time."

"Ever since the early days," Brenda agreed. "And we'll need to send a wreath from club funds."

"There'll be the funeral to attend, too. After we get back from Filey."

Joe clucked, and tested his microphone by tapping the head. Happy that it was working, he switched it off. "You two are just wishing all our lives away, aren't you?" He switched the microphone on again and faded the music out. "Evening, ladies and gentlemen. I know it's a little early but can I have your attention for just one minute please."

The hubbub died down and all eyes turned on him.

"I have a sad announcement to make," Joe said, his voice bouncing back at him from the wall speakers. "For those who may not know, Nicola Leach was knocked down by a car last night as she came out of the Foundry Inn. The driver didn't stop and unfortunately, Nicola was pronounced dead at the scene. I'm not going to go on about what a wonderful person she was. I didn't know her that well, personally, but she had been a member of the club from the very early days, and she will be missed. We will send a wreath from the club and a couple of members will be nominated to represent STAC at the funeral. For now, I'd like us all to spare a minute's silence in memory of Nicola." He switched his microphone off.

The room fell silent save for the clatter of bottles and

glasses from the bar where the landlord was stocking the chillers.

Joe did not time the impasse, but when he felt that justice had been done to Nicola, he switched his microphone on again. "Thank you, ladies and gentlemen."

The buzz of conversation rose, flooding the room again.

From the floor, Captain Les Tanner, resplendent as ever in his regimental blazer and tie, asked, "Have the police arrested anyone, Murray?"

Joe, who usually took great delight in antagonising the Captain, answered through the microphone. "I spoke with my niece, Detective Sergeant Craddock, this morning and she told me that although there was a witness, neither the driver nor his vehicle have been traced."

"Drunk, I'll bet," Tanner snorted.

"That's the feeling, Les."

"Ought to be hung." Tanner turned and walked stiffly away.

"Silly old sod," Joe grumbled, putting down the microphone and turning up the music again. He watched Tanner rejoin his open-secret lady friend, Sylvia Goodson. "We'd still be hanging kids for nicking sweets if he had his way."

"Whereas you'd only give them a public flogging, wouldn't you, dear?" Sheila teased.

"And cut their grubby little hands off," Brenda giggled.

Joe delivered a grunt that could have been a complaint or a laugh. "Hanging's too good for the thieving swine." He consulted his play list, and switched on the microphone again. "All right, all right, all right. Let's get the evening under way with a trip back to the sixties and Manfred Mann's *Do-Wah-Diddy-Diddy*."

Music burst from the speakers and the dance floor remained ominously empty. Joe was not worried. This early in the evening, those wishing to strut their stuff were few and far between. Aside from a few hardy souls, it took time for alcohol to loosen inhibitions and ageing joints.

"Gemma didn't believe a word you said, then?" Sheila

asked as Joe settled down with his traditional half of bitter.

"She's quite happy to go along with most of what I said, but she won't accept that this woman was involved or that the hit on Knickers-off was deliberate."

"It is a bit extreme, Joe," Brenda commented. "And Gemma's ideas sound quite reasonable to me."

Joe eyed her sourly. "They would."

Without rising to his bait, Brenda asked, "Why would anyone want to knock her down deliberately?"

"I don't know," Joe replied. "I just get this feeling about it, that's all. The only person who might know isn't here. Mavis. See, you had to be at the Foundry Inn to see what I saw. Nothing. From where people usually wait for taxis, you can't see a damn thing. So this Harrison woman had to be in a position where she could witness everything, and that means either standing on that narrow pavement outside the pub, or in front of the Sanford Park Hotel."

"Or wandering past on the other side of the road," Sheila ventured.

Joe had been thinking about the problem all afternoon and the moment Sheila spoke, he shook his head. "If she was on the other side of the road, she would have said she was outside the pharmacy or the baker's, not the pub. No, she was on the Foundry Inn side. And that name tells us more than you may think, too. Let's imagine the scene. She's stood there, she sees Knickers-off mowed down and the first thing she thinks of is, 'Good God, I need a false name for the filth'? It doesn't sound right to me. No, she had that name planned in advance, and as far as I can see, there's only one reason for it. Killing Nicola was intentional, and everything was thought out in advance."

"In that case, I repeat, why would anyone want to kill her?" Brenda insisted.

Joe shrugged. "Let's think about it. Nicola is known for playing around with men, and from all I gather she wasn't too choosy, either. Now suppose she's been messing with some woman's husband, and the woman is determined to get her own back."

"Joe, this is Sanford," Sheila protested, "not 1930s Chicago. You don't run a woman down in cold blood simply because she's been sleeping with your husband."

Brenda chuckled. "At least I hope not."

Joe scowled. "Man mad."

Heading off the potential argument, Sheila asked, "So what is Gemma doing?"

"Nothing," Joe replied. "It goes down as a road traffic accident, a hit and run, manslaughter or whatever they want to call it, and they pursue routine inquiries. And as usual, they inquire in the wrong areas."

Brenda frowned. "How do you mean?"

"They'll go looking for a Land Rover with a part of its bull bars missing. In other words, they'll be looking for the driver and his vehicle."

The two women exchanged puzzled glances.

"Where should they look?" Brenda demanded.

"The victim," Joe said. "You always look at the victim, see what he, or in this case, she, can tell you."

Sheila chewed her lip. "That's for murder, Joe, not manslaughter."

He stared candidly at her. "And how else would you describe deliberately running her down?"

As Manfred Mann reached the final verse, Joe selected the next track, Lulu's *Shout* and as the first track faded, he led the next one in. He cast a jaundiced eye over George Robson and Owen Frickley, and Julia and Alec Staines jiggling around the almost empty dance floor, then cast his gaze further afield, to the entrance where Mavis Barker had just entered with a tall, stout man Joe did not recognise.

"There's Mavis now," he said, pointing her out.

She was difficult to miss. Short and tubby, she tended to dress in the most outrageous outfits, tonight sporting a black, low-cut dress which showed the canyon-like V of her cleavage, and ended short of her chubby knees.

"She's with Eddie Dobson," Sheila said.

"Who?" Joe asked.

"Eddie Dobson. He was in the café this morning." Sheila

tutted in frustration at the blank look on Joe's face. "I've told you about him often enough."

"I'll go get Mavis," Brenda laughed. "You tell him it like it is, Sheila."

While Brenda went off, Sheila lectured Joe. "Eddie joined about two or three months ago. He's recently moved to Sanford, or something. Originally from Rotherham and he's either divorced or widowed, I can't remember which. Anyway, virtually from the moment he joined us, he's been trying to get on the Filey trip."

"Oh him."

"I get the feeling that he's very lonely, Joe, and he wants to make new friends." Sheila's face fell. "Sad thing is, with Nicola dead, there is a space on the bus."

"Yes," Joe agreed, "but Nicola and Mavis were booked into a double room, and unless the Beachside is a knocking shop, I don't think the management will take kindly to this Eddie Dobson hopping into bed with Mavis."

"So you still can't squeeze him in?"

"Not without ringing Filey and doing some negotiating, I can't." Joe watched Brenda make her way around the dance floor with Mavis in tow. "Why the hell does he want to come anyway? Filey's not the liveliest place on earth."

"I told you, I think he's lonely."

"If I was lonely, I still wouldn't go to Filey." Joe beamed a greeting at Mavis. "Hiya. Listen, Mavis, we were all sorry to hear about Nicola."

Mavis shrugged. "I'm gonna miss her." She grinned showing large gaps in her teeth. "I offered to take Brenda under my wing, teach her a thing or two, but she's turned me down."

"I'm not in your league, Mavis," Brenda admitted with a smile.

"You didn't see the accident?" Sheila asked before Joe could return a ribald comment.

Mavis shook her head. "A coupla blokes were chatting us up. Feeding us booze, y'know. Nicola was well tanked up when we left, and she was walking it home. She didn't have the money for a taxi cos she was saving her dosh for Filey. She'll have been all over the place walking after all that drink, so it doesn't surprise me that she got hit."

"Joe has the feeling that it was deliberate," Sheila said. "What do you think, Mavis?"

"I think Joe spends too much time on his own, that's what I think. He needs a woman in his life, and I mean a proper woman, not like Alison." Mavis grinned again, directly at Joe this time. "I'm always looking for a bloke with a bob or two."

Joe made no effort to suppress a shudder. "Pass," he said. "You don't think there might have been some woman determined to get back at Knickers-off?"

"What? By running her down? Stop looking for problems, Joe. It was an accident, pure and simple." Mavis looked around the room. "Right, I'm gonna see who'll buy me a glass or two. See you later."

"See," Sheila declared as Mavis wandered off to pester Cyril Peck. "Even Mavis thinks you're silly."

"I'm reserving judgement," Joe said. "I'll go to the bar. When this track finishes, it's *Nights in White Satin*."

He skirted the dance floor to the bar, stopping occasionally to pass a comment with members, queued for several minutes until Mick Chadwick served him with a half of bitter, a port and lemon for Brenda and a glass of lemonade for Sheila, then made it back to the dais as the Moody Blues number came to end. He noticed that Sheila was talking with Eddie Dobson, but paid them no mind as he announced the next track, *Jesamine* by The Casuals.

With the music under way, Brenda wandered off to dance with George Robson, and Sheila nudged him. "Joe, Eddie has a request."

"Just write it down, pal," Joe invited, "along with the dedication, and I'll play…"

"Nought to do with music, matey," Eddie interrupted.

Joe looked him over. A tall and stout man, with large, flushed features, what impressed Joe most was the size of Eddie's fists. They were like hams, and each wrist was decked with tattoos. He was not the kind of man Joe would like to meet down an alley on a dark night.

"What is it, then?"

"Filey," Eddie replied. He pronounced it fah-lee. "I was thinking, like, if yon woman who was run over was going to Filey, there'll be a place on the bus now."

Joe scratched his head. "You're not letting the grass grow under your feet, are you?"

"Whey, there's nought neither you nor me can do for her, is there? You've got to take whatever opportunity comes your way, haven't ye?"

With so many members in the room, Joe felt sufficiently emboldened to observe, "You don't mind my saying, but you seem awfully keen to get to Filey."

"Ahm a fisherman, see, and there's good fishing off the Brigg."

"All right, Eddie, let me tell you how it is. We have 36 rooms booked for 71 people. Now Mavis and Nicola were in one room, and there's no way the hotel would let you literally share Mavis' room. I'll have to ring them tomorrow, and see if they have a spare single. And this is short notice so I'll need the full amount off you tomorrow. That's…" Joe turned to Sheila. "How much?"

"One hundred and twenty five pounds, Eddie."

"I can have it for you," Eddie replied. "If I stop by your place tomorrow, would that be all reight?"

"Yeah, but make it late morning," Joe advised. "Gimme time to speak to the Beachside."

With a smile and a nod, Eddie went back to the bar.

"Where did you say he was from?" Joe asked.

"Rotherham," Sheila said.

Joe watched Brenda stop Eddie and speak with him. Then Brenda smiled broadly and Eddie carried on to the bar. "Rotherham? Not with an accent like that, he isn't."

Chapter Four

Thursday morning brought no sign of an end to the heat wave, now into its fifth day. In the kitchen of the Lazy Luncheonette, Lee worked with the back door open and a pair of freestanding fans blowing in an effort to create a cool airflow and combat the stifling heat. The ultraviolet Insect-o-cutor seemed to be working overtime dealing with the invasion of flies and large insects, which, so it appeared to Joe, were as desperate as any other species, to get indoors, out of the searing sunlight.

In the dining area, Joe, too, was using tall fans to keep his customers cool, while complaining about the cost of electricity they consumed.

When the early rush was over, Joe stood on the pavement enjoying a smoke, and compared notes with his long time friend and neighbour, Ramesh Patel who owned the minimarket, and both agreed that the weather had seen a massive rise in sales of soft drinks and ice cream, while Dennis Walmsley from the hardware and DIY shop, busy setting up some of his stock on the pavement, confirmed that he had been forced to order more of the same freestanding fans that Joe was using in the Lazy Luncheonette.

With his cigarette break over, Joe stepped back into the café, and took his seat at the table by the counter. There were only a few customers in and Sheila had gone out with the sandwich order, while Brenda had finished helping Lee with the washing up and was preparing tea for herself and Joe.

"Have you arranged cover for the weekend, Joe?" she asked as he took out his mobile phone and the Sanford 3rd

Age Club's booking confirmation from the Beachside Hotel, Filey.

"Lee's wife, Cheryl, is coming in with her friends, Franny and Pauline."

Brenda sat down and placed a beaker of tea before him. "As long as we're covered. Those dray men will go through the roof if the place is understaffed."

Eyes darting from the letter to the mobile as he tapped in the individual numbers, Joe tutted. "You think I don't know how to run my own place? I told Sheila to warn Ingleton's that the sandwich order may be a bit late tomorrow and Monday." Punching in the final number, he hit the green, 'connect' button and put the phone to his ear.

The moment it began to ring out, it was answered. "Good morning, Beachside Hotel, Kieran speaking."

"Ah, good morning," Joe replied, trying to inject some enthusiasm into his voice. "My name is Murray, I'm Chairman of the Sanford 3rd Age Club and we have a booking with you for tomorrow until Monday. I wondered whether we could make an alteration to the booking."

The young man sounded doubtful. "I dain't knah, sir. It's a bit late."

"I appreciate that," Joe said, "but one of our members who was supposed to be coming with us, passed away quite suddenly, yesterday. What I'd like to do is change the booking. That's all."

"One moment, sir. I'll put my mother… the manager on."

There was a thump as the young man put the receiver down, and for a few moments all Joe could hear was a muttered conversation between him and someone else, before the rattle of the receiver being picked up again.

"Good morning, Mr Murray. It's Sarah Pringle. We spoke back in April when you first booked."

"I remember," Joe said, and repeated his request.

"If it's only a case of changing a name, there's no problem," said Sarah, when he had finished. "We can deal with it when you arrive."

"It's more complicated than that. The person who, er,

died, was a woman, booked into a twin room with another woman, and it's a man who wants to take her place." Joe laughed. "I know seaside places have a reputation for illicit, er, goings on, but…" Joe trailed off.

"I can assure you, Mr Murray, the Beachside does not promote promiscuity," Sarah said tartly.

Joe removed the humour from his voice. "Yeah, well, so you see the problem. I just wondered whether you could accommodate the chap in a single room?"

"Could you hold a moment, while I check?"

She put the phone down and Joe drank some tea.

"You need to get to the cash and carry today," Brenda said. "Make sure Lee is well stocked on sundries like sweets and cans."

"The minute Sheila gets back and I can find the time," Joe replied.

"And have you told Cheryl how to bank the takings?"

"Yes. Anything else? Would you like me to apply for planning permission for a rooftop garden?"

"I'm just…"

With the sound of the receiver picked up at the Beachside, Joe held up a hand to silence Brenda.

"Mr Murray?"

"Mrs Pringle?"

"Right. Yes, we can accommodate your client, but there will be a single room surcharge of fifteen pounds."

"That's his lookout, not mine."

"And I'll need payment now by debit or credit card."

Joe tutted. "Just a minute while I dig it out." He put the mobile on the table and took his battered, brown leather wallet from his back pocket. The thing was so old, the leather shone in the overhead lighting. "You're a witness to this, Brenda," he said. "I'm paying Eddie Dobson's bill so when he comes in and pays up, the money is mine." He picked the phone up again and gave Sarah his credit card number.

"That's gone through okay, Mr Murray," she said at length. "Now, if I could just have the client's name, please?" Sarah asked.

"Dobson. Edward Dobson."

There was a pause, after which, Sarah said, "That's all taken care of Mr Murray. I'll look forward to seeing you and your party tomorrow."

"Yeah, yeah. Thanks." Joe cut the connection and tossed the phone on the table. Taking another swallow of tea, he dug out his tobacco tin and began the task of rolling a cigarette. "That's done. Eddie can get his fishing in, now. Brenda, you have the tickets for the Abba show, don't you?"

She nodded and finished her tea. "Stashed away where no man would dare to look for them."

Joe scowled. "Except George Robson and three dozen others."

Brenda's smile faded as Sheila came through the rear door, her face set grim. "What's up, ducks?"

"That flaming car of Joe's." Her angry eye rested on the man. "I thought you were going to clean it out yesterday afternoon?"

"I was, but I got sidetracked with other business and forgot. Anyway, what's wrong with it?"

Like Brenda the previous day, Sheila picked several grey hairs from her tabard. "It is disgusting. My hair isn't grey, neither is Brenda's, so it must be yours."

He waved away the argument. "I'll deal with it, right? When I have a minute."

The doorbell trilled and Gemma entered, ending the threat of all-out war.

"Why do I get a feeling of déjà vu?" Joe asked. "Morning, Gemma. Want some tea?"

She shook her head. "Haven't time. Do you have Bluetooth on your phone, Uncle Joe?"

He nodded, much to the surprise of Brenda and Sheila. "Lee and Cheryl showed me how to use it," he explained. Turning to Gemma, he asked, "Why do I need it?"

"You wanted to hear the 999 call from Cora Harrison." Gemma held up her phone. "You said, and I quote, 'I know people who'll tell you not only what kind of engine it is, but probably who built it'. The call is on here."

"And have you listened to it?" Joe demanded.

Gemma tucked in alongside Brenda, opposite Joe. "Yes. Our people have analysed it and they agree with you, she was in some kind of vehicle. They could hear the engine in the background. They've suppressed the woman's voice so you can hear the engine, and they're working on a more detailed analysis but that'll take a few days. I thought, since you offered, I'd let you have a dabble with it, see if your mate really can tell you who built it."

Joe worked through the menus of his phone as he talked. "I'll wander over to Broadbent's with it, and see if one of their older men can tell me anything." Activating the Bluetooth, he nodded at his niece. "Gimme the file." Joe watched the file transfer and when it was done, he dropped it into his pocket. "Have you learned anything more overnight?"

"Hmm. A little," Gemma nodded. "The bit of bull bar Vinny Gillespie found near the Sanford Park Hotel had traces of Nicola's clothing, skin and blood on it, so it definitely came from the vehicle that hit her, and it gives us a clue as to the type of vehicle. The post-mortem is today and we're waiting for the report so we can judge the position of her external injuries, which will give us the approximate height of the bull bars on the vehicle."

"And how will that help?" Brenda asked.

"Fitted to vans, they tend to be quite low," Gemma replied, "but on four-by-fours, Land Rovers and the like, they're higher up. For the moment, we think it's a four-by-four." She smiled at her uncle. "It tells us that Cora Harrison was a witness, and not involved."

"Why?" Joe demanded.

"We're assuming, like you, that she gave us a false name, Uncle Joe. If she was in the vehicle that hit Nicola, she would have given us a false description of it, too."

"Not necessarily," Joe argued. "Rover isn't the only company to make four-by-fours."

"Whatever," Gemma sighed. "Listen, Uncle Joe, all this

is strictly unofficial. When I spoke to my boss, he said he didn't mind you listening to it, but no one else can know what it's about. All right?"

Joe smiled crookedly. "I'll tell 'em it's my car."

***

Broadbent's Auto Service Centre was the largest factory and employer on Doncaster Road Industrial Estate, and coincidentally, the largest accident and service centre in Sanford. Joe's father had known the company's founder, Ken Broadbent in the days when the company first set up, just after the end of World War Two.

Broadbent's had come a long way since the days of a run-down shed and scrub of land near the old foundry. Their premises were clean, modern, and contained the latest in technology to aid the mechanics in their diagnostic work.

Walking in through the gates, Joe noted a range of cars and vans parked in the yard. Some belonged to the staff, some were waiting for service or repair and some had prices in the window. Broadbent's had never been slow to maximise their profit opportunities.

While most visitors or customers would report to reception, Joe Murray was not most people. He walked past the glass fronted office, waving to the counter hands, and stepped into the workshop.

Technicians were working on various vehicles. Damon Allbright, the youngest apprentice in the place, therefore the one detailed to collect sandwiches from the Lazy Luncheonette, stood beneath a Nissan Micra, which was raised on a hydraulic ramp allowing the lad access to the exhaust. In the far corner, two fitters had the bonnet of an ageing Ford Ka raised and were gunning the engine. Other men stood at benches stripping down bits of engine, yet more had the body panels off vehicles, and more than one technician had oxy-acetylene burners lit for welding or cutting.

He found Harry Needham perched on a bench, scanning

the racing pages of the *Daily Mirror.* A big, beefy man, covered in a matt of dark hair, Harry sported a full beard and a hooked nose, which Joe knew had been caused by a van door flying open and not, as Harry often claimed, by a stray punch in a bar fight.

On seeing Joe, the face behind the beard split into a broad grin. "Hey up, it's Joe Murray. What's up, Joe? Lost a fiver in that scrap heap of yours and figure we've nicked it?"

"Up yours" Joe replied and ranged himself alongside Harry at the bench. He looked out across the workshop. "Keeping you busy, Harry?"

"Six days a week, Joe." Harry rubbed his thumb and forefinger together. "Making plenty of moolah, mind."

"And losing it all on the nags?" Joe nodded at the newspaper.

"I win now and then."

"More then than now, I reckon."

Harry folded the newspaper away. "What do you want, Joe? Looking for new wheels?"

"There's nothing wrong with my car," Joe protested.

Harry laughed. "Nothing that a match and a gallon of unleaded wouldn't put right. At least you'd be able to claim on the insurance."

"Did I tell you once to get knotted? Tell me summat, Harry," Joe pressed on before Harry could dig into his fund of cynical retorts, "Can you tell what kind of vehicle is running just by listening to a recording of the engine?"

Harry roared with laughter. "Do me a favour. Who do you think I am? Mystic Meg? I might be able to tell you summat about it, but I couldn't pin it down that well."

Joe offered his phone. "It's an mp3 track. Just have a listen will you?"

Harry frowned at the workshop. "Too noisy out here. Come into the office."

He led the way from the workshop into the mechanics' rest room where they sat at one of the large, wooden tables dotted around the floor. Harry started the recording and put it to his ear.

Joe had already listened before leaving the Lazy Luncheonette. As Gemma had promised, the police acoustic technicians had muted the woman's voice to a level just below the threshold of hearing, so that the noise of the engine came through louder.

"Bad piston slap on that," Harry muttered, "and there's some bint talking, but I can't hear what she's saying."

"That's deliberate," Joe told him.

Harry listened further and while he waited, Joe feasted his eyes on a tyre company calendar where the July model bared magnificent breasts for the camera, and urged the oglers to take her and the tyres she was selling.

"You need a life, Joe," he muttered to himself.

Harry passed the phone back and Joe slipped it in his pocket.

"Diesel," the mechanic said. "Bad piston slap, too. Most engines when they're cool have a bit of slap on them, but the driver's running through the gears, so you have to figure that it's coming up to operating temperature., and with a noise like that, it really needs attention." He screwed his eyes, his gaze intent on Joe. "What's this all about?"

"Like you, I'm a betting man. I bet a pal that you could tell me what kind of vehicle it was."

"Looks like you've lost your bet, then," Harry retorted. "Get your wallet out and pay the man."

Joe ignored the dig at his legendary skinflint habits. "Piston slap?" he asked.

"In an ideal world, the piston should move straight up and down," Harry explained, "but often there's a bit of leeway and it causes the piston to rock sideways, and it slaps the side of the pot. As the engine warms up, it's less noticeable because the piston expands and the oil runs freer."

"You mean more freely," Joe corrected him.

"Let's make a deal. You listen to what I'm telling you and you don't correct my English," Harry said.

"And what do I get out of this deal?" Joe demanded.

"The benefit of my experience." Harry paused a moment. "Tell you what, though, it's an old motor. Maybe a van."

Joe's eyebrows rose. "Go on?"

"On a modern vehicle, there's so much acoustic cladding that you wouldn't hear that much engine noise."

"The recording has been enhanced, so you *can* hear the engine," Joe told him.

"I guessed that," Harry said, "but even so, you're hearing too much. I can hear the driver shifting the gears, and yet the engine noise almost drowns it out. No, Joe, trust me. It's an old motor, maybe a van."

"Or a Land Rover?" Joe prompted.

Light dawned in Harry's eyes. "You know, you may just be right."

Walking back to the Lazy Luncheonette, and crossing Doncaster Road, Joe rang his niece and reported his findings.

"It is only an opinion, though, Uncle Joe," she said.

"Yes, but I'm still hedging bets in my favour," he told her. "I still think this Cora Harrison was in the Land Rover that knocked Knickers-off down."

"And she was so sorry she rang us to tell us about it?" Gemma complained. "Sorry, Joe, but it doesn't quite add up to a cold-blooded hit and run, so you're wrong on one count or the other. Anyway, thanks for chasing it up. I'll wait to see what our sound lab boys say and let you know."

"You know I'm off to Filey tomorrow?" Joe said, stopping outside the café.

"I have your mobile number. I'll bell you. All right?"

Joe cut the connection, tucked the phone back in his shirt and rolled a cigarette.

Sucking the carcinogens gratefully into his lungs, he pondered Gemma's words. She was right. If running Nicola Leach down was deliberate, Cora Harrison would not bother to ring the police and report it. So if Harrison was in the vehicle that hit Nicola, it had to be an accident.

"Unless she had a motive for ringing the law," Sheila suggested when Joe brought his companions up to speed ten

46

minutes later.

With the time coming up to 11:30, the first of the lunches were now ordered and customers began to arrive. Joe stationed himself at the counter, filled the large, stainless steel teapot, pen and numbered notepad at the cash register and began to take orders.

Over the years, they had developed their own shorthand to cope with the rush. SKP meant steak and kidney pie, SKPU was steak and kidney pudding, SEC, sausage, egg and chips (one of the favourites amongst the working people who came in). While he took orders and dished out beakers of tea, Sheila hurried back and forth between the tables and the kitchen delivering the orders, while Brenda took Joe's notes through the serving hatch and assisted Lee in preparing the meals. Dirty plates and cutlery were racked up in the dishwasher or, when that was full and working, on the side of the sink. To an outsider, the system would appear chaotic, but it worked and had done so for umpteen years.

And while he worked, his financially adept brain totting up figures, his fingers scribbling notes, taking money, giving change, pouring tea, Joe conversed equally well with the customers and his crew.

"What possible motive could she have for ringing the police?" he asked, as he passed an order through the hatch, and took a ten-pound note from his customer.

"I don't know," Sheila replied, leaning on the doorframe by the kitchen entrance, waiting for the order to be filled.

From the kitchen Brenda called out, "Maybe she wanted Nicola's seat on the Filey trip."

"Well if she did," Sheila observed, "she was too slow. Eddie Dobson moved faster." She watched Joe scribble out an order for an all day breakfast, and pour tea for his customer. "You're the one with the suspicious mind, Joe. In fact, you're the one who started all this. As far as the police were concerned, it was a simple drunk driving hit and run."

"They don't think anything different even now," Joe said, handing over more change and facing his next customer, a grubby man dressed in Sanford Borough Council overalls.

"What are you having, sport?"

"Cheese on toast, Joe, and a fiver out of the till."

"Stop pratting about, man," Joe grumbled. He scribbled COT on a note and passed it through the hatch while Sheila collected the first meal and walked out into the dining area to deliver it. Pouring tea for his customer, holding his hand out for the cash, when Sheila returned, he said, "I can't think of any ulterior motive she might have had for belling the cops. All I'm saying is, when you look at the big picture, the accident looks more like a deliberate act and she was in on it."

And how are you going to prove that?" Brenda called out, passing the all-day breakfast to Sheila.

With the café door opening more frequently, and a queue beginning to form, Joe sped up his delivery at the till. "We need to find out who she is and why she had a downer on Knickers-off," he called back, "but right now, we're up to our neck in customers, so let's concentrate on the job at hand, huh?"

The lunchtime rush was an event they could predict with near-perfect accuracy. It went on until 1:30, after which the customers died to a trickle, allowing the staff to concentrate on the majority of the cleaning down. Cooked meals stopped at two, and Lee went home, leaving Joe and his two female companions to deal with the final few customers and the last of the cleaning before locking the doors at three.

With the wall clock registering 2:55, and the last of the day's customers departing, Joe was thinking about locking up, when Eddie Dobson appeared.

"Cutting it fine there, squire," Joe commented, ushering him to the table near the counter.

Red-faced and breathless, Eddie apologised. "Sorry, shipmate, but the bus services in this town ain't the best, and I hit a queue in the bank." He dug into his shabby suit and retrieved a faded, black leather wallet.

"There's a slight complication," Joe told him. "I got you in all right, but the hotel have demanded a surcharge for altering the booking."

Eddie appeared doubtful.

"It's only another fifteen pounds," Joe hurried on. "They had to change Mavis Barker to a single room and put you in another single."

"Ah, right, I see." The colour flushed to Eddie's cheeks. "Bit of a bugger that. See, when you told me a hundred and twenty five, that was all I drew from the bank. I ain't got much more on me. I mean it's no problem," he hastened to add. "Ah've gorrit, like, but I just ain't gorrit wi' me. Can I owe it you?"

His natural propensity for keeping the books balanced, Joe hesitated, but Brenda chirped up.

"Course you can, Eddie. You're not going to leave town for fifteen pounds, and believe me, Joe will hound you for it."

Joe puffed out his breath, while Eddie smiled and handed over the money he had with him.

Joe counted it twice, flipping the occasional note over to ensure that the Queen's head was uppermost on all of them. Then he began to count it again.

While he did so, Eddie Dobson looked around the empty dining room. "Wow. You're a writer, too?"

Frowning at the interruption, Joe followed Eddie's gaze to the racks of books ranged on shelves around the café, and the notice above them: *The Joe Murray Casebooks*.

"I'm a private detective in my spare time," he said, and Eddie grinned as if he thought Joe was joking. "Seriously," Joe pressed on. "I've solved any number of minor crimes in this town."

"And one or two major ones," Sheila said from the doorway where she was sweeping the floor."

"Every time I solve a case, I write them up and have them published through the internet," Joe concluded.

"And do you sell many?" Eddie asked.

"I don't sell any," Joe replied. "Well, I do, but only as ebooks. The print copies stay here for my customers to read." He nodded at the money. "Now, can I count this?"

Eddie fell silent, Joe thumbed through the notes again,

and satisfied that it was all there, tucked the money in his pocket.

"All right, you're officially on board," he declared. "The fee includes your ticket for the Abba tribute show in Scarborough on Saturday night. We have the tickets, and we'll issue them on Saturday when we leave Filey for Scarborough. The coach leaves the Miner's Arms at eight tomorrow morning and we should be in Filey between half past nine and ten o'clock. We'll give you the official itinerary when we're moving, but the only fixed thing about the weekend is the Abba show. You know where the Miner's Arms is?"

Eddie pointed to the outside and towards Sanford. "About half a mile along there?"

"The very place," Joe agreed. "Eight o'clock tomorrow morning. Try not to be late."

Smiling happily, Eddie left the café and Sheila locked the doors behind him. Joe finished his beaker of tea, moved to the back of the counter and pulled the drawer from the cash register.

"If you two wanna clear off, I'll count the takings and go to the bank. And I'll see you both tomorrow morning."

"And don't you be late, Joe," Sheila warned.

"Joe? Late?" Brenda laughed. "Not while Eddie Dobson owes him fifteen quid."

Chapter Five

Friday morning dawned and for the 6th day running, there was not a cloud in the sky.

Sweating and breathing heavily in the still air, clad only in jeans, trainers, a short sleeved shirt and an ageing, pale green fisherman's gilet (he insisted he needed the pocket space the garment afforded) Joe walked along Doncaster Road dragging a small suitcase behind him.

He had risen at 5:30, as he did on every other morning. He even helped his nephew Lee, and wife Cheryl to prepare for opening, then leaving them with instructions on running the café during his absence, he had retired to his 1st-floor flat where he showered and changed before setting out.

It was the first time in many a year that Joe had left the café on a business day, and the thought filled him with dread. Lee, a former prop for the Sanford Bulls Rugby League team, was an excellent cook, but notoriously clumsy, and Joe fretted on the number of plates the lad would break over the weekend. Cheryl was better organised, and he could trust her with the financial side of things, but that was a responsibility Joe did not enjoy leaving to anyone else. He did it himself, as a consequence of which on those rare occasions when something went wrong, he was the only one to blame.

As he trudged along Doncaster Road, muttering under his breath at the uncomfortable heat and the oppressive fumes from the queue of traffic built up at the twin sets of lights, he had his first sight of the 70-seater bus from Sanford Coach Services pulling onto the car park at the Miner's Arms and suddenly, he felt glad to be away from the Lazy Luncheonette. He was looking forward to a few days at the seaside, and even the problem of Nicola Leach's death, the kind of mystery he loved to get his teeth into, could be pushed to the background until Monday.

Not that he was yet convinced there was mystery. There were questions which needed to be answered about Cora Harrison, but they were secondary to the sudden elation at the prospect of a weekend on the coast.

"It's too hot," Brenda complained when he joined her and Sheila on the car park.

The two women were busy checking the members onto the bus as they arrived.

"And in January you were complaining it was too cold," Joe retorted.

Many people were already on the coach, some settling down to read or sleep, others fiddling with the overhead airflow controls. Bus driver Keith Lowry, the man designated to most of the Sanford 3rd Age Club outings, was busy stacking suitcases into the coach's underslung storage area. Dressed only in dark, uniform trousers, with a white shirt and navy blue, company tie, he too complained when he slid Joe's small case into the luggage rack.

"You people never get it right, do you? If it's not freezing cold, it's boiling hot."

"Shut it," Joe ordered. "Your boss makes a fortune out of us, and you don't do too badly."

"I deserve it," Keith said. "Hauling a bunch of old crumblies like you all over the country." He delivered his opinion with a broad grin. Tall, tubby and fair haired, Joe guessed him to be in his late thirties or early forties. He had been with Sanford Coach Services for as long as Joe could remember, and to his credit, he knew the roads and routes well, and he knew most of the STAC members like they were his family.

"Are you staying with us in Filey?" Joe asked.

Keith shook his head. "If you'd scheduled another couple of outings on the weekend, I woulda been, but with only the Abba show in Scarborough, the boss reckoned you wouldn't need a bus on site for the duration."

Joe frowned. "So how do we get from Filey to Scarborough tomorrow night? The deal was you would take us."

"He's sub-contracted it to a local firm out there," Keith explained. "They'll pick you up from your hotel Saturday, between six and six thirty, run you to Scarborough and bring you back about half ten, eleven o'clock." Keith grinned again. "Give you time for a pint after the show."

Joe clucked. "What makes you think I'll be able to afford to drink? Do you know how much this gig is costing me personally?"

"Come off it, Joe. You'll need a cooling beer after watching them Abba sorts. There's a rumour you have pictures of the blonde all over your bedroom wall."

"I may have, but this isn't the real Agnetha. It's just a look-alike." Joe moved to the front of the coach, where Sheila and Brenda were studying the clipboard on which was a list of members expected. "How are we doing?"

"About half a dozen to come," Sheila replied.

Joe took out his tobacco tin. "I must have time for a last gasp before we set off." He began to roll a cigarette. "Is your bloke on?"

Sheila glared. "Who do you mean, 'my bloke'?"

"Eddie Dobson."

"Eddie," Sheila snapped, "is not my bloke. He's a club member like all the others. And yes, he is on." She handed the clipboard to Brenda and climbed on the coach.

"Well done, Joe," Brenda said. "That's got the weekend off to a flying start."

Joe licked the gummed edge of the cigarette paper and completed the smoke. "Too bloody touchy. The pair of you."

"You know how sensitive Sheila can be. She's never bothered with any man since Peter died." Brenda narrowed a quizzical gaze on him. "Which makes me wonder what you might have been up to since Alison left."

Joe tucked the thin tube in his mouth, and lit it. Hissing out a lungful of smoke, he said, "And unlike Sheila, I won't snap at you. I'll just tell you to mind your own bloody business."

Brenda shuffled herself intimately close to him and grinned. "Go on, Joe. You can tell me. I'm broad-minded."

"So I've heard. Now back off, you're crowding me." His mobile sounded for attention. Taking it from his pocket and checking the menu, he read *unknown number*. "This'll be Gemma," he said, and made the connection.

"Uncle Joe? It's Gemma."

Joe silently congratulated himself on his perspicacity and took another drag on his cigarette. "Hi, sugar, what's up?"

"Just thought I'd let you know, we got the report back from our acoustics boys this morning. The 999 call? They agree with your man. Cora Harrison, or whatever her name might be, was inside a vehicle and the engine was a diesel, with some mechanical problems, which don't make any sense to me."

"Piston slap?" Joe asked.

"That's exactly what it says here," Gemma congratulated him. "It's still means nothing to me. Anyway, from the balance of various sounds, the sound engineers judged that the vehicle was an older one with less sound insulation than more modern cars and vans. They also suggest it sounds like a van or, as you said, a Land Rover."

Joe beamed a smile, causing Brenda's eyebrows to rise. "I told you. Always listen to your Uncle Joe."

"It still doesn't mean she had anything to do with the accident," Gemma insisted. "That would be very difficult to prove without witnesses. And it still doesn't give us a lead on whether she gave us a false name or who she really was if she did."

"Very suggestive, though, isn't it? If I were you, I'd look into Nicola and her activities. That's where you'll find the answers. Listen, Gemma. We're on our way to Filey in a few minutes, so I'll catch up with you on Monday afternoon."

"Hokey-cokey. Have a nice weekend."

Joe slipped the mobile back in his pocket and pulled on

his cigarette again. "See," he beamed at Brenda, "Harry at Broadbent got it dead right."

Five minutes later, with Les Tanner and Sylvia Goodson the last to arrive and board the bus, Brenda joined Sheila on the front seats, Keith got behind the wheel, Joe took the jump seat across the aisle from the driver, and to a muted cheer from the passengers, the coach pulled out into the heavy, rush hour traffic of Doncaster Road.

Joe half turned to look at his two companions. "Pass me the mike, please Sheila."

Her face still prim and irritated, she reached up, detached the PA microphone from its clip and handed it down to him. Joe switched it on, tapped the head to ensure it was working and then began to speak.

"Morning, people. We're a minute or two ahead of schedule, but the traffic will probably eat that up long before we get to Filey. We're due at the Beachside Hotel about ten o'clock, or maybe a little earlier. When we get there, the drill is as it always is. Check in, drop your bags in the room and the day is yours. Don't forget, I've arranged with the hotel management for us to hold a sixties disco tonight in their bar. We start about eight thirty. Tomorrow, your time is your own, but the bus will leave the Beachside for Scarborough at about half past six. The show begins at eight. Keith tells me there'll be a little time after the show for a drink before we go back to Filey. Then on Sunday, you have all day to yourself and we're running a *seventies* disco in the Beachside. We have to check out of the Beachside before ten on Monday morning and we leave Filey at noon."

"What about tickets for the Abba show, Murray?" Les Tanner called out.

"Sheila, Brenda and I have them," Joe replied. "We'll issue them on the bus from Filey tomorrow evening."

"Do you not think we're capable of looking after them ourselves?" Tanner goaded him.

"Considering you work at the Town Hall, I wouldn't think you're capable of looking after a receipt for my laundry."

Someone laughed and Tanner turned his vexation on them, allowing Joe to return to his ad-hoc announcement.

"Sheila and Brenda will be passing out printed itineraries when we get on the motorway away from this stop-start traffic. Just a reminder to you all. None of this is compulsory, but you've paid for it, so it's all up to you." He switched the microphone off and handed it to Sheila, who clipped it back in place. "You got the itineraries?"

Sheila patted a document folder on her lap. "They're in here." She had put aside her irritation with him. "What did Gemma have to say about Nicola?"

"Not much," Joe replied. "Just that Harry was right about the vehicle."

"And you still think this Harrison woman was involved in the accident?"

Sitting down again, fastening his seat belt, Joe turned his legs to the side so he could look at the two women as he spoke. "All I'm saying is it's suspicious and it should be investigated. If I hadn't piped up over this, they'd have chalked it down as a hit and run and investigated it half-heartedly, as manpower permitted. I've given Gemma grounds for looking deeper into it."

"You're talking nonsense," Brenda insisted. "They don't have a clue who this woman really is, do they?"

"No, but there are ways and means of finding out," Joe insisted.

"Name one," Brenda said.

"CCTV," Joe retorted quick as a flash. "This is the Big Brother age, Brenda. There are cameras all over Sanford. All they have to do is check the footage of those cameras the Land Rover might have passed after it hit Nicola, and see whether there are *two* Land Rovers, or a Land Rover and a van."

Brenda looked to Sheila for support. "Will they do that?"

"Well, they might," Sheila agreed. "Peter was an inspector in the traffic division, you know, and they treat hit and run deaths as manslaughter unless there's evidence to indicate otherwise. Joe has opened up a potential can of worms, and it's possible that they'll go to a lot more trouble on the off chance that it may be murder. It would be up to the Superintendent in charge at Sanford, but he would probably need more than the theories Joe is putting forward." She gave the matter some consideration as Keith turned the bus onto the M62, heading East. "I think they may look into Nicola's, er, love life and see if there is any possible motive. It's all a bit thin."

Brenda laughed. "If they look into her love life, it won't be thin. Her bed-hopping would make War and Peace look like a Betterware brochure."

Sheila opened the document folder and took out the wad of itineraries. "Why did this witness tell them it was a Land Rover, Joe? Surely if she was involved and prepared to lie about her name, she would have lied about that, too."

"You're forgetting the bit of the bull bars that young Vinny and his mate picked up near the scene of the accident. It was a four-by-four. Remember?"

Passing about half the sheets to Brenda, Sheila said, "I don't mean that. I mean how can you say that she was involved?"

Joe shrugged. "We won't know until they can track her down."

Brenda's face became slightly more serious. "I can point to one of Nicola's men."

"You can? Who?" Joe demanded.

Brenda unclipped her seat belt as the coach accelerated along the motorway. Standing up, the thin stack of itineraries in her hand, she said, "Eddie Dobson."

***

At 9:45, after manoeuvring his vehicle through the narrow, tortuous streets of Filey, Keith finally pulled up outside the gates of the Beachside Hotel.

It was a misnomer. Situated at the far end of The Crescent, the place was actually a hundred yards or more from the sands. For anyone coming out of its gates and crossing the road, there was a stepped path that ran down the steep hill to the promenade, and even then the beach was a good 20 feet lower down.

A four-storey, white-fronted building, built sometime in the 1920s or 30s, its sheer size made it stand out amongst the various hotels and holiday apartments in the immediate vicinity. Despite its distance from the sands, the front terrace, immediately outside the dining room and lounge bar, granted magnificent views across the calm waters of Filey Bay from the Brigg in the north to Speeton Point in the south. It had an instant, calming effect on Joe and, he noticed, most of his fellow travellers. Julia and Alec Staines sat on the low, white painted walls, taking the sun and watching Keith pass Eddie Dobson's single suitcase to its owner. George Robson, Owen Frickley and Cyril Peck were chatting near the gates, probably weighing up which pub they would tackle first, and while he rolled a cigarette, Joe basked in the sunshine and serenity.

But something was nagging at him. Something, he knew, was not quite right.

Les Tanner, complimentary for once, interrupted his train of thought. Collecting his suitcase from Keith, he said, "A fine place, Murray. An improvement on your usual cock-ups."

"How did you make Captain in the army?" Joe asked. "Were you promoted on the Peter Principle?"

Tanner turned and walked stiffly away to join his lady friend, Sylvia.

"Berk," Joe commented after the Captain's departing back.

"Les annoying you again, is he, Joe?" Brenda asked.

"He's the only man I know who can get up my nose just by breathing the same air as me."

"What's the Peter Principle?" Brenda wanted to know.

"You have someone in middle management who is so inefficient that he's almost dangerous," Sheila explained. "He's difficult to fire, so you promote him even higher where, thanks to the inertia of those below him, he can't do anymore damage."

"Similar to me leaving Lee in charge of the Lazy Luncheonette. I'd have to promote him above me to save money." Joe looked around at the melee of club members crowding the drive. "Excuse me a minute, Brenda. I just need to speak to Eddie Dobson." Joe ducked and weaved his way through the crowd and caught up with Eddie by the hotel entrance. "Eddie. A word?"

Eddie came out of the throng and off to one side. "What's up marrer?"

"Coupla things. First, can I remind you, you owe me fifteen pounds?"

Eddie's face turned beetroot red. "Oh, crikey. I'm sorry, Joe, I forgot all about it." He dug into his pocket and brought out his wallet. Opening it, he showed it to Joe. There was a single debit card tucked into the slots, and two empty compartments at the rear. "I'll get to the bank once we've checked in, and catch you later in the day."

"Sure, sure. Long as you don't leave town." Joe grinned. "Second thing. I've been told that you had a bit of a fling with Nicola Leach."

Again Eddie blushed. "Well, we went out a time or two. I dain't knah if you knew her well…"

"In the Biblical sense, no, but I knew of her reputation."

"Aye, well, we had a bit of thing for a few weeks, but she wasn't the kind of woman to stick with one man."

"So you weren't out with her the other night, at the Foundry Inn?"

Eddie shook his head. "I'm a bit short of readies at the moment, Joe, and I used most of me money for this trip. I never went out on Tuesday."

"Okay. No problem thanks, Eddie. I'll catch you later, and don't forget the fifteen notes. I just like to keep the books straight."

Watching the queue waiting to get into the hotel, his eyes flashing above the door to a chocolate coloured notice which read, *William Pringle, licensed to sell intoxicating liquors for consumption on the premises*, then switching to the plaque awarded by the *Good Accommodation Guide*, the nagging doubt came back to Joe. Was it something missing or something extraneous? Had talking to Eddie helped or hindered?

He never got the opportunity to exchange views with his friends. The check-in process was slow and ponderous and when he received several complaints from his members, Joe approached Sarah Pringle.

"You've taken thirty-six of my rooms," she told him, "and there are only the three of us on reception."

A slim, mousy woman in her mid 50s, Joe found himself ambivalent in his attitude to her. A short head of fair hair framed her long face, and he guessed she would be attractive if she had ever learned how to smile. Her busty upper half, and, as he would discover when she emerged from behind the reception counter, her shapely legs would have made her the perfect date for a middle-aged man like himself, but the dour set of her face told a different tale.

Her son, Kieran, looked nothing like her. In his early 20s, he was a tall and muscular young man, not in the same league as, say, Lee, but nevertheless, lean and fit. If he was not as big and bulky as Joe's nephew, he was just as slow-witted, and seemed incapable of making decisions for himself.

Alongside Kieran was Billy Pringle, whom Sarah introduced as her older brother. A stocky and cheerful man, with a hooked nose, his jowly features flushed with sweat and, so Joe assumed, worry as he worked his way through the booking process. He was a man, Joe concluded, not accustomed to administrative procedures.

"We're a comparatively small hotel," Sarah went on, "and we cope as best we can, but when we get a large party like yours coming in, delays are inevitable."

"And your bosses won't spring for extra staff?" Joe asked.

Sarah gave him a withering stare. "My brother and I own the Beachside, Mr Murray."

In the light of this announcement, she rose several rungs

in Joe's estimation. "My apologies," he said. "I run a café in Sanford, and I know what it's like trying to balance staff levels against profits. I get the same earache from my customers when my place is busy and they have to queue up. Is there any way we can help?" he asked.

"I dain't knah," she replied. She eyed a stack of registration slips, then grabbed a handful. "If you could give these out to your members and have them complete them before they get to the counter, we might make a bit of progress."

"No problem," Joe agreed.

With the nagging feeling coming back to him, Joe handed out the forms.

Inevitably, they speeded up the checking in process and within a quarter of an hour, he was unlocking the door to room 202, while Sheila and Brenda went into room 208 directly opposite him.

"We'll see you on the front terrace for tea in about ten minutes, Joe," Sheila said.

After the grand front, and the decorative panelling of reception, the room was a disappointment. Small and basic, the single bed, centred on the rear wall, was flanked by a wardrobe and dresser, and the en suite shower and toilet was cramped, but well lit.

Joe flopped his small suitcase on the bed, opened it, took out the few clothes he had brought with him, hung them in the wardrobe, and then pulled out his netbook computer. Looking around, he could see nowhere to set it but the dresser, and instead chose to leave it in one of the lower drawers.

Ambling over to the window, he parted the net curtains and looked out on the rear of the hotel.

Despite its art deco front face, at the back it was like any other establishment. A narrow, poky yard cluttered with beer crates and empty barrels stacked around, awaiting the arrival of the dray lorry, and wheelie bins waiting for the weekly call of the refuse vehicle. Some of Mrs Pringles' private washing hung out on a line and while Joe watched, a chambermaid came out of the rear door, ducked under the shirts hanging on the line, and tossed a bag of rubbish into a large capacity bin.

The sun was shining on the front of the hotel, casting dark shadows over the rear, but further back, the narrow streets were bathed in the sunlight of another scorching day. Looking over to his left, he could see the tourists making their way along the street, crowding around the windows of cafes and souvenir shops, or making their way down to the sea front; young families and older couples, the mainstay of Filey's summer visitors, cluttering the pavements, with the occasional delivery vehicle negotiating the throng.

Something troubled him, but no matter much he tried to distract himself by looking out on the town, it would not come to him. Ensuring he had his Fuji compact camera, his tobacco and lighter, he took his key, and stepped out of the room.

Richly carpeted, but plainly decorated, the second floor landing had that graveyard air of quiet about it, disturbed only by the padding of his trainers on the Axminster. Waiting for the lift, with only a freestanding fire extinguisher to distract his attention, he looked over a couple of pictures adorning the walls. Reproductions of artworks, one was a view of Filey Bay from Coble Landing, the other a stylised landscape of the Brigg.

"What would you expect to find in a Filey hotel, Joe?" he muttered as the lift arrived.

Passing through the dining room and lounge bar, Joe paused and ordered tea, then passed out onto the terrace where Julia and Alec Staines were already enjoying the sunshine with their coffee.

"Great place, Joe," Julia congratulated him. "Just what we needed."

"Glad you appreciate it, Julia."

Choosing a table away from them, sitting down so he could face the sun, he dragged the ashtray towards him, took out his tobacco tin and rolled a cigarette. A light, onshore breeze tickled his crinkly hair and when the waitress delivered his tea, he felt almost at peace with the world.

Almost.

Something still troubled him. Something was not quite right.

His usual practice in such circumstances was to let his mind freewheel, allowing some space for whatever the problem was to jump into, but that was not working. He could not even identify the source of the problem: Nicola Leach or Filey.

"Summat wrong, Joe?" Brenda asked, joining him.

He came back to reality and looked around. "Where's Sheila?"

"Ordering tea and cakes." Brenda smacked her lips and sat alongside him. "Why so anxious?"

He shrugged and drew on his cigarette. "Something is wrong, but I can't think what it is."

She smiled. "It's all right. The hotel don't send any of your details to the taxman."

"What?" Joe realised she was taking a rise out of him and chuckled. "No, no, it's nothing like that."

"What then?" Brenda put an arm round his shoulder and hugged him. "Come on, you can tell Auntie Brenda all your problems. I promise they'll go no further than you and me and the world wide web."

He shrugged her off. "If I knew what it was, it wouldn't be bothering me, would it?"

Brenda dug into her handbag and came out with an antiperspirant. "Nothing to do with Nicola is it?" she asked spraying her forearms.

Joe watched a speedboat skip across the waters, leaving a broad wake in its trail. "Could be," he said. "I told you. I don't know."

"You're not still worried about upsetting Sheila earlier?"

He snorted. "I wasn't worried about upsetting Sheila at all, never mind now. She knows I didn't mean it the way she took it, and you two are always pulling my leg."

"Only she can be quite touchy about men," Brenda

reminded him. "She really is not interested in relationships at all."

"You're not listening, are you?" Joe demanded. "I'm not remotely concerned about you or Sheila having a moody on you, but there's something nagging away at the back of my mind, and I don't know what it is. Something I should be realising, but I'm not. It's no problem. It'll come to me."

Chapter Six

Standing on the podium in one corner of the Beachside's lounge bar, Joe mopped his brow and surveyed the scene before him.

A mirrorball bounced the multi-coloured lights of his disco around the room where they reflected from many shining pates on the dance floor. Couples danced, some locked together, others jiggling face to face, one or two wriggling alone, most were dressed in clothing that had last been fashionable when Harold Wilson was Prime Minister, and all had that ridiculous air of elders reliving their youth. The entire room had the surreal atmosphere of an underground 60s club taken over for a grandparents' evening. The bizarre lyrics of Traffic singing *Hole In My Shoe* added to the sense of unreality.

Without exception, the club members were around when the title was first released, and a good number probably bought it. "Nineteen sixty-seven the summer of love," he said.

"I have an idea it was a hit a lot later than the summer, Joe," Sheila responded.

Wearing a pair of denims and a white T-shirt that declared, 'I'm a third age rocker', he sweated in overpowering heat. "I don't know where they get the energy to dance from."

"You mean you don't know where they get the energy from to dance."

Joe narrowed his eyes on Sheila and tutted. "That doesn't make any more sense than the way I said it."

"It wouldn't." Sheila picked up a handheld, battery operated fan, switched it on and wafted it before her face.

After tea on the terrace, they had spent the remainder of the morning ambling round Filey, the women enjoying a little retail therapy, Joe grumbling along behind them. At intervals they met other club members on the street: George Robson and Owen Frickley heading into the Three Tuns, Les Tanner and Sylvia Goodson coming out of a fancy goods shop, Sylvia holding a carrier bag. Joe and Les took the opportunity to verbally aggravate one another again, Sylvia showed Sheila and Brenda a couple of china ornaments she had just bought. Further down the street, they met the Staineses coming out of a clothing shop. Joe and Alec idled away a few minutes waiting for the three women to stop chatting before they moved on, nodding hello to Eddie Dobson as he walked into a hardware and fishing supplies store, and then bumping into Cyril Peck and Mavis Barker as they made their way into the Belle Vue Hotel for a midday drink.

Joe treated his two companions to lunch in a restaurant, after which they spent the afternoon on the beach, soaking up the sun with thousands of other holidaymakers.

Joe took many photographs, often complaining, "I wish I'd brought my Sony. This compact is too limited."

Whatever troubled Joe earlier in the day continued to haunt him at intervals, and he had not yet solved it. There had been no word from Gemma (not that he expected any) and therefore, no progress on the death of Nicola Leach.

"I think that's what's bothering you," Brenda had said. "You've persuaded yourself that it was a deliberate act, and you can't prove it."

"I'm willing to back off on that," Joe confessed, "but only because what I'm really saying is it doesn't add up." A note of enthusiasm entered his voice as he went on. "Let's put it together. Knickers-off comes out of the Foundry Inn and staggers along the pavement on her way home. As she passes the Sanford Park Hotel's car park, this Land Rover comes out and mows her down then drives off. Cora Harrison is riding shotgun in a similar vehicle, sees it and dials 999. While she's doing so, she digs into her diary or something, and comes up with a false handle. And all this is in the space of the few seconds that it takes her and her… I dunno, lover, let's say, to pass Nicola lying dying in the road. It just doesn't add up."

"She may have stopped, Joe," Sheila pointed out.

"The vehicle was moving when she made the call," he retorted. "And all right, so they could have stopped, checked Nicola and then drove off because they don't want to get involved, but all the same, it's hooky."

Brenda was dismissive. "That's the trouble with you, Joe. You don't know what it's like to have a bit on the side. Personally, I'd have done just as Sheila says. I'd have stopped, checked on Knickers-off and when I realised I could do nothing for her, I'd order my man to scarper, and then bell the filth while we were moving." Her cheery features became sad. "Poor Nicola. She may have been a bit fast and loose, but no one deserves that."

"Amen," Sheila said, and Joe echoed the sentiment.

"Couldn't agree more, which is why I think we have a duty to shove our noses in, see if we can't track down the driver and this Cora Harrison."

"And how are we gonna do that?" Sheila asked. "Send for Batman?"

"Logic," Joe insisted. "These people make mistakes. All we need to do is pick them out."

They had left the beach at four and returned to their hotel, where Joe took an hour's nap before showering, shaving and throwing on his sixties clothing for the evening.

After an excellent meal of lamb cutlets, which considerably raised Joe's opinion of the Beachside, they retired to the lounge bar, where he set up the disco.

"It's a good do, Joe," Sheila approved, bringing him back from his memories of the day. "A fine start to the weekend."

Joe clucked again and took a swallow of ice-cold lager. His grumpy features twisted into a grimace of malevolence. "Lager. Baby beer. Give me a pint of Guinness any day."

"You could have had a pint of Guinness," Sheila pointed out.

"Too hot for Guinness," Joe grumbled. He picked up on her previous announcement. "And it should be a good do. Do you know how much the manageress, that Sarah Pringle, charged us for the hire of the room? She said along with the additional bar staff and all the cleaning up, not to mention the extra electricity they'd use running the disco gear, she would have to charge me a 'substantial fee'." He described speech marks in the air with his fingers as he pronounced the last two words. "Substantial fee? I'm sure the Lazy Luncheonette cost less."

Sheila frowned. "Club funds pay for it, Joe. It's not as if the money comes out of your own pocket."

"Yeah, well, I'm a businessman, aren't I," Joe reminded her, "and business is there to make a profit. Even the club. I know we put the money back in for the members, but we have to show a profit, and you don't make a profit by spending on unplanned, er…" He struggled to find a simile and couldn't. "Spending," he concluded.

Sheila let out a weary sigh. "What are we going to do with you? We came here to enjoy ourselves for the weekend. Stop whining about Nicola Leach and money, and let your hair down."

Joe glanced out across the crowd on the dance floor to remind himself of their balding heads. He ran a hand through his own curly mop. "Well at least I've still got some hair to let down."

"It's just a shame you don't get out of the Lazy Luncheonette often enough to spend some of that fortune you have stashed away." Sheila wafted her fan again. "Where is Brenda? I need her by my side if I'm really going to rattle your cage."

Joe's eyes left the dance floor and checked out the bar area where he quickly picked out Brenda Jump. She was difficult to miss. Dressed in a short, dark skirt, topped by a vivid scarlet blouse with an orange, silk scarf at her neck, she looked like an advertisement for gloss paint.

She sat at the bar with Eddie Dobson. Perched on a bar stool, his belly hanging over the waistband of his jeans, his weather-beaten skin glistened with sweat in the raw heat of the lounge.

"She's over there," Joe reported, "buttonholing that new guy."

Sheila peered across the room. "Oh. Eddie. Poor man."

"Yeah, poor man," agreed Joe. "Brenda hitting on him like that."

Sheila pursed her lips primly. "That's not what I meant, and you know it. He's just got out of the forces. A single man. Doesn't have a soul in the world."

Joe tutted sadly. "And just when he thinks things can't get any worse, Brenda sets her sights on him." He eyed Sheila. "This morning, you took the hump because I called him 'your man'. Fair comment, maybe I shouldn't have said it, but you certainly seem to know a lot about him."

"That, Joe, is because I talk to people. I don't simply bend their ear while I moan about money and Nicola Leach."

With a grunt that could have been agreement or dissent, he drank the remainder of his lager. "I'd better go rescue him from Brenda. You want another drink?"

Sheila nodded. "Just a glass of lemonade, please, Joe. With ice."

Joe was about to step off the podium when the progress of the music permeated his ears. "It doesn't have long to go, Sheila. Next track is The Monkees, *I'm A Believer*."

She looked anxiously at the laptop computer's screen display, a seemingly endless list of tunes. "Where is it?"

Joe had already stepped off the podium. "Track seven, seven, one," he called back.

At least he thought it was 771. Unlike so many of the club members, whose ages ranged from 50 to 85, his mind was as sharp as ever, but if the numbers were not prefixed by a "£" sign, he sometimes struggled to recall them.

He skirted the dance floor nodding to one or two people. Tanner, looking resplendent in his grey flannels and regimental blazer, danced ridiculously with Sylvia Goodson, and nearby, Alec and Julia Staines were smooching. As frisky a middle-aged married couple as he had ever come across, but smooching? To *Hole In My Shoe*? As Joe passed around the edge of the floor, Mavis Barker gave him the glad eye. He returned a grumpy smile and looked away. True to form, the woman was dressed in an outrageous, lime green trouser suit that perfectly captured the theme of the weekend, but which, thanks to her short, dumpy figure, made her appear as a grotesque leprechaun wiggling its bottom in pale imitation of a jitterbug barely paying lip service to the musical tempo.

Although he would never admit it to anyone, as a founder member and chairman of the Sanford 3rd Age Club, it was a matter of some pride that his discos were the highlight of the week, and tonight, as a leader into the Abba weekend, was extra special. The 70 or so people who had come along for the weekend were like Joe; they preferred their music, their beer and their partners from that magical era between the beginning of the end of the Beatles and the birth of punk rock.

Arriving at the bar, he stood behind Brenda and signalled for service.

"The club is just wonderful, Eddie," he overheard Brenda say as she waved an arm at the dance floor. "Many of our members joined as couples, but we have our share of divorcees and widows. We've had plenty of engagements and marriages, too; members who were like you; alone."

Joe nudged her in the back. She looked over her shoulder and smiled. "Oh hello, Joe."

"You want a drink?" he asked. "Only Sheila was looking for you."

"Port and lemon, please, and I'll be over in a minute." She turned quickly back to Eddie Dobson. "Eddie, you know Joe, don't you? Club chairman. Runs the Lazy Luncheonette on Doncaster Road."

"I was there yesterday," Eddie reminded her and Joe made a mental note to watch how much Brenda drank.

"Of course you were."

Eddie gave Joe a wan smile.

"How you doing?" Joe greeted the club's newest member. "Your room up to the mark?"

Eddie grinned. "Why, I dain't knah about that, shipmate, but I've been in worse places."

Joe felt the same way, but with Kieran Pringle waiting for his order, Joe turned his attention from Brenda and Eddie Dobson, leaned into the bar and raised his voice over the music. "Pint of lager, glass of lemonade with ice, and a port and lemon."

"You want ice with that?" Kieran asked.

Joe fumed. "Didn't I just say so?"

The young man scowled. "I meant the port and lemon, sir." Kieran imbued the word 'sir' with just enough stress to indicate that what he really meant was 'prat'. Joe considered taking him to task but decided against it. He nodded instead.

While Kieran busied himself getting the drinks, Joe concentrated on a laminated certificate tucked between the optics. It showed a photograph of Kieran but the writing on it was too small to read. All Joe could make out was the flamboyant heading, NYSAA.

"What's that stand for?" Joe asked when Kieran placed the drinks in front of him. "New Youth Service & Argumentative Awards?"

"If that's what you wish, sir. Eight pounds sixty three, please."

Muttering mutinously on hotel bar prices, Joe handed over a ten-pound note and while waiting for his change, he spotted a clipboard at Brenda's elbow, two sheets of A4 paper attached to it, and a wad of theatre tickets under the clip.

"We have some really great evenings, you know," Brenda was saying to Eddie. "Apart from the weekly disco at the Miners Arms, we arrange plenty of outings; shopping trips to places like York and Chester and Sheffield, and a full weekend outing every three months. Last summer we went to Stratford for a Shakespeare festival, didn't we Joe?"

"Yeah and that was a bloody disaster, wasn't it?" Joe complained as Kieran returned with his change.

"Some of us," Brenda said haughtily, "enjoyed it."

"And one of us fell asleep during Hamlet's big number," Joe reminded her, winking at Eddie Dobson. "Give me Inspector Morse anytime. So, Eddie, you're not a Sanford native?"

The big man shook his head. "Rotherham, originally. Just done my twenty-two in the navy, but couldn't find work, so I moved up to West Yorkshire." He frowned. "Not much more work there, either."

"Not since they closed the pits and the foundry," Joe agreed. "But I'm sure you'll find something." He took his change from Kieran, checked it, and eyed the theatre tickets again. "Listen, Brenda, let me take those from you before they get covered in spilled booze."

Brenda looked irritated. "I do not spill drink."

"I didn't say you did…"

Joe trailed off. Something was not right. *Hole In My Shoe* had finished and he recognised the introduction to Terry Scott's *My Bruvver*.

"Oh, sh… sugar. I told her to put on *I'm A Believer*."

Snatching the clipboard from under Brenda's elbow, he tucked it under his arm, picked up the drinks and scurried back to the podium, crossing the dance floor this time, to the muted protests of one or two dancers.

"Damned inefficient, Murray," growled Captain Tanner.

"Shut up, you old fool, and get out of my way," snapped Joe.

He leapt onto the podium put the drinks and clipboard on the table behind Sheila and jabbed the laptop keyboard to stop the music.

Picking up the microphone, he apologised. "Sorry about that, folks." His voice boomed around the room. "Technical difficulties." He ran the cursor down the screen, selected the correct track and pressed the 'enter' key. Presently the sound of The Monkees came through the speakers. Joe turned angrily on Sheila. "Are you trying to make me look an idiot?"

Sheila refused to rise to his irritation. "Oh I think you can manage that on your own, Joe." Sheila picked up her lemonade and drank gratefully from it.

"What?"

"You said seven, seven, one and that's what I played," she pointed out.

"I meant seven, seven …" Joe checked the computer listing, "two. Didn't you read the screen first?"

"No. I just pushed the numbers in."

Joe shook his head sadly. "Saints preserve me from dim witted women and randy widows."

This time, Sheila took immediate offence. "Who's a randy widow? I'll have you know that since Peter died I've never…"

"Not you," interrupted Joe. "Brenda. She's chatting that poor sod up at the bar and he has the kind of look on his face that you see on those prisoners going to the guillotine in the old movies. Pleading for mercy."

Sheila gave a silly chuckle. "Poor Brenda. Poor Eddie." She fanned herself again. "You have to understand, Joe, when Colin died, he left Brenda financially secure but she had no children. She was alone in the world after thirty years of marriage and constant companionship. Widowhood is more difficult for her. That's why she comes onto men." Sheila sighed and gazed wistfully through the panoramic windows. "I have my son and daughter, I have Peter's brother and his wife, my sister and her husband. I have people around me and I don't feel the need of a new partner."

With a grimace, Joe sipped his fresh lager. Through the windows, the last of midsummer sunlight had disappeared and the long spread of Filey beach lay bathed in shadow. To the north, the cliffs of Carr Naze still shone in red light, but where they tapered off to the Brigg, that finger of land jutting out into the North Sea, the low-lying rocks were all but invisible.

"I'm just nipping out for a smoke," Joe said. "This time, check the titles and put on whatever you think. You know how to do it."

"Yes, Joe, I do. And if you'd said that last time, we wouldn't have had Terry Scott."

Joe stepped out onto the terrace, drew in a deep breath of the cooler air, and sat down at the nearest table. Taking out his tobacco tin, he quickly rolled a thin cigarette and lit it, the flare of his Zippo highlighting his face against the gathering dusk.

Billy Pringle came out of the lounge and skirted the tables, collecting empty glasses and bottles. He worked his way around the perimeter of the terrace, coming to Joe last. With a cautious glance back into the lounge, he dug into his shirt pocket and came out with a half-smoked cigarette.

"Any danger of a light, marrer?"

Joe pushed his Zippo across the table, Billy put his glass and bottle carrier on the ground, lit up and handed the lighter back. Puffing out a cloud of smoke, he sat with Joe.

"You don't mind, do you?"

"Be my guest," Joe replied. "Does your sister disapprove?"

Billy shook his head. "It's not that. She smokes herself, but with us being so busy, if she catches me sneaking a quick drag, she'll hit the roof."

Joe smiled. "Sheila and Brenda are the same with me, back home, and I own the damn place." He drew on his cigarette, and took a wet of beer. "You're not usually this busy then?"

"Season doesn't officially start for another two weeks. When the kids break up for the summer holidays. So we're usually only busy on a weekend. We're booked solid from the middle of this month clear up to the end of September, but of course, we don't run discos in the lounge. Well, we do, but it's only now and then, and usually because we're asked to arrange them for parties like yours." Billy took another puff of his smoke. "You run a hotel, do you?"

Joe shook his head. "Café. The Lazy Luncheonette. Sounds a lot grander than it is, but it's a good little business. Must be a struggle to make a big place like this pay its way."

"Nah, not really," Billy said. "The mortgages are paid off, so we own the bricks and mortar. I'm just a bar and cellar man, really. Sarah's the business brain. She bought the place with her first husband, and when they fell out and divorced, she called me in. That was, oh, nigh on twenty-five years ago. She knows what she's doing, you know. Employs me and our... her son, Kieran, and one or two others permanently and brings in temps when we need 'em. You know. When we're full."

"Makes sense to keep it in the family," Joe agreed. "I employ my nephew as my cook, and Sheila and Brenda as my assistants, and when I need them, I call on casual labour, just like you." He narrowed his stare on the other. "You're the licensee."

He nodded. "Administrative set up more than anything. I've held the licence ever since I started here. Sarah is listed as the hotel manager, but booze is my department. If anything goes wrong, it's my neck on the chopping block, not hers. That way, the hotel can still function." He stubbed out his cigarette. "It also means I can go to the cash and carry for emergency supplies if we need them." He laughed. "And that happens more than you might imagine." He stood up and stretched. "Ah well. Better get back to it." He picked up his carrier. "Catch you later."

Joe took a final drag on his smoke, crushed it in the ashtray and returned to the disco and the dancing couples making merry to the music of The Trogs and *Wild Thing*. Brenda had left the bar and was making her way around the floor. She had stopped and was chatting to Mavis Barker. A pair of widows on the hunt for fresh, male blood, Joe thought.

He glanced at the bar and frowned. "Curious."

Sheila had been in a mental void, tapping her fingers in time to the rhythm of the music. When Joe spoke, she snapped back to the present. "What?"

Glass in hand, Joe waved it in the direction of the bar where Eddie Dobson had detached himself from his seat and was in conversation with Sarah Pringle, the manageress.

She had changed from her austere business suit, and now wore a short skirt and dark blouse. Her hair, he noticed, was different, too. Darker; set differently.

"That Eddie Dobson guy, talking to the Pringle woman," said Joe. "Almost like he knows her."

"You and your mind. Sex-obsessed, that's what you are," Sheila chuckled. "There's nothing odd about it. Mrs Pringle is quite a sociable woman when she's not talking to you about the cost and difficulties of running a hotel. As you would know if you'd ever spoken to her about anything other than the cost and difficulties of running a café."

Joe's malleable features transfigured themselves into a mask of irritation. "I know there's nothing odd about him talking to her. After Brenda, even talking to that idiot son of hers would be a relief. No, it's not that. It's… well, look at his hand." Again he gestured.

It was such a surreptitious movement that only the sharpest of eyes would have noticed, but as he stood close to Sarah Pringle, Eddie Dobson handed something to her.

"Looks to me like he was handing money over," said Joe. He raised his eyebrow at Sheila. "What's it for? Services she doesn't advertise."

Sheila tutted. "That's just the way your mind works. I'm sure there's a perfectly reasonable explanation."

"Yeah. Like I said. Services rendered." Joe sat down. "I'll tell you something else, too. You know he keeps saying he's from Rotherham?"

"Yes?"

"He isn't. He's from round here."

"And how do you know?" Sheila demanded.

"Remember the other morning in the café? I had to tell Lee off for not speaking as he'd been brought up to speak, and he said his dad taught him to say 'no worries'. That's because Lee was born in Australia, and it's the way they speak. Next time you talk to him, listen to the way Eddie speaks. His accent and dialect are exactly the same as Sarah and Billy Pringle's."

***

With the time coming up to one in the morning, Joe left the final track of the night, Engelbert Humperdink's *The Last Waltz,* playing and once more stepped out onto the terrace for a last cigarette.

There were few people left in the lounge. Alec and Julia Staines were smooching to the music… again… Tanner and Sylvia were waltzing, George Robson was chatting up one of the chambermaids in the far corner, while Sheila and Brenda were helping Billy and Kieran Pringle tidy up the room.

Lighting his cigarette, gazing out across the lights of the bay, and out to sea, winking lights from moored ships came back at him. A few stars twinkled in the night, but the moon had disappeared somewhere over Speeton Point. It was still warm but a light breeze tickled his cheeks as he smoked his cigarette.

"I've lived here all my life and I still find it a peaceful sight."

Joe turned his head to his right, and found Sarah Pringle stood alongside him. Once more he took in the dark head of hair and realised she was wearing a wig.

She must have noticed him looking. "Vanity," she said. "As I get older, more and more grey shows at the sides. When I'm off duty, I put this on."

"It suits you," he said.

Sarah smiled and lit her cigarette. Joe silently cursed himself for not offering her a light.

"How was your first day in Filey, Mr Murray?" she asked.

"Pleasant," Joe said. "And please call me Joe.

"I'm Sarah."

"It's good to meet you, Sarah." Joe sighed. "Despite all the problems this week, we had a good day, today."

"Problems?"

"I told you on the phone yesterday that one of our members had died."

77

"Oh. Right. A friend?"

Joe shrugged. "Only in the sense that all the club members are friends. I didn't know her that well." He smiled modestly. "I have a reputation as a private detective, Sarah, and Nicola's death is, er, problematic. The cops think it's a drunk driving thing, but I'm not so sure."

Most of his words seemed to pass over her. "A private detective, eh? I don't think we've ever had a real detective stay with us before."

Joe laughed. "I'm not a real detective. Just an enthusiastic amateur. I notice things, you see. Things that other people don't see. My niece, a Detective Sergeant with the Sanford police, thinks she has it sewn up, I poke my nose in and suddenly they have a lot more questions they need answering." He turned to face her. "Why are we talking about me? Tell me about the joys of running a hotel in Filey."

Now Sarah laughed. "If I did that, Joe, that lovely hair of yours would all fall out."

Chapter Seven

Licking his thumb and forefinger, Joe counted through the stack of tickets for the third time. Satisfied that there were only 70, he picked up Brenda's clipboard and ran a finger down the list of names, his lips moving soundlessly as he tallied them up.

At length, he tossed the clipboard back on the table, took out his tobacco tin and cigarette papers and quickly rolled a cigarette. Jamming the slender tube between his lips, he flipped open the top of his Zippo lighter and flicked the wheel with an irritable movement of his thumb. A large flame leapt from the wick. Joe placed his hands around it as if protecting it from a non-existent wind, and drew deeply on the tobacco. Closing the flip-top, he dropped the lighter on the table, exhaled the smoke with a loud hiss, and took a swill of tea from his cup.

"Well?" Across the table, wearing a conservative knee-length skirt and flowered blouse, Sheila demanded an answer.

Joe did not immediately oblige. Instead, deep furrows lined his brow. He puffed agitatedly at his cigarette and toyed with the lighter on the tabletop. With a shake of the head, he picked up the clipboard and began to run through the list again.

Saturday morning had dawned with no change in the weather. Over an excellent full English breakfast they had looked out through the panoramic windows of the Beachside's dining room, across Filey Bay bathed in sunlight beaming down from a cloudless sky.

Joe had taken a few moments out to remind everyone that the bus left for Scarborough at 6:30 that afternoon, then the club members had gone their own way. While Joe and Sheila moved out onto the terrace, Brenda returned to their room to change into something cooler than the skirt and top she had put on for the day.

For the last half hour, Joe and Sheila had sat out on the terrace, enjoying the morning sun, checking, double checking the itinerary, Joe making calls on his mobile phone to ensure that both the bus and the theatre were ready for their arrival (as well as ringing home to make certain that Lee and Cheryl had not burned the café to the ground). Now his attention wandered to the uninterrupted view across Filey Bay as if expecting it to solve his problem.

There was nothing out in the real world to suggest a solution to his arithmetic. It was 9:45 Saturday morning and even at this comparatively early hour Filey beach was once again busy with families taking advantage of the heat wave. Children and teenagers bathed in the safe waters, a couple walked their several dogs, the animals splashing and playing in the shallows, one or two fisherman were on their way back in their cobles, landing the morning's catch. There had been a flurry of excitement an hour or so back, when the inshore lifeboat rushed from its station and out into the sea, turning to the north and the far side of the Brigg, but aside from that, little had changed and nothing he could see would alter the results of his repeated counts.

He had had a poor night's sleep. The surprise of Sarah Pringle complimenting him upon his grey locks had energised his imagination, and when sleep finally came, the lager had woken him a few times to visit the bathroom. Sometime around three, he'd been woken by the sounds of an argument on the floor below. A loud, metallic thump ended the argument and Joe drifted off to sleep, only to be woken again just after four by the noise of a diesel engine revving out back. He made his window in time to see an ageing, dark blue Transit van pull away up the narrow backstreet, a set of metal ladders strapped to its roof rattling as it made its way along the silent streets.

After visiting the lavatory again, he went back to bed, but

the disappearing van had turned his mind to the death of Nicola Leach, and he found sleep reluctant to come. At length, he managed a further hour before finally getting up at half past six.

Now, sat on the Beachside's terrace, the morning sun already too hot, he felt tired and more irritable than usual.

"Well?" Sheila demanded more insistently.

A police car had just driven in through the hotel gates and stopped by the entrance. A young, uniformed constable climbed out, putting his peaked cap on his head as he retrieved something from the passenger seat. Throwing a polyester rucksack onto his shoulder and tucking a rod and line under his armpit, he locked up the car and made his way into the hotel.

"Well, Joe?"

Sheila's repeated direct question pulled Joe back to his faulty arithmetic. "What?" he asked.

"You've added them up again, again and again. Where are you up to?"

Joe tossed the clipboard down, took another deep drag on his thin cigarette and waved vaguely at the table. "Seventy tickets, seventy-one people. We are a ticket short. I'd better ring the box office and tell them. We need to arrange a replacement and let them know to keep an eye out in case the other's been stolen."

Sheila shook her head and her shower of fair curls wobbled attractively around her pretty features.

"Joe, Brenda and I counted those tickets when they were first delivered to the café. There were seventy-one."

"I know, I know," he agreed. "But where's the odd one?"

Sheila shrugged, and there was something about the casual disregard of the gesture that caused Joe to wonder why he had never made a pass at her.

Brenda stepped from the dining room into the sweating air. She had abandoned her long skirt and blood red top in favour of off-white shorts and a thin white T-Shirt which showed her bra. The sight reminded Joe of precisely *why* he had never made a pass at Sheila. It was the same reason he had never made a pass at Brenda. The women did *everything* together. He couldn't hit on one because he'd never be able to get rid of the other.

Brenda sat alongside Sheila, and helped herself to a cup of tea. "Trouble at t' mill?" she asked, taking in Joe's irritated features.

"He's a ticket missing," said Sheila.

"He's been a ticket short of the full book for years," Brenda observed with a wicked grin.

"A ticket for tonight," Joe rasped.

With a sly smile, Sheila commented, "I think he's slipped it to Sarah Pringle and arranged to meet her after the show."

Joe growled something incomprehensible.

"Hang on. A ticket missing?" asked Brenda. "For the show? Tonight?"

Joe gave her a mock round of applause. "We're not talking about a ticket for the Orient Express, are we?" He held up his wedge of tickets. "Seventy seats for the Abba Tribute Show." Putting them down, he held up the clipboard. "Seventy-one names on the list. One of the tickets is missing."

"It's not missing," Brenda laughed. "I gave it to Eddie Dobson."

In an effort to quell his irritation, Joe stubbed out his cigarette, drank his tea and filled the cup from a stainless steel pot. Stirring milk and two sugars into the drink, he fumed at Brenda.

"I have just spent the last half hour going through this list more times than you've had hot dinners and now you turn up and have the brass nerve to tell me you gave a ticket to Eddie Dobson?"

Brenda ignored his tetchiness. Both women routinely ignored his liverish temper and here in Filey, he had no one upon whom he could vent it, unlike home where he could take it out on his nephew, Lee.

"We were in the bar last night, remember? I asked Eddie if he fancied a day in Scarborough or Bridlington, with us." Brenda took in Joe's livid gleam. "Well, the poor man lives all alone, he has no real friends, so I thought he might enjoy a day out with pleasant company."

Sheila gave a girlish giggle. "Joe? Pleasant company? Oh, Brenda, you can't half tell them."

The women dissolved into silly laughter while Joe ignored Sheila's dig at his infamous irritability. "You still haven't told me why you gave him the damn ticket."

Brenda choked back her laughter. "Well," she explained more soberly, "Eddie didn't want to come shopping with us. He said he planned to go out onto the Brigg and spend the day fishing. I reminded him that the bus leaves for Scarborough at half past six, but he said he'd be out on the Brigg all day and he might not make it back, so he asked if he could have his ticket and he'd make his own way to Scarborough and I said, okay. I didn't think you'd mind. In fact, I didn't think you'd *care*."

"I don't," Joe agreed, "but don't you think you should have told me?"

"I was going to, but we were boogying the night away and cleaning up in the lounge until the wee, small hours, and I forgot."

"Saints preserve me from middle-aged women trying to recapture their lost youth." Joe tutted, and gathered together his tickets and clipboard. "That clears up another mystery, too. The money I thought I saw Eddie giving to Mrs Pringle, last night." The women were mystified, and Joe revelled briefly in his superior, deductive skills. "He's going fishing for the day, what will he need?" He chuckled evilly at their puzzlement. "A packed lunch," he announced and their faces lit up.

"You mean you didn't ask her last night when you were getting acquainted on the terrace," Sheila asked in an effort to cover her admiration for Joe's sleuthing skills.

"Only short of going down on one knee and proposing, from what I saw," Brenda agreed.

Joe ignored their taunts. "Now we've cleared up some of our problems, we've only Nicola Leach's death to worry about, so let's make a move," suggested Joe. "You dragged

83

me to Filey, away from my business, and I'm supposed to be enjoying myself. So far, all I've done is sort out the rooms, sort out the meals, sort out the disco, sort out the tickets for tonight's show and wasted an hour trying to find a missing ticket that wasn't missing in the first place. So, where do you want to go? Bridlington or Scarborough?" Joe got to his feet.

Sheila's eyes were on the dining room door, a few yards away, where Sarah Pringle was in whispered conference with the police officer, both casting occasional glances in their direction. "I don't think we're going anywhere for the moment, Joe. It looks like this chap may want a word with us."

Joe and Brenda looked around as the policeman nodded his thanks to the manageress and strode out to join them. He carried his cap in one hand, the rucksack in the other, while the rod and line were tucked under his arm.

"Good morning, sir, madam, madam," he greeted them. "I'm PC Flowers, North Yorkshire Police."

"Really?" asked Joe. "I could have sworn you were auditioning for a TV show."

Flowers looked puzzled.

"Just ignore him," suggested Brenda. "He's always like that."

"Yes, madam," said Flowers. "May I ask, are you the organisers for the party from Sanford?"

"The Sanford 3rd Age Club," Sheila said grandly. "Joe's the chairman, I'm membership secretary and Brenda is the treasurer."

PC Flowers put his cap on the table behind them, dropped the rucksack on the paved terrace and rested the rod and line on it. Reaching into his breast pocket, he took out his notebook.

"Could I have your names and contact addresses, please?"

Brenda opened her mouth to comply, but Joe silenced her with an upraised hand. If anyone was going to deal with the law, it was him. "Names and addresses? What for?"

"I'll come to that, sir."

"Yes," Joe assured him. "You'll come to it now. I've met your sort of copper before. Give 'em your name and address and the next thing you know, they're turning up with Environmental Health trying to do you for dumping chip fat in the dustbins. Tell us what it's about."

Nonplussed by Joe's aggression, Flowers scratched his head. "Well, it's a bit sensitive, sir." He paused a moment, either marshalling his thoughts or plucking up courage. "Do you know a man named Eddie Dobson?"

"Eddie? Again? He's certainly the centre of attention just lately. Yeah, we know him. He's one of our members." Joe looked pointedly at Brenda. "He's one of our members with a ticket for the Abba show." He transferred his gaze, now more suspicious than angry, to the rucksack. "What about him?"

Flowers cleared his throat. "Well, sir, I'm afraid I have bad news. There's been an accident and he's missing. We believe he may have died."

Joe, still standing, ready to leave, sat down suddenly and quickly, Brenda gasped and Sheila said, "Oh, dear lord."

In the stunned silence following the announcement, Sarah Pringle arrived with a fresh tray of tea things, and Flowers tucked himself into the spare chair alongside Joe. Brenda poured four cups of tea from the pot, while Joe, his hand shaking, rolled another cigarette.

With tea dispensed, Flowers took control. "Now, ladies, sir, let's start again, eh? Your names and a contact address."

"I'm Joe Murray, this is Brenda Jump and that's Sheila Riley."

Flowers wrote quickly. "And a contact address or telephone number?"

"The Lazy Luncheonette, Doncaster Road, Sanford," said Sheila.

Flowers was confounded once more. "Lazy Luncheonette?"

"It used to be Joe's Café," said Joe. "My place. I changed the name four years ago when these two," he nodded at

Sheila and Brenda, "persuaded me to go upmarket. Here. I'll give you my card." He reached into his hip pocket, took out an old, shiny and battered brown leather wallet, and retrieved a business card from it.

Flowers studied the ornate lettering.

Joe Murray Catering
The Lazy Luncheonette
Britannia Parade
Doncaster Road, Sanford.
For all your catering needs.

Tucking the card under the elastic strap of his pocketbook, the policeman took a drink of tea. "Right. That's that sorted. May I ask, how well do you know Mr Dobson?"

"I don't," Joe confessed. "I've seen him a time or two at the weekly disco, and he's caused us some hassle these last few days because he wanted to come to Filey, but aside from that he liked to keep to himself."

"He has no relatives?"

Joe shrugged and puffed on his cigarette. "I neither know nor care."

"He hasn't," Sheila asserted with a disapproving glower at Joe. "I canvassed him when he first moved to Sanford. He came into the café and we got chatting. He wasn't a particularly chatty type, but I recall him telling me he'd just come out of the navy and he moved to Sanford to look for work. I persuaded him to join STAC."

Flowers frowned again. "Stack?"

"S-T-A-C," Brenda spelled the letters out. "The Sanford 3rd Age Club."

"Ah." Flowers made more notes.

Joe drew heavily on his cigarette. "So do we know what's happened?"

"Mr Dobson was fishing out on the Brigg, sir," reported the police officer, "and apparently slipped and fell in the sea. The currents are quite strong there, especially when the tide's on the ebb, as it is now. One of the other anglers raised the alarm, and the inshore lifeboat was called out, but by the time they got there, his body was probably washed out to sea. There were red smears on the rocks, which looked fresh, and may have been blood. We won't know about that until samples are analysed. If so, it seems likely that as he fell, he struck his head on the rocks and was dragged under. Without a body, he's officially posted as missing, but we're not hopeful of finding him and I think we can take it that he's dead."

Listening to Flowers, Joe recalled that he'd seen the inshore lifeboat rushing off across the waters, a long dinghy leaving a broad wake in its trail as it skipped over the surface like a stone across a pond.

"And no one saw nothing?" he asked.

"One or two of the other fishermen noticed him when he first arrived." Flowers consulted his notes again. "They described him as a tall gentleman dressed in baggy jeans and an overlarge T-shirt, carrying a wax jacket."

Joe shrugged and relit his cigarette. "I never saw him this morning, so I don't know how he was dressed. How can you be sure it was him?"

"Well, we're not, sir, but the bag has an identification label bearing his name." Flowers patted the rucksack. "When we checked the contents, we found the key to room 102 inside. The moment I asked Mrs Pringle, she knew who I meant and pointed me to you."

"A tragic accident," Sheila commented.

"It looks that way, madam. No one saw him actually fall, but one or two people heard him cry out. Obviously, by the time they got to his pitch, he was gone." The constable drank more tea. "Tell me, do you know if he was particularly worried or depressed about anything? I only ask because most anglers know how treacherous the rocks can be and they take extra caution when they're walking out to their pitches. An experienced angler would know to tread carefully, but if he had something on his mind, it could account for him slipping."

Joe shrugged. "Being divorced or separated is depressing, being divorced or separated and living in

Sanford is enough to make anyone suicidal. You don't think he jumped, do you?"

Flowers mirrored the shrug. "Anything's possible, sir. We don't think there are any suspicious circumstances surrounding the incident, and we certainly don't believe there was anyone else involved. My inquiries are merely routine." The officer's brow creased. "You said a moment or two ago, sir, that Mr Dobson seemed to be the centre of attention. Could I ask what you meant by that?"

Joe laid a beady eye on Brenda. "We were talking about him last night, at the disco. He was a bit of a wallflower, and we're going to Scarborough tonight, for the Abba Tribute show, but he didn't want to come with the rest of us on the bus. He was gonna make his own way there."

A solemn silence fell over them, each lost to their own thoughts.

Sheila broke it. "There was no one on shore who saw anything?"

Flowers shook his head. "He was on the north side of the Brigg, madam, the side that looks towards Scarborough. When the lifeboat got there, they reported a few people walking along Gristhorpe Sands, a good half mile away, and our lads are out there now, but I haven't heard anything yet." Flowers finished his tea. "Could I ask a favour? I need to leave his personal effects with someone so they can be passed on either to him, should he return, or to whatever family he may have had. Would you mind taking them?"

Brenda nodded. "Of course."

Flowers stood up and tucked his notebook away. "Thank you, madam, sir, madam. I'll take my leave of you. And please accept my, er, condolences, I suppose. It sounds as if you people were the closest he came to friends."

The policeman left and the three STAC members sat in brief silence.

"What an awful thing to happen. First Nicola and now Eddie." Tears welled in Brenda's eyes. "Oh dear. I think I'm going to..." She reached into her bag for a tissue and Sheila patted her comfortingly on the shoulder.

88

Joe looked away. Women who cried always made him feel guilty.

"Cheer up, Brenda," Sheila encouraged. "After all, we don't know for sure that he's dead, do we?"

Joe almost commented, but caught himself in time. That cop was sure Eddie was dead, and so was Joe.

His eye fell on the rucksack, a large affair of woven polyester in drab, army green, with an identification label set into the front pocket. Written by an erratic hand, the label read *Eddie Dobson*. Its various pockets bulged and there was a small, folding stool strapped to it.

Shifting the tea tray and cups out of the way, Joe plucked the rucksack from the flagstones, grunting with the unexpected weight, and dropped it on the table in the space he had just created.

Unzipping the main compartment, he removed a sturdy, black case and flipped open the lid revealing bite alarms and their leads. Pushing that to one side, he investigated further, taking out packs of lures, hooks, spare lines, a high-speed reel, and other angling items, until the compartment was empty.

A frown creased his already wrinkled brow. Turning the carryall round, he opened the two side pockets, took out a pair of chain mail gloves from one and a wallet of pirks from the other. His frown deepened. Slowly, methodically, he went through every compartment in the bag, and finally sat down again, chewing thoughtfully on his cigarette.

"That's odd." His cigarette had gone out. Relighting it, he asked, "Brenda, did you say he was going to be out on the Brigg all day?"

"That's what the man told me," she replied, "and you, yourself, said he paid Sarah Pringle for a packed lunch."

Joe's puzzlement increased in proportion to the number of wrinkles on his forehead. "Yeah, and that's what's odd."

Sheila and Brenda exchanged knowing glances. They had heard that tone before in Joe's voice and it usually spelled a mystery.

"What's odd?" ask Sheila.

"I've been in catering all my life. There isn't nothing I don't know about it. Now here's a man who's gonna spend all day sitting on wet rocks dangling his rod and line in the sea. He's gonna be out there, over half a mile from land, a good mile from the nearest shops and yet, look."

He tilted the bag forward so they could see its contents.

"No packed lunch. No thermos, not even a bottle of water or a bar of chocolate. Not a single item of food. It's almost as if he knew he wouldn't be coming back."

Chapter Eight

The two women greeted Joe's announcement with cautious stares. Drying her eyes, Brenda helped herself to another cup of tea, slopping milk across the plastic table and the upper flap of the open rucksack. Sheila fussed over the spillage, mopping it with a serviette, while Joe chewed on his cigarette stub and studied the carryall's contents spread across the tabletop.

"Maybe he already ate them," Brenda suggested. "Or maybe someone took them after he fell in."

"Oh naturally," Joe sneered. "You see someone fall in the sea and the first thing you think is, 'right, I'm having his sandwiches.' Talk bloody sense, woman."

"Perhaps," Sheila ventured, "he intended coming back from the Brigg to get something to eat."

Joe waved a frantic arm at the searing day and clear sky. The sun glistened on his leathery skin, and added weight to his irritation. "So what you're saying is, he goes out for eight hours' fishing, it's a scorching hot day, and yet he doesn't even have a bottle of water with him? It doesn't make sense. And have you ever walked out onto the Brigg?"

Sheila nodded. "Years ago, when the children were young and Peter and I brought them here on holiday."

"Then you should know how bad it is underfoot," said Joe. "It's a good half-mile from the shore, and like that cop said, the rocks are jagged, slippery, and difficult to get across. It's not the kind of journey you wanna make twice or three times in a day. You think he's gonna walk out, walk back to get a brew and a butty, walk back again, walk to the shore for a pee and another brew a couple of hours later? Naw. He knew he wasn't coming back, and that says he was out to commit hari kari."

"I think you'll find it's called hara-kiri," Sheila corrected him, "and in Japanese it's a vulgar term for the practice of seppuku."

Joe snorted. "I've got a puzzle on my hands and she gives me a lecture on Oriental etiquette. Whatever you want to call it, it doesn't make any sense. Everything he did tells us he was going to commit suicide, but if he was going to top himself, why did he pester Brenda for his ticket?"

Brenda blushed. "Well, he didn't really pester me. It just… sort of… came up in the conversation. At the disco, last night."

Joe understood at once and fumed. "I had it right the first time, didn't I? You hit on him and nagged the pants off him. What did you say?" Joe put on a high, squeaky voice, supposedly imitating Brenda. "I'll get you a seat next to me at the show." In his normal voice, he went on, "the bloke got so fed up of it, he asked if he could have his ticket so he could make his own way there and keep away from your clutches."

Brenda's rose colour deepened. "Something like that."

Joe shook his head and began to scan the bag's contents once more. "No wonder the poor sod felt like committing suicide. With Sheila nagging him to join the club and you trying to get him between your sheets, I'm surprised he didn't throw himself under the bus before we left Sanford."

Brenda took instant umbrage. "For your information, I wasn't trying to get him between my bed-sheets. What do you take me for?"

"Man mad."

"I am not man mad," Brenda defended herself. "I'm just young for my years."

Joe disagreed again. "You're a randy old widow."

"I am not old."

"What the hell makes you think he'd be interested in you, anyway?"

Brenda stared defiantly. "I knew about him and Nicola, and I may not be in her league, but I could give her a run for her money."

Joe suppressed further comment and concentrated more finely on the bag's contents. He scanned them, checked the bag again, looked through the collection of fishing accessories, opened up the plastic case of bite alarms and checked that too, before turning his attention back to the bag, running his hand around the interior to feel for hidden compartments.

"What are you looking for, Joe?" asked Brenda, determined to get back at him. "His will?"

"You're a woman," Joe replied, still scanning the items. "You wouldn't understand."

"That," Sheila disapproved, "is sexist."

Without looking up from his search, Joe said, "Don't use that word in front of Brenda. Don't use any word that has the letters s-e-x in them. You'll distract her."

Sheila giggled. "Good job she doesn't come from Middlesex then, isn't it?"

Brenda took the jibes in good part and chuckled fatly. Smacking her lips, she looked hungrily at Joe. "One night with me, Joe Murray, and…"

Joe cut her off as he sat down again. "You know, I've never been into fishing, but this bag of tricks is all wrong. There's no bait and no knife."

"Knife?"

He nodded, sucked on his cigarette and found that once more, it had gone out. "Every fisherman carries a good, sharp knife." Raising his backside slightly off the chair, he fished into his trouser pocket for the Zippo lighter. "You need it for gutting the fish, you need it for cutting away tangled lines. That kind of thing. A good, fisherman's knife makes a Swiss army knife look as common as a hacksaw blade." He lit the cigarette.

"Well perhaps it was in his pocket," suggested Sheila.

"Could be," Joe conceded, "but like I said, there's no bait. What do you think he planned? The fish would come up and shout 'take me, I'm next'? You don't go fishing without giving the little tykes something to chew on. I'm telling you, this guy was no fisherman. He just wanted to look like one so he could throw himself off the Brigg." Crushing out his cigarette, he went on, "This stuff looks brand new, too. Yesterday, when we were wandering round Filey, I spotted him going into a fishing tackle shop and…" He slapped a hand to his forehead. "Oh my God, that's it."

The women were surprised. "What?" Brenda demanded. "What's it?"

"Remember something was bothering me yesterday? Well that was it." The excitement of a successful deduction building in him, Joe rolled a fresh cigarette. "When I spoke to him in the Miner's Arms the other night, I commented on how keen he was to come to Filey, and he said he was a fisherman. Yet, when he got of the bus yesterday, he had only the one suitcase with him. If he was a fisherman, where was his gear?"

"In his case?" Brenda suggested, more in hope than conviction.

"Brenda," Sheila said, "you do not pack an eight foot fishing rod in a three foot suitcase."

"Correct," Joe agreed. "These are expensive toys, and even the sort that break down into short sections won't fit into a case. So he bought it all yesterday, and looking at it, he hadn't much of a clue what he was buying. He was no angler, which means he had another reason for wanting to be on the Filey bus." He stared meaningfully at them. "Perhaps he was so desperate to be on the bus that he arranged for Nicola Leach to be mowed down."

The two women greeted this announcement with shocked stares.

Joe was unmoved. "Think about it. You've just reminded us, Brenda, that Knickers-off had a bit of a thing with him. He's been pestering to get on the Filey trip since the day he joined the club. Knickers-off gets it, and the same evening he's there chasing her seat."

He stared out across Filey Bay from Speeton Point a few miles to the south to Carr Naze and the Brigg a mile or so north of them. Carr Naze jutted out half a mile, a low hill, dropping off sharply at the seaward end where it became the Brigg and continued for several hundred more yards barely scratching the surface of the sea. At the landward end, the bay waters were flat, mirror calm, but beyond the Brigg, the sea splashed and frothed over the projecting rocks, and anglers could be seen perched among the rock pools waiting patiently for that telltale waggle of the float to signal a bite.

The fine, sandy beach was busy with families, children building sandcastles, chasing Frisbees, paddling in the safe shallow waters. Along the smart promenade, groups of people made their way slowly along in the baking sun, and out to sea a fishing coble plodded towards the bay, bobbing on the slight swell.

"Why would he be so desperate to come here?"

Sheila's question brought Joe back from his mental impasse. "What? I don't know. We need more information on Eddie Dobson and I think we should start at the shop where he bought this gear." He gestured at the rucksack.

"This is all a bit, er, airy fairy," Brenda commented.

Sheila agreed but only so far. "It does seem odd, but I think Joe is extrapolating too much when he links Nicola's death to Eddie's."

Brenda grinned. "I didn't know you could extrapolate, Joe."

"Yeah, well, I have hidden depths."

Sheila half turned in her seat and like Joe, she took in the view, but concentrated her gaze on the far reaches of the Brigg where the anglers sat. She could see several men, police divers presumably, busying themselves at the water's edge. "Perhaps," she suggested, "the knife and bait are still out there. On the Brigg."

Joe followed her gaze. "Yeah, and maybe they're in the pockets of those navy blue uniforms."

The moment he said it, Joe regretted it. Inspector Peter Riley had died suddenly and unexpectedly of a double heart attack five years previously. Sheila had put it down to the pressure of modern policing. The widow rounded on Joe, her soft brown eyes blazing, and he became humbly apologetic.

"Sorry, Sheila."

She wagged a disapproving finger at him. "The vast majority of police officers are honest, Joe. Peter was, and I've no doubts that constable Flowers and his colleagues are too."

Pouring oil on troubled waters, Brenda reminded them, "We don't actually know that Eddie did commit suicide, do we? Like Sheila said, we don't actually know that he's dead."

Her intervention was unnecessary. Having committed the *faux pas*, Joe would take Sheila's rebuke without response. He would not, however, accept Brenda's mindless optimism.

"Right, so what do we have? A guy who's been desperate to get to Filey with the club ever since he joined, and the minute he gets here, what does he do? He wanders a mile out towards Belgium, short of food, water and essential tackle, carrying newly bought fishing gear that wouldn't hook a goldfish from a bowl. Now assuming the cops haven't nicked it all, what could he have been doing? I know; he was spying on Scarborough. He was in the navy, wasn't he? But do we know which navy? Maybe he worked for the Russians, and he wanted to keep his eye on the Yorkshire Belle. Make sure she wasn't carrying sixteen inch guns on the foredeck."

"Grow up, Joe."

"No, you grow up. Eddie Dobson is dead. That's for sure. The cop didn't want to say it because he's not allowed to. Isn't that right, Sheila?" Joe paused to let Sheila nod. "I'm not saying for sure that he committed suicide, I'm simply saying it doesn't add up. None of it. And when I think about the circumstances of Nicola's death, it makes it all the more suspicious. It may all be perfectly innocent. He may not be involved in the hit and run, and he may have had a legitimate reason for going out there like he did, and it may have been an accident." He laid a gimlet eye on Brenda. "Maybe he was just getting away from you. All I'm saying is, he was no more a fisherman than me and I think the plod ought to be told, because for my money it really does look like murder back in Sanford followed by suicide here." He paused a moment. "Why don't we go into town, check with the fishing tackle shop, then go out onto the Brigg, and see what's going on?"

Neither woman looked particularly enthusiastic.

"I don't think the law would let us," said Sheila.

Joe waved at the far off Brigg. "They're not stopping the other fishermen, are they? This is England, remember. A free country. We can go where we like. Come on. It'll liven the weekend up."

Sheila and Brenda were saved the immediate decision when Sarah Pringle stepped out of the dining room and onto the terrace.

"May I just take those tea things?" she asked.

The two women stood up and back, away from the table. Joe hurriedly repacked Dobson's belongings back in the carryall.

"I was terribly sorry to hear about your friend," Sarah said.

"It's frightening, isn't it," gossiped Brenda. "I always say you never know what's round the corner."

Joe snorted but suppressed a sarcastic rejoinder about lorries and buses. "Sarah…" he trailed off under an amused stare from Brenda. "Mrs Pringle, did you see Eddie this morning?"

"He was the gentleman who ordered the packed lunch?"

With a smug grin at Sheila and Brenda, Joe silently congratulated himself on his perspicacity. "The very man," he declared.

"I didn't see him this morning," said the manageress. "He ordered his lunch yesterday, but he never came to collect it. However, I served seventy-one breakfasts to your party this morning, Mr Murray, so he must have been there."

Noting that Sarah employed the same level of formality as she had when addressing him as Chair of the Sanford 3rd Age Club, rather than the informal level of the previous night on the terrace, Joe racked his memory, trying to recall whether he had seen Eddie at breakfast. Then he remembered that he had been busy counting the theatre tickets and checking them against the passenger list.

He pressed Sarah. "And there's nowhere out on the Brigg where a man could get food or drink?"

The woman nodded to the view across the bay. "You can see for yourself. There's nothing beyond Coble Landing." She picked up the tray of tea things.

Joe stayed her. "Mrs Pringle, what would you say about a man who went out onto the Brigg for a day's fishing and took nothing to eat or drink."

"In this weather?" Her face was prim and stern. She looked sharply at Joe. "I'd say he was either out of his mind or on a very severe diet. Excuse me." She disappeared with the tray.

"See," Joe challenged his companions. "Even she thinks there's something odd about Eddie if he went out there without sandwiches and a flask. We should talk to the police about this."

Sheila tentatively agreed. "It does look as if he intended to commit suicide, and there's certainly something odd about it all, even if the link to Nicola is only spurious. Perhaps Joe's right and the police should be made aware." She looked to Brenda for agreement.

"Then let's go for a walk along Filey Brigg," Joe persuaded them. "If nothing else, it's cheaper than shopping in Scarborough."

Brenda sighed. "What do we have to do to get you to spend some of that money, Joe?"

Joe collected Eddie Dobson's belongings. "I've told you before. Money isn't for spending. It's for counting by candlelight at night as you eat your bowl of gruel. I'll just take these up to my room."

"Joe," suggested Sheila as they stepped back into the darker and cooler air of the dining room, "hadn't we better get Eddie's cases and clothing out of his room? The hotel may want it vacated."

"You can't smoke that in there," Brenda warned before Joe could answer Sheila.

Joe paused just inside the doorway, and threw his cigarette back out onto the paved terrace. With an impatient, 'tsk' Brenda picked it up and left it to burn out on an ashtray.

"Sheila," she said, "we don't really know that he's dead."

"No, he's dead," Joe asserted, "and Sheila is right. We should pack his cases." After a moment of thought, he moderated his opinion. "Even if he has survived, he's likely to be in hospital for a day or three, so we still need to get his stuff together. Come on. I'll have a word with Mrs Pringle."

Shuffling the rucksack to a more comfortable position on his shoulder, he walked through the dining room and into reception, where Mrs Pringle was on the telephone while her son, Kieran sat watching TV.

"Yes, sir?" the young man greeted Joe.

"Sorry to be a pain, but we thought you might need Eddie Dobson's room clearing out." Joe gave short, sharp, cynical laugh. "He's not gonna need it no more, is he? I wonder if I could have the key? We'll get his gear together and move it into my room."

Kieran vacillated a moment and looked to his mother for guidance.

"I'm terribly sorry to hear that, sir," said Mrs Pringle into the telephone, casting a glance in her son's direction. "Leave it with me and I'll get it arranged for you." She put the receiver down, gave Joe a surly half smile and raised her eyebrows at Kieran, who proceeded to explain Joe's request. Picking the key from the rack behind her, she smiled again in a sweet and wholly false manner. "I'm sorry, sir, but there are times when I despair of him." She nodded to indicate her son.

"You don't need to explain, Mrs Pringle," Joe assured her. "My brother's kid works for me and he's about as much use as chocolate teapot."

She handed over the key to room 102. "If you'd be so kind as to let me have it back when you've finished."

"No problem," he agreed. "Twenty minutes."

Sheila and Brenda emerged from the dining room as Joe made his way to the lift. Cramming into it, Sheila pressed the button for the first floor, and a minute later they emerged onto a broad, richly carpeted corridor, their footsteps muffled in that curious silence that was the hallmark of hotel landings.

Along the corridor, Joe turned the key in the lock and they stepped in.

Aside from a suitcase resting on top of the wardrobe, there was nothing to indicate that the room had been occupied. The bed was neatly made, and when Joe checked the small bathroom, it too was pristine, shaving gear and toothbrush neatly stacked in tumblers on the washbasin.

He took down a bottle of *Givenchy Pour Homme* aftershave lotion, removed the cap and sniffed at it. He recoiled in disgust. "Expensive crap," he muttered. "Give me *Old Spice* any day."

While Sheila opened the single wardrobe and Brenda concentrated on the three drawers of the dresser, Joe dragged the suitcase down onto the bed, and opened it up. He allowed the women to begin packing Eddie Dobson's few items of clothing, while he strode to the window and looked out over the rear of the hotel.

It was exactly the same as the view from his room, one floor above, and the only difference he could see now was a fire extinguisher left near the gates. As he looked down, one of the chambermaids, the same blonde he had seen from his window 24 hours previously, came out, tossed a bag into the large capacity bins, and looked up at the hotel. Joe almost waved to her, but changed his mind. That kind of gesture was too easy to misinterpret.

Instead, he cast his gaze further out looking on a typical English seaside town on a typical, English summer Saturday.

Not typical, Joe reminded himself. A member of their party was lost, presumed dead, drowned in the fast currents off the headland, and with each passing moment it looked more like suicide.

About to turn from the window, a glint caught his eye down in the corner, behind the net curtains. The nets were well bunched near the bottom of the window frame, but sunlight reflected from a window at the rear had picked out whatever was hidden behind them.

Pulling the curtains to one side, Joe found a key and at first assumed that it would fit the window locks, but there were no locks on the windows.

He picked it up and examined it. A double deadlock door key on a rabbit's foot fob. Joe glanced back at the room door, recalled that the lock had been a five-lever mortise, not a double deadlock. Why would anyone leave a door key on the windowsill, hidden behind the curtains? Was it anything to do with Eddie Dobson?

Logic told him that it must have belonged to a previous guest. Eddie Dobson's keys were somewhere under the waters of the North Sea in his jacket. They had to be. They weren't in the fishing basket.

"That's the lot," said Sheila, shutting the lid of the suitcase and fastening the straps.

Her voice snapped Joe out of his reverie. He slipped the key into his trouser pocket and, striding to the bed, picked up the case.

"Light," he commented.

"He didn't have much with him," said Brenda. "Pitiful really. Just a few items of clothing, a couple of paperback books. The sum total of his life. Oh dear…"

Tears pooled in the corner of her eyes and she sat down on the bed, suddenly unable to control her emotions. Sheila sat with her, putting a comforting arm around her shoulder.

Joe stood by feeling helpless and embarrassed. He picked up the fishing basket. "We'd better get moving."

They came out of the room and to the lift where Sheila caught her leg on an empty fire extinguisher bracket.

"I thought hotels were supposed to have fire extinguishers in their proper place," she grumbled, rubbing at the red mark it had left on her leg.

101

"It's out in the back yard," Joe told her. "I just saw it."

"Then someone should remind Mrs Pringle of it," Sheila griped.

"Leave it to Joe," Brenda grinned. "Oh, we heard you before you corrected yourself. Calling her Sarah. Barely known her twelve hours and already on first name terms. What were you up to last night, Joe?"

"I was praying," he replied. "I needed guidance on how I'm supposed to deal with an irritable widow and a sex mad one."

Chapter Nine

"Thank you, Mr Murray." Sarah took the key and hung it back on her board.

"No problem." Joe said. "I always take personal responsibility for keys. Mrs Pringle, when we were in the disco last night, I noticed Eddie handing you something."

Sarah's ears coloured slightly. "He was paying me for the packed lunch."

Joe gave her a crooked smile. "I'm sorry. I didn't mean that to sound like it did. You didn't know him, then?"

Sarah shook her head.

"With everything happening I've been thinking about Eddie a lot this last hour."

"Obviously." Sarah appeared mollified. "I said out on the terrace that he'd ordered a packed lunch and he paid me for it last night."

"But he never collected it?" Joe asked.

"I believe I said that out on the terrace, too." Sarah's hard features narrowed. "Is there something wrong?"

"Yeah, there is." Joe hastened to reassure her. "Oh, it's not you. It's Eddie. Why would he order a packed lunch, then not bother picking it up? Especially considering he was at breakfast this morning... so we're told."

"All I know, Mr Murray, is what I told you earlier. I served seventy-one breakfasts this morning. He must have been there."

"And you didn't know him?"

"I just said, I've never met Edward Dobson in my life," Sarah replied.

"Yeah, right, thanks." Joe turned to leave, and then thought again. "Oh, Mrs Pringle."

She had already moved on to other duties and turned back with a sigh. "What is it, Mr Murray?"

"I'm in the same business as you. Catering. I run a workman's café in Sanford."

"Yes, you told me that, too."

"Yeah, well, it's just that I was looking out through Eddie's window while we were packing away his gear, and I noticed you had a dud fire extinguisher stood in the back yard." He grinned crookedly. "I don't know what your fire people are like but if Sanford is anything to go by, they'll book you for that."

She clucked. "Those engineers are as bad as the dray men. It's a replacement. One of ours was taken for servicing yesterday and he didn't have a spare. He must have dropped it off early this morning. Thank you, Mr Murray. I'll have Kieran attend to it."

Satisfied that he had done his duty by a fellow business proprietor, Joe stepped out into the heat of the morning, and joined his companions for a stroll into Filey.

They skirted up the side of the hotel and round to the rear, where a dark blue Transit van was now parked. Joe checked the roof rack as they approached the rear. No ladders.

Passing the van, the driver's door suddenly opened and Joe almost walked into it.

Billy Pringle climbed out full of apologies. "Hey up. Sorry, marrer. I shoulda checked me mirrors."

"No problem, Billy," Joe reassured him. "Was that you pottering about at five this morning?"

"Could have been," Billy agreed. "I was down the wholesale markets for half past three. Fresh veg for the dinners, you know."

"Right," Joe nodded. "And you need ladders for that?"

"Ladders?" Billy frowned. "Oh, those. No, I borrowed 'em last week from a mate." He threw an arm up at the hotel. "Gutters needed clearing. I took 'em back this morning while I was on me way to Scarborough. Why? Did I wake you?"

Joe nodded. "Noisy little bugger, your van."

Billy grinned. "Sorry, mate."

"Ah, don't worry about it. I'm used to being up at that time of day. Catch you later, Billy."

"Aye. When I've caught up on me sleep."

With a smile, Joe hurried on to catch up with his friends.

Making their way into Filey, Sheila and Brenda walked ahead of him, checking out the shop windows. Sheila had also changed from her skirt and blouse to a pair of shorts and a T-Shirt, and Joe envied them. He wished he'd brought shorts along. He spent a little time looking at the options in various shops, but as the price of umbrellas rose on the threat of rain, so the cost of even a pair of football shorts had gone up with the heat wave, and even though his two friends pressured him, he would not open his wallet.

"I didn't come here to get mugged by opportunist shopkeepers," he told them.

"You're a shopkeeper… of a kind," Brenda pointed out.

"Yes, but I don't hike the price of cans in this weather, or meat pies in winter."

Ambling further along the street, while the two women pressed on, checking out souvenir shops, women's clothing and shoes, Joe paused at Irwin's Hardware and Angling Supplies and puffed at a cigarette.

Looking over the window display, the shop had more to do with angling than hardware. Rods were stocked upright in racks, leaning towards the window, and beneath them were alarm sets, lures, a selection of reels and sundry items of clothing and luggage.

Crushing his cigarette on a wall-mounted stubber, Joe stepped into the shop to the double trill of the doorbell.

The interior was more cluttered than the window. Joe found himself walking beneath hanging displays of clothing and confronted by more racks of rods, displays of reels, lines, lures, and sitting incongruously amongst them all, bolts for doors, packs of wood screws, budget priced tools and more expensive ones.

He eyed a rucksack similar to the one Flowers had left

with them at the Beachside. *Greys Apollo: ideal for the serious angler. £44.99,* read the sign beneath it.

"Morning, squire. Another grand one, eh?"

A large jovial face greeted Joe when he turned to the counter. Joe judged him to be in his fifties, his skin bronzed and weather-beaten, hands like shovels, broad and powerful shoulders hidden beneath a thin jumper. Like Joe, the man had no hint of a paunch, but unlike Joe, he was immense, not small and wiry.

"How are you doing?" Joe greeted.

"Long as this weather keeps up, I'm deeing fahn, me old mate. What can I do for you? Looking for a bitta tackle, are you?"

Joe shook his head. "The only thing I know about fish is how to deep fry them." He smiled to show he was only joking. "No. Fact is, you had a guy in here yesterday who bought an awful lot of tackle."

The genial smile disappeared and a look of forbidding came to the grey eyes. "What goes on between me and mah customers is nobody's business but ours."

"I appreciate that," Joe said, "but the cops have just been to see me. This bloke fell off the Brigg early this morning. Plod reckons he drowned."

"Do they now? Well, all the same, it's no business of yours what he was doing here yesterday."

Joe switched tack. "I guess you're Mr Irwin."

"Jonny Irwin."

You been trading here long?"

"Thirty years."

"And you obviously know your stuff."

"You'll not find anyone in this town who knows more about angling off the Brigg, but it's still nought to do with…"

Joe cut Irwin off. "The bloke's name was Eddie Dobson. He told me he was a keen fisherman. Would you describe him like that?"

"He was a customer. That's it."

"Yeah, I get that, but you saw what he bought, and when

106

I looked it over, my guess is he'd never been near a fishing rod in his life."

The eyes narrowed further, the mouth twisted into a menacing grimace. "I dain't khah what all this has to do wi' you. What goes on between me and mah customers is nay concern of yours. Now if tha's not here to buy summat, get out."

"Don't get your knickers in a twist," Joe said. "I'm just trying to clear up the death of one of my members."

Irwin frowned. "Members?"

Digging out his wallet, Joe took a club card and handed it over. "The Sanford 3rd Age Club. I'm Chairman. You should consider joining something like that, Irwin. It does wonders for your social skills."

There was no mistaking the blaze of fury in Irwin's eyes. "Get out."

"I'm going," Joe agreed, "but before I do, tell me how many fish Dobson was likely to catch when you didn't sell him any bait."

"I dain't sell bait. Now bugger off afore I throw thee aht."

Joe shrugged. "I'll be back. Or if not me, I reckon the police will when I tell them what I know."

Irwin was not impressed. "And I'll tell them the same as I've telled thee. It's nobody's business but mine."

Joe ignored the hubris and walked out into the sunshine.

Looking up and down the street, he spotted Sheila and Brenda on the far corner at the junction with Murray Street. Wondering idly whether he had ancestors from the Filey area who were responsible for the street name, and coming to the conclusion that it was unlikely, he caught up with his friends.

"Any joy?" Brenda asked.

"Yes," he replied. "I've found the perfect bloke for running the Lazy Luncheonette when I'm not there."

In answer to their quizzical stares, he gave them a rundown of what had transpired in Irwin's.

Sheila pursed her lips. "Hmm. It sounds is if you're right

about him being a match for you, but I see nothing suspicious in his behaviour. Trader, customer relationships are confidential."

"Yes, well, we'll have to see what the law thinks of that, won't we."

"How do you mean, Joe?"

"I think we should take that walk along the Brigg and report to the police."

***

The light breeze ruffled Sheila's hair, but did little to suppress the searing heat of mid-morning, and by the time they had reached the Beach Café, a quarter of a mile from the town, they were all feeling the strain.

The two women sat on a bench, looking out to sea, getting their breath back, while Joe mooched, eager to be moving on.

"It's all right for you," complained Brenda. "You were drinking baby beer last night." She mopped her brow with a handkerchief. "I was on proper drink."

Sheila sprayed a dash of *Chanel* on her wrists. "It's all that excellent cooking at the Lazy Luncheonette. It keeps Joe fit, doesn't it Joe?"

Joe snorted. "Yeah, yeah, very funny. At this rate, by the time we get to the Brigg, the tide will be in."

He wandered a few yards to the next bench, reading the brass commemoration plate on it, then returned to them and studied that plate, before back tracking to the previous bench and reading that.

"Town full of goody-goodies," he grumbled as he rejoined the women. "Edna Taylor, Albert Pennig, Ronald Beckton."

"What are you moaning at, Joe?" demanded Sheila.

"The benches." He waved at them. "Each of these seats is dedicated to some old fuddy-duddy who lived in this town."

"It's a common enough practice," said Sheila. "Some of the benches in Sanford Memorial Park are dedicated to former councillors and charity workers."

Brenda chuckled and got to her feet. "There won't be one dedicated to Joe then, will there? His idea of charity is letting someone put a collection box on the counter, and then emptying it into his till."

"I do my share," said Joe, leading off towards The Landings. "I keep you two off the streets, don't I?"

"I could take offence at that, Joe," said Brenda. "I've never been on the streets."

Joe opened his mouth to deliver the obvious comment, but changed his mind and walked on ahead of them.

The smart, refurbished promenade, with its neatly flagged paths and carefully tended lawns, ended where the road turned sharp left back into the town, and Coble Landing began. Here was a line of shops and cafés, the lifeboat station, and a sharply inclined concrete path leading down to the beach.

It was a busy little area. Many people milled around the shops, bars and cafés, and cars clogged some of the access, amongst them several 4x4s, including an ageing Land Rover.

"No bull bars, Joe," Sheila said, when he examined the front grille.

Joe looked over the paintwork, and agreed with her. "No. You're right, but there's fresh paint and a dent in the front bumper that's been straightened out.

"You gonna make me an offer for it, or are you thinking of nicking it?"

Joe looked up from the front of the vehicle into a familiar face. A large, round face, the skin bronzed and weather-beaten, huge hands, broad and powerful shoulders hidden under a thick, fisherman's jumper. No hint of a middle-aged spread, and he was huge.

"Do I know you?" Joe asked.

"Ah dain't think so. Ah'm just wondering what you're doing looking at mah motor."

Joe refused to be intimidated. "Do you have a brother? Runs the fishing tackle shop in town?"

"Our Jonny? What of him?"

"You obviously both went to the same charm school."

"Now listen, smartarse…"

"Two days ago," Joe interrupted, "a vehicle like yours ran over a friend of ours and killed her. Yesterday, your brother sold a load of fishing tackle to another friend of ours, and he fell in the sea and drowned this morning. What have you got against the Sanford 3rd Age Club?"

"I dain't knah what you're talking about. Now get away from my truck."

Joe walked on after his companions. Looking over his shoulder, he warned, "The cops will get to know everything we know."

"Joe, stop it," his friend urged. "People are staring."

"If they don't have anything better to do with their time, let 'em stare," Joe insisted.

A stout man stood in their way. Not much taller than Joe, rotund, a flat cap covering his thin hair, he was dressed in bright orange overalls. "Your lass is right, matey."

"What do you mean?" Joe demanded.

"You shouldn't look for trouble with Ivan Irwin or his brother. They have a habit of dealing with it in an old fashioned way."

"Well someone should tell them they shouldn't look for trouble with Joe Murray. He has a habit of calling on his friends in the police force to help him out."

Brenda tugged at his shirt and they wandered on.

A couple of rusty old tractors stood by, festooned with strong chains and sets of single axles on which the fishing cobles would be rested so they could be towed from the water's edge to the landing.

Joe and his companions made their way down to the beach where they paused again, to get their breath back.

"What do you make of all that?" Joe asked.

"That fisherman?" Sheila asked. "A nasty piece of work. That's why I told you to come away. There are times, Joe, when I think you deserve a good smack on the legs, but I wouldn't want to see you end up in hospital after getting into a fight with a man like that."

Another tractor was out in the shallows, the driver hooking his chain to an incoming coble, while the fisherman stacked his catch in ice boxes in the prow.

"And you were asking for it, Joe," Brenda said as the aged vehicle slowly hauled the boat from the water and across the sands. "Accusing him of running Knickers-off down, like that."

"I didn't actually accuse him," Joe said as the tractor laboured up the ramp.

"As good as," Sheila countered. "We're eighty miles from Sanford. What on earth makes you think he would have been there on Tuesday night?"

"He annoyed me," Joe declared. "Now are we gonna get a move on?"

They set off once more for the most northerly point of the beach and the landward end of the Carr Naze.

From there, a rough path led along the base of the cliff until they reached the spur of rocks thrusting out into the sea.

"Interesting legend behind the Brigg," said Sheila taking Joe's hand as she stepped between the treacherous rocks and intermittent pools of water. "They say that the Devil dropped his hammer into the sea while he was making the ridge," she gestured up at the towering cliff. "Then he dipped his hand into the sea to get the hammer back, and when he pulled his hand out, he found he'd picked up a fish instead and shouted, 'Ha, Dick', and that's how the Haddock got its name."

Helping Brenda across a difficult patch of rock, Joe tutted. "Where do you get this twaddle?"

"It's legend, Joe," Sheila insisted. "Myth. Fireside stories from the days before TV, radio and newspapers."

Joe was not convinced. "Well, if you ask me, it was an insurance fiddle. The Devil claiming for a lost hammer that was hidden in the back of his van."

Both women laughed.

From the far end of the Brigg, where Constable Flowers

and a couple of colleagues were stationed, keeping back sightseers, they had a fine view of Gristhorpe Sands, Cayton Bay and, seven miles to the north, Scarborough with its harbour and prominent lighthouse. To the south, they could now see the cliffs at the furthest point of Flamborough Head, and looking back the way they had come, Filey sat slightly north of centre of the fine, sandy bay.

A number of anglers were still fishing on the south, Filey side of the Brigg, but Joe noticed instantly that there were none on the north side; not just in the area where Eddie had gone into the sea and where the police now kept people back, but all along the length of the spur, there were no anglers.

"Better catches on the other side, sir," Flowers explained when Joe asked. "You can fish this side, but the waters are fast and your chances of a bite are a lot slimmer. Usually only really skilled anglers fish this side. On the south side, you're inside the breakwater formed by the Brigg, and the fish come there to feed." He waved at the north side in general. "But to be honest, we have divers down there, and we don't want anglers snagging them."

"Sounds like another fireside tale for the kids before radio," muttered Joe logging the information in his agile brain.

"Sir?"

"Nothing. It's just that a lot of things don't add up, Constable, and I think you're possibly dealing with a suicide."

Busy wiping mossy weed from his boots, Flowers looked sharply up at Joe. "What makes you say that?"

Patiently, Joe explained his findings and conclusions. Flowers listened with equal patience, occasionally asking questions to clarify one point or another, and when Joe had finished, he ruminated on the matter for a few moments.

Eventually, he said, "I can see where you're coming from, sir, but it's largely circumstantial. I'd need more concrete evidence than that before confirming suicide. But I will make a note of it all in my report. The CID bods can make their minds up whether they want to investigate further."

"I tried asking around at Irwin's tackle shop in the town, but he gave me the bum's rush."

Flowers laughed. "Ivan or Jonny?"

"Jonny. We met Ivan at Coble Landing, and he was none too pleasant, either."

Flowers smiled again. "This is a close-knit community, Mr Murray, and people like the Irwins are very protective of it. It's bluster, most of it, but they can be serious trouble if you're not careful."

"Well, anyway," Joe concluded, "We thought you ought to know all this."

Flowers was eager to encourage him. "No, sir, that's all right. Despite what most people think, the police are always glad of the public's help, no matter how trivial things may seem."

The head of a police diver appeared in the water, close to the edge of the rocks. He held up his arm clutching a wet and bedraggled coat.

"Mike," shouted one of the officers on the rocks. "We've got something."

"Excuse me, sir," said Flowers, and hurried off across the slippery surface to join his colleagues.

Joe and his two companions watched as the garment was passed onto land, its pockets searched, a wallet removed and that too searched, before the coat, wallet and its contents were carefully placed in separate, seal-easy evidence bags.

A grim-faced Flowers approached them. "I wonder if any of you could identify this."

They looked it over, a wax cotton coat in dark green with a twill lining.

"Like I said earlier, I never saw him this morning," said Joe.

"How about the wallet then?" asked Flowers when the others said nothing.

Again they were unable to comment.

"Anything in the wallet?" asked Joe?

"Just this, sir."

Flowers held up the evidence bag for them to see a white, laminated card bearing the legend, *Sanford 3rd Age Club*, beneath which was a passport sized photograph and the member's name: *Edward Dobson.*

From somewhere behind Joe, Brenda burst into tears.

Chapter Ten

The day moved on quickly. Returning to Filey from the Brigg, they caught the bus to Scarborough, Joe complaining at the cost of the fares when he had a perfectly good car back in Sanford, and they arrived in the area's premier resort just before two.

"We'll be on the sea front tonight," Joe told them, "and time is getting on. Why don't you just do your shopping in the town?"

They agreed and headed for the Brunswick Shopping Centre on the Westborough pedestrian precinct, where Joe elected to stay outside.

"Keep your phone on, Joe," Sheila urged.

"In case we need a pack mule," Brenda chuckled.

While they disappeared into the shopping mall, Joe took a seat on a nearby bench, savouring the sun on his skin, while he enjoyed a cigarette and permitted his agile mind to run over the strange events of the last few days.

Eddie Dobson's disappearance had overtaken Nicola Leach's death, but his brush with Ivan Irwin over the Land Rover had brought Nicola back to the forefront of his mind, and the more he thought about it, the more he became convinced that the two deaths were linked. Brenda had linked Eddie to Nicola and now the pair were dead.

"I don't like coincidences," he said to his two companions when they came out of the Brunswick Centre half an hour later, "and we're wading in them."

Ambling along Huntriss Row, towards the monolithic Grand Hotel, Brenda asked, "are you suggesting that Knickers-off and Eddie were up to something that got her killed and persuaded him to jump into the sea?"

"Maybe he didn't jump," Joe suggested. "Maybe he was pushed."

"Not according to Constable Flowers," Sheila countered. "He said there were no suspicious circumstances and no one else was involved."

"No," Joe disagreed. "He said he didn't *think* anyone else was involved."

"All I can say is it must be something really bad," Brenda said, pausing to study the window display of a craft shop. "I do like some of these African wood carvings."

"Most of them are turned on lathes in Leeds," Joe argued. "What do you mean it must have been something bad?"

They reached the end of the narrow, pedestrian lane, with the Grand Hotel, its four domed spires framed in the afternoon sun, standing over to their left.

"I know a little café over there," Sheila said. "Let's have a cuppa."

While they manoeuvred their way through the throng of afternoon traffic and people, Brenda said, "Let's be brutally honest about this, Nicola wasn't much better than a tart. I reckon I'm fairly freewheeling, but she makes me look like a Trappist Nun."

"You mean Trappist Monk," Joe said.

"She means Trapistine Nun," Sheila corrected them both.

Joe sighed as they crossed the public car park outside the Grand. "Get to the point, Brenda."

"What I'm saying is, Nicola would have to commit a murder before she'd show any regret."

"Now there's a thought," Sheila said, leading the way to the left hand corner of the Grand and the upper station of the funicular railway that ran down to the promenade. "Suppose Eddie killed Nicola and then decided he couldn't live with the guilt, so threw himself into the sea off the Brigg."

Joe fumed as they made the café by the funicular station. "Why don't you order toasted teacakes and leave the deducing to me?"

They took a table outside, and ordered the teacakes.

116

"Go on then, Joe," Sheila said while they waited. "What's wrong with my idea?"

"The pudding is over-egged," he said and rolled a fresh cigarette.

He refused to yield to any more questions until their tea and teacakes were delivered, and then, while they ate, he explained his reasoning.

"As Brenda pointed out, Nicola wasn't known as Knickers-off for nothing. Let's assume that she's had a bit of a thing with Eddie and let's say she was blackmailing him."

Sheila shook her head and swallowed a large bit of teacake. "Nicola would not do that."

"I didn't say she would," Joe agreed, "but let's assume it, anyway. It gives us a nice motive for Eddie to mow her down. From there you're assuming Eddie gets a bad attack of guilt and decides to do away with himself. Why, then, did he bother with the fishing gear? It's obvious he's no fisherman. Why didn't he just go out during the night and throw himself in the sea? Come to that, why bother with Filey at all? Why not just stick his head in the gas oven, or swallow a bottle of paracetemol with a bottle of scotch?" He finished his teacake, washed it down with a mouthful of tea and took out his tobacco again. "I'm linking the two deaths. I've no real evidence for that, but I'm doing it, and for me Eddie killed Nicola, or he arranged it, so he could get on the Filey trip. He had some motive for coming here, and he needed to come with the Sanford 3rd Age Club."

"And what could that motive be?" Sheila asked.

"If I knew that, I'd be able to tell you everything."

Brenda finished her teacake, licked her fingers, wiped her mouth with a serviette and looking from one to the other of her two companions, asked, "Why does a toasted teacake always taste better when someone else has prepared it?"

On Brenda's rhetorical question, Joe's creased features darkened. "Here we are discussing murder and suicide and she's on about toasted teacakes."

"I'm changing the subject, Joe," Brenda argued. "All this

talk of death. It's depressing."

"All right. Are you saying there's something wrong with my toasted teacakes?" he demanded.

"No. It's just that they're tastier when someone serves them to you."

"I suppose," said Sheila from behind her teacup, "it's the general indolence of holidays. We all like to be waited on, and that adds to the ambience of a toasted teacake. And, of course, because we spend so much of our time actually making these things, we have an insight into the preparation that allows us to enjoy them on more levels than your average customer. Rather like one artist can appreciate the work of another on more levels than the casual viewer."

Joe snorted. "I don't see many of my toasted teacakes hanging on the walls of Sanford Art gallery." Pushing aside his teacup, he rolled a cigarette, jammed it between his lips and lit it. "You know what I don't understand?"

Across the table, Sheila tidied the cups, saucers and detritus of their afternoon snack. "I should think there are a lot of things you don't understand, Joe. The principles of artistic perspective, for example, Schröedinger's cat…"

"I've never seen art made of Perspex," Joe interrupted.

Alongside him, Brenda was equally puzzled. "And what's to understand about whoisit's cat?"

"Schröedinger's cat was a theoretical exercise in quantum physics designed to demonstrate the uncertainty principle," Sheila explained.

Their blank stares clearly told her that Joe and Brenda were completely at sea.

With a world-weary sigh, Sheila explained, "Basically, you seal a cat in a box and attached to the box is a canister of poisonous gas and another piece of equipment that emits an atomic nucleus that may or may not decay in one hour. If the nucleus decays, it will emit a particle that triggers the gas, if it doesn't the gas will not be triggered. The experiment is set up so that chances of decay or not decay are exactly fifty-fifty. When you open the box you will see either a dead cat or a living cat. It…"

"Isn't this a bit cruel to the cat?"

Sheila took in Brenda's concerned stare, and hastened to explain. "There isn't really a cat, Brenda, it's a hypothetical exercise only."

"How does the cat breathe if the box is sealed?" demanded Joe. "I mean, the chances are it would run out of air if the box wasn't large enough."

"And did they put milk in for it?" Brenda wanted to know. "If the RSPCA found out there'd be hell to pay. Sealing cats in boxes with poisonous gas. It's not right."

Sheila gave up the ghost. "Let's forget about Schröedinger's cat. Tell us what it is you specifically don't understand, Joe."

Taking a deep drag on his cigarette, he tuned in his lively mind. "That cop. Flowers. He asked us whether we recognised Eddie's jacket, and then his wallet, and yet, he had a STAC membership card in there. He *knew* it was Eddie's so why ask us to confirm it?"

Again it was Sheila who had the explanation, and to her relief it was simpler than quantum physics. "The police need as many forms of positive identification as they can get," she advised them. "It's all right saying they've found a wallet containing his membership card, but for all they know, the wallet could have been stolen, that could be the thief's coat and Eddie Dobson could be laid beaten up in hospital or something."

"Ah."

"Right."

A short silence intervened. Joe screwed up his malleable features again.

"I'll tell you what is a much more important question. Why did Eddie take a coat with him in the first place?" He gestured around them. "It's been hot enough to fry eggs on the pavement for the last week and there's no change in the forecast for at least another day or two. Why would he want a coat?"

The two women sat in awe of him. After a slightly longer silence, Joe realised they were waiting for him to supply the answer.

"Well, I don't know, either. I was asking the question. It doesn't mean to say I have the answer." He checked his watch. "It's almost half past three. Shouldn't we be getting back to Filey? Dinner's at five and the coach comes at six."

The other two agreed, Joe paid the bill and they ambled away from the cliff top, up into the town centre, towards the bus station. They waited patiently at a crossing for the lights to change in their favour. When they did so, Joe stepped out, only to be dragged back by Sheila as a red van tore past.

"Idiot," Joe cursed, and studied the back of the van. *Scarborough Gases, serving the licensed trade since 1965.* "He'll be serving time for dangerous driving when I've done speaking to his bosses."

"You should watch where you're going, Joe," Sheila told him. "I always taught the children that just because a traffic light says stop, you should not assume that drivers will stop."

Ten minutes later they boarded a bus, Joe grumbled about not being allowed to smoke, while Sheila and Brenda sat on the rear, face-to-face, bench seat comparing their purchases.

As the bus turned off the main road, onto the A1039 into Filey, Sheila asked, "Joe, are we going to tell the others that Eddie is, er, you know?"

"Dead," growled Joe. "You mean dead. Right? Why do we have a problem using the word, dead? Huh? He's dead. There's nothing we can do about that, so we shouldn't be troubled about using the word."

"All right," interjected Brenda, "but are we going to tell everyone else?"

The bus bumped over a level crossing and plodded on to Filey town centre, Joe gave the proposition brief thought and then shook his head.

"My feeling is no, we don't tell 'em. At least, not tonight." He picked up the doubt in their eyes. "Look, we're all going out tonight to enjoy ourselves, to take in a show. We booked it months ago, and we've all been looking forward to it, right? Right. Do we want to spoil the evening for everyone else? We three know. That's enough for now. My feeling is we should leave it until tomorrow morning and I'll let everyone know at breakfast."

"And put them off their bacon and egg," grumbled Brenda.

"It didn't put you off your toasted teacakes," Joe pointed out and stared out of the windows. Passing the front of the Star Inn, he spotted Sarah Pringle coming out, alongside a tall, well-built man dressed in scruffy jeans and a shabby working shirt. Even without the fisherman's jumper, Joe recognised him as Ivan Irwin.

It was not only Ivan who had changed, but Sarah Pringle looked different, too. She had put on her wig, the one she had worn the previous night. In daylight, he could see the effect it had on her. Reaching her neck and shoulders, it appeared almost black and took several years off her age.

The pair were smiling over something.

"I'll bet he's telling her about how he tried to warn me off," Joe grumbled.

"Say again, Joe?" Sheila said."

He shook his head. "Nothing. Sarah Pringle and one of those Irwin brothers." He nodded through the window. "She's pinching a couple of hours off."

"Quite right, too," Sheila said. "You do it back home." Dragging their attention back to the debate, she said, "I think you're right, Joe. I think we should keep Eddie's death between ourselves for the time being."

Twenty-two minutes after leaving Scarborough bus station, the vehicle pulled into the small square of Filey terminus and they got off into hot afternoon sunshine, strolled along the main street and paused to study window displays in the various shops and stores. Under their joshing, Joe invested in a new tobacco tin with a grumpy cartoon face on the front, bearing the legend, *Don't hassle me, I'm having a bad day*, and they moved on.

Outside a gents' outfitters, the women paused and admired a Crombie overcoat.

"You should buy yourself one of those, Joe," Brenda

suggested. "They're smart and dressy."

"Oh sure," Joe sneered, his eye on the price tag of several hundred pounds. "It's just the kind of thing you need for serving a full English to a shop full of lorry drivers. Shall I take the bowler and cravat to go with it?"

Brenda clucked impatiently. "You don't understand, do you? It's not a case of function, it's appearance. It's all about being seen in it, letting people know you own expensive clothing." She walked on to catch up with Sheila who was now examining the goods on sale in a china shop.

Joe stared after her wiggling behind, thinking of all the times when he had been tempted to grab a handful of it. In her own way, Brenda could be a pain in the nether regions, but she was a good-hearted woman, hard working and utterly dependable. There were also those times when, without even being aware of it, she supplied answers to life's mysteries, and right now was one of them.

Eventually, they reached The Crescent, and meandered past grand, white fronted hotels and guest houses, harking back to a gentler, more refined age, and into the grounds of the Beachside. Walking into reception, where Joe collected the keys from Kieran Pringle, he passed the women theirs and followed them to the lifts for the journey to the second floor.

He paused at his door. "Don't forget. The bus leaves at half past six. I'll see you in the dining room at five."

He turned the key in the lock, opened the door, stepped in and stopped dead.

His single, battered suitcase was on the bed, open, its contents spread around the bed and floor. His travel alarm had been pulled apart, the batteries removed and tossed, along with the clock itself, on the bedside cabinet. The dresser drawers were open, his possessions dumped everywhere, and the wardrobe too was open, his clothing strewn about the floor.

***

"I can assure you, Mr Murray, that I trust my staff and none of them would do anything like this," Sarah Pringle said.

With Sheila and Brenda helping Joe tidy the room, Sarah had only just arrived back at the Beachside when they called her up to the room. While his two female companions collected and folded his clothing neatly back into place, Joe argued the toss with the hotel manageress.

She had changed again from the way he saw her in the town. Now dressed in her uniform skirt, blouse and waistcoat, minus the wig, her hair was pulled back and collected into a ponytail at the rear, tightening the skin at her temples, where the touches of grey she had spoke of could be seen amongst the dark brown.

"So you're saying it's one of your guests?" Joe demanded.

"I have fifty rooms, and your party has taken three quarters of them. None of my other guests are likely to know who you are, or that this was your room, and in addition there are no other reports of rooms being broken into, so I would suggest you look at your own people."

Joe felt his gorge rising. "Listen, Mrs Pringle, I know my people. I run the club for God's sake. These are honest folk and I'd trust 'em with my life... maybe not my wallet, but certainly with my life."

Mrs Pringle was no so easily persuaded. "Are you certain you locked your door?"

"Hey, lady, I'm a businessman, same as you. I *always* lock doors." He crossed the room and checked the lock. "It doesn't appear to have been forced, but then..." He twisted the deadlock back and forward. "Someone with the right skills could have tripped it with a credit card."

Sarah Pringle turned bright red. "Mr Murray, are you suggesting that I routinely provide board and lodgings for burglars?"

"Would you know if you did?" Joe demanded. "I don't

123

recall you asking me what I do for a living and even if you did put burglars up, do you think they're gonna tell you?" His voice dripped bile and cynicism. "Right, Mr Smith, what do you do when you're not sneaking off for a dirty weekend with your secretary, also known as Mrs Smith? Oh, I break into other guests' rooms and rifle them for goodies."

His sarcasm was lost on Sarah. "If you are unhappy with my hotel, or the way I run it, then I suggest you call the police."

Joe thrust his hands deep into his trouser pockets. "They've got enough to be doing looking for Eddie Dobson's body." His fingers closed around a rabbit's foot fob and the attached keys and a frown furrowed his brow. "I wonder…"

"I beg your pardon."

"No. Nothing. All right. As long as you know about it so that if there's anything missing, my insurance company can come back to you for confirmation."

Mrs Pringle pulled herself primly upright. "In that case, I shall bid you good evening and I hope you enjoy the rest of your stay in Filey."

"I don't see why we should. It ain't been much cop so far." Joe watched her leave and then joined Sheila and Brenda tidying his effects.

"I've a travel iron with me, Joe," said Brenda, neatly folding his best trousers. "I'll press your jacket and pants before we go out."

"Thanks, Brenda."

"I think this needs ironing too, Brenda," said Sheila, draping his white shirt on a hanger. "Why would anyone want to break into your room, Joe? Everyone knows you never leave your wallet anywhere."

Joe shook his head. "It wasn't a robbery. Well, not in the usual sense of the word, it wasn't."

Both heads turned quickly to stare at him. "What?" Brenda demanded.

"They were not trying to rob me. Look at the place." He

124

threw out an arm towards the dresser. "My netbook is there. The battery's been taken out of it, but it's still there, and so is the computer. They even pulled the batteries from my alarm clock. They weren't looking for money and they weren't after things they could sell on the black market or down the pub. They were looking for something small and easily hidden."

"What, then?" Sheila asked.

Joe fingered the keys again. "It certainly wasn't my wallet. Your room hasn't been touched?"

They shook their heads.

"So how did they know I had it?"

Chapter Eleven

At five thirty, after their early evening meal, they retired to the terrace where Joe could enjoy a cigarette. Still high in the cloudless sky, the sun had disappeared over the right shoulder of the Beachside, providing pleasant shade from the searing heat.

Wearing a pair of freshly pressed, dark, casual trousers and white, short-sleeved shirt, much to the dismay of his companions Joe had also opted to put on his thin, pale green and shabby fisherman's gilet.

"I need the space," he had told them, dropping items like his tobacco tin, cigarette lighter, mobile phone and wallet into the garment's many pockets.

"You told us you were no fisherman," Brenda pointed out, "so why are you wearing a fisherman's wossname?"

"I have a pair of pit boots at home, but I've never been a miner," Joe retorted.

Enjoying the cooler air of the terrace, while Sheila and Brenda chatted excitedly about the coming show, Joe chewed on his cigarette, the day's puzzles weighing and preying on his mind.

Three tables away, Les Tanner sat with Sylvia Goodson and Alec and Julia Staines. They joked and laughed as they chatted and Joe guessed that, like he and his two women, they were in a state of high anticipation over the evening's entertainment.

The roar of a rough diesel engine assaulted his ears. A dark red van turned right and up the side of the hotel. Looking over the potted plants on the hotel's balustrade, Joe could just make out the top of the letters 'S' and 'G', enough to tell him it was one of Scarborough Gases'

126

vehicles. He heard it slow down, and then disappear around the rear of the hotel and it reminded him of the puzzling location of the key.

He stood up. "Won't be a minute, just wanna check on something."

He walked from the terrace, through the hotel gate and turned right, then right again, up a residential street of guest houses and small hotels. Cars choked both sides of the road for as far as he could see, but there were few people about. Most of the holidaymakers would be back in their digs, he guessed, either enjoying or getting ready to enjoy their evening meals.

Walking up the slight hill, he turned into the narrow street at the rear of the Beachside, and found the Scarborough Gases van, its rear doors wide open, parked near the hotel's rear entrance. It was full of gas canisters of varying sizes and markings. As he neared the van, the driver emerged from the hotel's rear yard carrying a couple of empty cylinders.

"All right, boss?" the driver asked.

"Coulda been worse if you'd hit me in Scarborough earlier today."

"Not me, gaffer," the driver said placing the cylinders in the van and strapping them into place. "Haven't been back to the depot since ten this morning." He grinned at Joe. "We have a dozen vans out and about, you know." He collected two full cylinders and hurried back into the hotel.

Joe stood at the gates, looking up at the hotel. The errant fire extinguisher had been removed from the rear yard, but using the large refuse bin and the washing line he had seen from Eddie's room as guides, he looked up at the first floor. A drainpipe ran up the wall close to what he believed was Eddie's window. Was it possible? Could someone have climbed up there?

Joe turned to leave and the driver emerged from the hotel again, this time carrying a standard, black cylinder and two painted bright yellow.

Joe laughed. "What are they for? Lemonade?"

The driver chuckled and secured the cylinders in his van. "Scuba diving, them, boss. Billy and his lad, Kieran are members of the local club. Shows you how much money there is in running hotels, eh?" He patted the scuba tanks. "These things cost a bloody fortune."

"Why yellow?" Joe asked. "Another one of these crazy European rules?"

"Nah, mate," the driver replied, slamming the doors. "There are rules for the labels and the tank shoulders, but divers like them painted yellow cos they're easier to see underwater. See ya." The driver grinned again. "And watch out for our lads when you're crossing the road. We're all nutters."

Joe watched the van drive off and then retraced his steps to the front terrace, his agile mind mulling over the things he had learned.

"So, does the master have a solution?" Brenda asked.

Still mentally trying to slot together the pieces of the jigsaw, Joe gazed absently across at the Staineses, Tanner and Sylvia. It was only the slightest of movements, made under the table, but Joe saw Tanner pass something to Sylvia. The Staineses could not have seen it because they were too close, but Joe understood immediately and nudged Brenda for her to see.

She chuckled. "The key to his room, I'll bet."

"Was he really a Captain?" Sheila asked, keeping her voice low. "As long as I've known him, he's worked at the town hall."

"Territorial Army," Joe said, putting a light to his cigarette. "Toy soldier. Playing war games outside York two weekends outta three."

"The Territorials are usually the first to be called up in an emergency," Sheila pointed out, "and they get the same training as regular soldiers, albeit on a part time basis."

Joe chuckled. "Looks like he'll be getting the same fringe benefits as regular soldiers tonight. Why do they bother trying to keep it secret? Everyone knows they're at it." He checked his wristwatch. "Pushing six. The buses will be here soon." He lapsed into a brooding silence and toyed with his Zippo lighter, turning it end over end on the table.

"What is wrong with you, Joe?" Sheila demanded. "We're used to your miseries at the café, but why so glum now?"

"It's this Nicola Leach and Eddie Dobson business, and someone breaking into my room," he replied. "I can't get it out of my head." He half turned in his seat. "Brenda, when you were chatting Eddie up last night…"

"I was not chatting him up," Brenda cut him off. "I was simply being friendly."

Joe puffed out a cloud of carcinogens. "When you were being friendly with him last night, did you find out what he did for a living?"

Brenda shook her head. "He was in the navy for years. He told you the same thing. But he never told me what he did, and I don't know what kind of work he was looking for."

Joe's crumpled features split into a broad smile. "The navy. Of course he was. Now I wonder…"

***

The memory of Abba's music still ringing in their ears, Joe, Sheila and Brenda, along with several hundred others, emerged from Futurist Theatre onto Scarborough seafront.

"Oh look, it's still daylight," Brenda said.

Joe checked his watch. "Only half past nine. The sun's not gone down yet and the bus doesn't leave until half ten. Keith said we'd have time for a beer after the show. Shall we?"

They agreed and turned left, ambling along the promenade, its pavements crowded with summer tourists, families seeking a late snack or waiting for children by the funfair rides on the beach. Evening revellers sought their next watering hole, and the lights of souvenir shops and amusement arcades cast an almost festive glow onto the twilight pavements.

While Joe mused silently on the day's events, his two companions compared notes on the performance.

"Did you see the girl playing Agnetha?" asked Sheila.

Brenda nodded enthusiastically. "I thought she was very good. She looked the part and she had a marvellous voice."

"Oh, yes," agreed Sheila, "but did you notice the size of her bottom?"

"About the size of Norfolk," said Joe, snapping out of his reverie.

"Trust you to spot that," Brenda chuckled. "Mind you, I wouldn't have said Norfolk."

"West Yorkshire, perhaps?"

Sheila's comment dissolved both women into girlish giggles.

Opposite the harbour, where the speedboat which took passengers out for a ten minute, high-speed ride across the bay, was tying up after its last trip of the day, Joe led the way into the Lord Nelson.

The bar was crowded, the karaoke in full swing. To one side, in an appalling, gravelly voice, a young man crucified, *You've Lost That Loving Feeling* causing Joe to comment, "If he sang to her like that, I'm not surprised she went off the boil."

Sheila and Brenda found seats as far away as possible from the music while Joe threaded his way through the crowds at the bar.

It was fully ten minutes before he was served, by which time the wannabe singer had moved off the dais, and been replaced by a young woman who, in an ear-shattering falsetto, belted out *Send In The Clowns*.

Placing a gin and tonic before Sheila and a Campari and soda in front of Brenda, Joe sat down with his half of bitter, took out his tobacco and rolled a cigarette, his face screwed up in disgust at the noise of the karaoke.

"I dunno about sending in the clowns, they wanna send in the lawyers and prosecute her for describing that racket as singing."

"You can't smoke that in here," Sheila warned.

"I know, I know. I was just rolling it for when we leave."

"What on earth is wrong with you, Joe?" demanded Brenda. "You sat sulking through the show, almost as if you didn't enjoy one minute, and I thought you liked Abba."

"I'm still preoccupied," he explained. "Nicola and Eddie Dobson... again. And I do like Abba."

"What's your favourite number?" Sheila asked.

"*Money, Money, Money*, I'll bet," chuckled Brenda.

The women laughed, across the pub the young woman ceased her caterwauling and Joe took offence.

"As it happens, you're wrong. My favourite Abba track is… oh God, that's it."

Sheila exchanged a frown with Brenda and said, "I don't remember that title."

"No, no. Don't you see?" Joe urged them with an intense stare. "The police found Eddie Dobson's wallet, but there was nothing in it other than the STAC membership card."

Once more the women looked at each other. Brenda turned back to Joe. "Yes. What about it?"

"No money," Joe declared. "He went out this morning and he had no money, no credit cards, nothing, except maybe a little small change in his pocket. He had no food or drink with him and no money to buy any. What kind of man does that?"

Sheila answered slowly. "One who doesn't need either, and what kind of man *knows* he won't need money?"

"One," echoed Brenda, "who knows he isn't coming back?" The tears formed in her eyes again. "Oh dear, I think I'm going to…"

Sheila patted her hand and Joe took a celebratory sip of his ale.

"It's more complicated than that," he told them when Brenda had calmed down. "Eddie Dobson wasn't committing suicide. He just wanted it to look that way. And that's the reason he wanted to look like a fisherman, and why he took his coat with him." He glowed with pride under their puzzled stares. "I guessed about his coat earlier, when Brenda said I should have bought that overcoat in

Filey because it has to be seen. It was the same with Eddie's wax jacket." He sat forward in an effort to help them follow his logic. "The cop, Flowers; he told us the currents on the north side of the Brigg were fast moving. Eddie needed to let them know what happened to him. His body will have been swept away on the currents, but his coat magically got tangled on the rocks and that's why he took it with him. He knew the police divers would find it. Oh yes. He wanted everyone to think he was committing suicide all right, but that's not what he was about."

He took another drink of his beer, and revelled in his deductive powers.

"Maybe," ventured Brenda, still puzzled by Joe's confidence, "he took the coat in case it rained and as he slipped, he grabbed at it."

Joe snorted again. "You ever heard of Occam's Razor?"

Brenda was puzzled. "Was it a twin blade or electric?"

"It was a statement," Sheila told her. "Basically, it said that you must not multiply logical entities without sufficient evidence."

"Correct," said Joe. "If you have Eddie clutching at the coat, you're clutching at straws." He waved at the windows and the outside world. "There's no hint of an end to the heat wave. Eddie would never have taken his coat with him."

"Perhaps he needed the pocket space," Brenda ventured. "Like you and your tramp's vest."

"It's a fisherman's gilet, not a tramp's vest," Joe grunted. "And you're off your rocker. He's carrying a rucksack the size of a small truck, and he's short of pocket space? And what happened to the stuff he was going to put in his pockets? Or do you think he'd keep the fish in there when he got a bite? And let's not forget, he put his room key in the bag. Again, he wanted it to be found so the police could track him down quick. No, he was out to make it look like suicide and carrying that coat, leaving the key in the bag, even ordering a packed lunch and not taking it, was all part of the game."

Silence fell between them. Across the bar, the same

young woman who had so screeched out *Send In The Clowns* now began to warble her way through *Somewhere Over The Rainbow*, much to Joe's irritation. He downed his drink.

"I wish she was singing somewhere over Manchester."

"Joe," asked Sheila, "why do you keep insisting he wanted it to appear that he committed suicide, but he didn't? You're hinting that he's still alive."

"He is. I'm sure of it. The van driver at the Beachside was collecting empty scuba diving tanks. Eddie Dobson was an ex-navy man. What's the betting he was a frogman in the navy? He wasn't carrying money because even the most experienced diver may lose it. Besides, if he had notes in his wallet, they'd have been ruined. He left the wallet in the wax jacket to make sure it would be found. This smacks of a bigger insurance scam than the Devil's hammer."

Sheila chewed her lip. "If you're right, then he could well have arranged Nicola's death."

"Which probably means he wasn't working alone," Joe declared.

"Call me thick…" Brenda began.

"You're thick," Joe interrupted with a grin.

She scowled. "How does this implicate him in Nicola's death?"

"Let's assume this is a big insurance fiddle," Joe began. "He wants to fake his own death so someone can claim on his life insurance and then divvy up the spoils. Let's also assume he was trained as a frogman in the navy. The easiest way to do it is somewhere where the lifeboats won't get to him quickly enough, and Filey is perfect for that, but only on the north side of the Brigg. Remember, Flowers told us the waters are calmer on the south side. And no matter what he said about coming from Rotherham, like I told you earlier he was actually from this area."

"His accent," Sheila said.

"Correct," Joe agreed. "He talked the way these people do. He's probably from one of the villages round here. That means he can't do it from here because someone may recognise him. He needs to be away from this area altogether. So he moves to Sanford. Then, as luck would have it, he discovers that the Sanford 3rd Age Club is on a summer trip to Filey. It's perfect for his purposes. But he can't get on the trip. It's full. So he needs to create a seat on the bus. He hits on Nicola. She was easy anyway. He has her bumped off, then comes hassling us for her seat. And we took him along. When he gets here, he buys the fishing gear, tootles along the Brigg this morning, makes sure no one is paying attention and throws himself in the drink. Either he or his accomplice has already stashed the scuba tanks under the rocks. He leaves the coat tangled there, grabs the tanks and swims to shore, where his buddy is waiting for him." He took in their impressed gazes.

"He'd need help," Sheila said.

"Yes, and I know who," Joe retorted. "Billy and Kieran Pringle."

Their surprise told him he had hooked his audience. "I just told you. Before we got on the bus tonight, I went round the back of the hotel and I was talking to a driver from Scarborough Gases. He told me that both Billy and Kieran are scuba divers. What would you need if you were pulling this kinda scam?" Joe grinned. "Scuba divers. He had one of them waiting under the water this morning, with a set of tanks for him."

"It all seems a little obvious, Joe," Sheila said.

"Obvious to people like us, yes, but not to the local cops because they believe he's had an accident or committed suicide. I'll tell you something else, too. Billy owns a dark blue van. You saw me talking to him this morning. Cora Harrison rang the cops from a van, didn't she?"

"Or a Land Rover," Brenda corrected.

"A van is favourite," Joe argued.

"And that van would have had to have been in Sanford on Tuesday night," Sheila pointed out.

"Yes, but it has wheels and an engine, Sheila, so it's not difficult for it to get to Sanford. Oh, and talking of Sanford, do we know where Eddie lived?"

"The East Side Estate, I believe," said Sheila, "but I'd have to check the club records to be certain. Does it matter?"

Joe fished into his pocket and came out with the key. "I found this on Eddie's windowsill when we cleared out his room this morning."

"And what does it fit?"

Joe shrugged. "I don't know for sure, but I'm willing to bet that it's the key to his flat back in Sanford. I can see how they had all this planned. They arrange for Nicola to be run down on Tuesday night, and Billy and this Cora Harrison, whoever she is, are in Sanford to witness it. Eddie is now on the bus to Filey. He goes out early this morning and chucks himself in the sea. Kieran or Billy is waiting for him, they get him back to shore and bring him back to the Beachside. Now, Billy's van woke me at four this morning. I saw it pulling away from the back street. My guess is, they were taking Eddie down to the Brigg, but get this, the van had a set of ladders on the roof. Eddie used those to climb out of his window so he wouldn't attract attention by going out the front doors. When I was talking to the gas delivery driver at the back of the hotel, I checked the layout at the rear. There's a drain running up the wall right by Eddie's room. Now let me paint you more of the picture. He gets back to the shore, then has his accomplice take him back to the Beachside where he climbs the drainpipe looking for his key, but it's already gone. I have it. Now he's right in it. He left his hotel key in the rucksack and he can't even get in for a change of clothing, never mind get back to Sanford. So he got in touch with the crew at the hotel and they raided my room looking for the key." Joe's eyes burned into them. "What do you think?"

There was a momentary pause while the singer finished her number and the crowded bar collectively ignored her.

"I think it's the biggest load of tripe I've ever heard," Sheila declared, and Brenda nodded her agreement.

Joe took another swallow of beer to hide his affront. He slammed his glass back down on the table. "What?"

"Earlier today you mentioned that you'd seen the inshore lifeboat making for the far side of the Brigg," Sheila pointed out. "Assume that was within fifteen minutes of Eddie going in, and what time was it? Nine-ish?"

"And Sarah Pringle served him breakfast at eight," Brenda pointed out.

"Yes. And?"

"Then where the hell was he going at four o'clock this morning when you saw the van driving away from behind the hotel?" Brenda demanded.

"Correct," Sheila confirmed. "But I go further. By the time he got back to the Beachside, it would be ten o'clock, possibly later. Do you seriously imagine he could shinny up the drainpipe at that time of day without being spotted? The streets were crowded, Joe. Someone would have seen him."

He drummed irritable fingers on the table. "All right, all right, so I was wrong about the drainpipe. Maybe he was hanging out in the street waiting for us all to go and then he'd sneak back into the hotel, up to his room and get his key back. Maybe that's what he did. That Sarah Pringle isn't around all day, is she? Remember when we got back to Filey this afternoon, and I saw her coming out of a pub with that Irwin bloke. And if she isn't there, it only leaves her son and we know what a dipstick he is. She told us. He'd be gormless enough to hand Eddie the key without question."

"But to do that, Joe, he'd have to walk back into the Beachside," Brenda argued. "Do you think he may have attracted some attention wandering around in clothes that are dripping wet?"

"It's scorching out there," Joe protested. "His clothes could have dried while he was being driven back."

"Brenda is right," Sheila said. "Clothing takes a lot longer than that to dry, even in this weather."

"Pah." Joe dismissed them with a snort, and polished off his half of bitter. The women followed suit.

"You talk about Occam's Razor, Joe," Sheila said as they made for the door and the balmy evening air. "You're trying to turn it into a lawnmower. You've dragged Billy Pringle and Kieran into this without a shred of evidence. They would have had to know Eddie, and yet you asked Sarah Pringle earlier whether she did and she said not. The simple solution is, Eddie Dobson died, and it was probably, but not certainly, suicide."

"And I'm sure I'm right," Joe argued. "It was an insurance scam. If he's alive, he got away with it. If he's dead, he didn't."

The thirty minutes since leaving the theatre had seen near night descend. They crossed the road to walk along the promenade by the sands, while away to the northwest, above the steep cliffs, the last vestiges of the high summer day were dwindling in an icy blue twilight. The searing heat had diminished, but it was still hot, and the light breeze coming off the sea worked to ease the oppressive air.

Joe lit his cigarette and they ambled back towards the theatre, where the coach waited for them. High up, the monument on Oliver's Mount, evoking vague reminders of Cleopatra's Needle, stood out starkly against the fading light and alongside it, a first quarter moon hung in the sky.

A jogger came towards them, dressed all in black, his head covered by a balaclava helmet and Joe chuckled sarcastically.

Joe laughed. "Just look at this idiot. Wrapped up like he's heading for the North Pole."

The two women said nothing but savoured the pleasant walk along the pavement and soft lapping of the sea against the shore.

"Oh look," said Brenda, "someone's starting a fire."

They paused and followed her pointing finger with their eyes. Over towards the Spa Complex, half a mile away, there was the telltale glow of flame.

"Beach bums," declared Joe. "Dossing overnight on the sands."

Sheila pointed further out to sea, where the winking lights of a ship could be seen. "Moored for the night. Remember the hymn we used to sing at school? For those in peril on the sea."

"No peril at this time of year," muttered Joe. "Seas are flat calm. Come on we'd better get down to the bus."

"You don't have to be so grumpy, Joe, just because you got it wrong."

"I'm used to being wrong," he riposted. "I work with you two, don't I?"

Everything happened so quickly, that it seemed almost unreal. The jogger burst through them, snatched at Brenda's bag. Determined to keep hold of it, she tightened her grip on the handle, the jogger tugged, tore the bag from her and ran on, Brenda fell to the pavement, Sheila cried out, and the jogger ran off. Leaving Sheila to help Brenda, Joe hurried after him.

While he ran, the jogger opened the bag and rummaged through it, casting aside makeup, hairbrush, driver's licence and her purse, until he finally risked a glance over his shoulder and found Joe bearing down on him, at which point he threw the bag away and put on a spurt.

"Stop him," Joe cried.

But rather than risk becoming involved, people stood back to let him pass. Up ahead, the fairground beneath the castle headland was still in full swing, its lights casting a cheerful glow across the harbour, crowds of holidaymakers still queuing for the Cyclone, the helter-skelter and Ferris Wheel.

The thief sprinted into the fairground, Joe followed at a slower pace, and scanned the crowds, seeking his quarry. He skirted the queue for the helter-skelter, mainly children, their parents waiting patiently at the exit, passed the Cyclone and Ferris Wheel, scanned the crowds around the few stalls, and children's rides, then made his way out of the fairground to a nearby café, where the staff of two were closing up.

By the gents' lavatories, his chest heaving with the unexpected exertion, Joe found a discarded balaclava, picked it up and after studying it for a moment, jammed it into his pocket before making his way back through the crowds to join the women. They had made it to the harbour, where they were picking up the last of Brenda's possessions and putting them back into her bag.

"He got away," Joe reported, his breath still coming in large gasps. "I'm too old to chase people like that."

"Well, he didn't get away with anything," Brenda said. "Not even my purse." Triumphantly, she held up the small, black leather clutch purse.

"Now don't you think that's strange?"

Joe's rhetorical question wiped the smiles from their faces.

"There he is running hell for leather and yet he goes through your bag as he's running and he doesn't steal nothing."

"Anything," Sheila corrected him.

"We've just come through an attempted mugging and she's still correcting my English. You know what I mean. He could have taken your cash and cards from the purse as he was running, but he didn't. Why not? Because like the bod who raided my room and could have nicked my computer, he wasn't after money."

"Then what was he after, Joe?"

He fished into his pocket and came out again with the key. "This… Again."

Chapter Twelve

By the time they got back to the Beachside, the excitement and stress of the evening were taking their toll on Brenda, and the two women declined Joe's offer of a drink.

"If it means anything to you, Joe, I know we're always poking fun at you, but I'm grateful to you for running after that thief," Brenda said.

"And I think you were magnificent," Sheila agreed.

"Isn't that what friends are for?" Joe asked.

Brenda kissed him on the cheek. "I need some sleep."

"Enjoy your nightcap, Joe, we'll see you tomorrow."

Watching them until they were safely in the lift, he took himself into the bar alone and ordered a half of bitter.

Waiting for Billy Pringle to give him change, Joe scanned the display along the rear of the bar and for the first time noticed a second NYSAA certificate, this one bearing Billy's photograph.

"Just admiring your certificates," Joe said when Billy handed him a fiver and change. "NYSAA. What is it?"

"North Yorkshire Sub Aqua Association," Billy explained. "I've been a member of years, and our Kieran has been diving since he was fifteen. He's an instructor now." Billy laughed. "When Sarah gives him enough time off to do any instructing. Ever done any diving?"

Joe shook his head. With a rueful grin, he said, "bitta ducking and diving, but nothing under water."

Billy's smile was one of pure enthusiasm. "Different world under the sea, mate. A magical world."

"Yeah, I've seen some of David Attenborough's films. Too many ugly fish for me, and I see enough ugly every time I look in the mirror."

Joe came away from the bar and looked for somewhere to sit. In one corner, Alec and Julia Staines sat with Mavis Barker and Cyril Peck. Julia, always a good looking woman and one who may have been a potential Mrs Murray if she hadn't fallen for Alec, waved to Joe in an invitation to join them, but he gave her a thin smile and shake of the head before ambling out onto the terrace with his beer.

The lights along the promenade twinkled in the night, out to sea he could see the lights of the same ships Brenda and Sheila had pointed out from Scarborough. The first quarter moon sat over Speeton Point and Flamborough Head and a few brighter stars shone from the night sky.

The click of heels on the terracotta paving slabs reached his ears. He looked to his left and the bar entrance, where Sarah Pringle stood, looking out across the bay.

"It's a peaceful time of night," she said.

"Very peaceful," Joe agreed.

She held a glass of brandy in one hand and a cigarette in the other. "May I join you?"

Joe gestured at the chair opposite. "Please." He took out his tobacco tin and rolled a cigarette. "We, er, were getting a little, er, heated earlier. Pity after we got on so famously last night."

Sarah nodded. "I was annoyed that someone could have gone into one of my rooms and robbed you. I was, perhaps, a little hasty with some of the things I said."

Taking out his Zippo, he offered her a light, lit his own cigarette and put the lighter on the table. Blowing a cloud of smoke into the night, he said, "I know what you mean. I run a business, too, remember. Nothing as grand as this, but the pressures are the same and I'm well known as Sanford's biggest grouch."

She smiled. "No offence, then?"

"Pax," Joe grinned.

A formal silence fell between them. Two strangers who knew little or nothing about one another. Joe thought it odd. Speaking with her the previous night, in exactly the same circumstances, he had found plenty to talk about.

Sarah seemed to sense his thoughts. "You've had a trying day."

He nodded. "And how. First Nicola and now Eddie. And one of my friends was just attacked in Scarborough."

"Dear me." The shock on Sarah's face belied the inanity of her comment. "What happened?"

Joe gave a brief account of the mugging. Sarah tut-tutted in all the right places and he sensed that the incident held no real interest for her.

"Well I hope the police get him," she said when Joe concluded the tale. "That kind of man is a scourge on our community."

Joe detected no conviction in her voice. She was, he guessed, echoing standard platitudes.

"Pardon me," she went on, "but you mentioned Nicola. Your wife?"

He couldn't help but laugh. "Me? Married to Knickers-off, er, sorry, Nicola? Not likely. I'm divorced, Sarah, and while Nicola wasn't a bad woman, she was a little too free with her favours, if you see what I mean, to make any man a good wife. Even her husband thought so." He sucked on his cigarette and picked up his lighter. "No, no. She was the member of our club killed in a hit and run on Tuesday night. I think I told you about her last night."

"So you did," Sarah agreed. "Good Lord. What is this world coming to?"

Slightly more sincerity this time, but still not enough to persuade Joe that Sarah was doing anything but making small talk.

Sarah crushed out her cigarette and swirled the brandy around in the glass. "This poor woman sounds a little like my ex-husband. He was, how did you put it, free with his favours, too."

"That's bad news," Joe responded with a lack of interest that matched Sarah's. "At least it's one problem I didn't have with Alison."

"No?"

"No. She just got fed up of working, working, working. I

142

tried to tell her it goes with the small business territory, but she wouldn't have it. Walked out on me about ten years ago. I've been on my own ever since."

"Alone?" With a naughty smile, Sarah took a slug of brandy. "With two fine women hanging on your arm?" There was a hint of more enthusiasm in her voice this time. She laughed. "Oh, I've seen you with your lady friends. Enough to make me jealous."

He smiled modestly. "I'm known for my powers of deduction, Sarah. Surprisingly, they're not difficult to develop, but yours are leading you to the wrong conclusion. Sheila, Brenda and I are good friends. They work for me and between us we run the Sanford 3rd Age Club, but you have my personal assurance that's as far as it goes." He stubbed out his cigarette. "One glance from Sheila would be enough to skewer any potential suitor, and Brenda... well Brenda is a smashing woman, but she prefers to keep more than one man dancing on a string at any given time. She's a lot more discreet than Nicola, but I know she's only looking for a good time, not a relationship, and I've never been a puppet for anyone. Apart from that, it would compromise our working relationship if I were involved with either of them."

Sarah's smile was more demure this time. "So there's hope for me yet."

With a broad grin, Joe wagged a warning finger at her. "Never trifle with an old fool, Sarah, or the old fool might be tempted to mix up a trifle with you."

"Who's trifling?" she asked. "It's not often that I get a good looking and available man like you staying here."

Joe laughed out loud and sipped more beer. "Good looking? Do me a favour. I'm a shortarsed, crinkly-haired, bad-tempered old bugger, and I don't have muscles in places where people don't know they have places. James Bond I am not. And I might run a busy café, but all the money I'm supposed to be worth is on paper, not in the bank."

"Don't sell yourself short, Joe," Sarah advised.

"Difficult, considering how short I am." he chuckled. "Five foot six, not six foot five."

Sarah swallowed her brandy. "Drink up and let me show you something."

Puzzled, Joe swallowed the last of his beer and followed her into the bar. They crossed the room under the watchful eye of Billy, through reception, and took the lift to the first floor. Unhooking the keychain at her waist, Sarah opened the door to room 101.

"Room 101," Joe noted. "Orwell."

Sarah faced him. "It's not your nightmares waiting in this room 101, Joe, but your desires."

And to his surprise, she kissed him.

**

Beyond the panoramic windows, the Sunday morning sky showed no trace of cloud, and the sun blazed onto the deserted beach, promising yet another day of unbearable heat.

It was a refreshed and rejuvenated Joe who joined Sheila and Brenda for breakfast at eight o'clock.

"You're looking very chipper this morning," Sheila commented.

Brenda, never one to resist a joke at Joe's expense, smiled savagely. "Remember that shilling he lost at the youth club Christmas party in 1971? He's found it."

Joe refused to rise. "For your information, I had a rather interesting night, last night, after you two cleared off to bed."

"Ooh," Sheila giggled. "Who was the lucky woman?"

"I'm saying nothing more than that," Joe replied tucking into his full English.

Joe had declined Sarah's invitation, despite her efforts to press him.

"I'm flattered," he told her, "but you've had one or two drinks and it's not the best way for two people to get to know each other."

Instead, they returned to the ground floor, and he sat with her in the hotel office, and dazzled her with accounts of his previous cases. And Sarah did not appear too disappointed. She was rapt with interest in his progress, or rather lack of it, in the killing of Nicola Leach and the supposed death of Eddie Dobson.

Making his way quietly back to his own room just after one in the morning, he'd slept well and woke full of determination to get on with the task at hand. He knew Eddie was still alive and since Joe had the key to his Sanford flat, he had to be somewhere in the Filey area.

First however, there were formalities to be dealt with. After finishing his breakfast, pushing his plate to one side, he stood up and rattled a knife against a carafe of water in the centre of the table.

Across the Beachside Hotel's dining room, having dispensed with their morning meal, the members of the Sanford 3rd Age Club fell silent and honed their collective attention on their chairman.

"As you know, I don't go much on speechifying, but I have a couple of announcements to make. First, coming back on the bus last night, a few of you were asking about the bag snatch. Let me assure you, Brenda is fine and the thief got away with nothing."

"He was probably after the recipe for your meat pies, Joe," called out Alec Staines, and many people laughed.

"Waste of time," commented George Robson. "The recipe's divided into three. Sheila has half, Brenda has half and Joe has the Pedigree Chum."

Joe rattled the glass again through the laughter. "Yeah, yeah, all right. Let's get serious, people. I have another announcement to make, and this one isn't so pleasant." He cleared his throat. "Yesterday morning, there was an, er, accident out on the Brigg. Eddie Dobson was out there fishing when he apparently slipped and fell into the sea. I'm sorry to have to say that his body was not found."

As he anticipated, the announcement was greeted with various gasps of astonishment, but mostly by awed silence.

"We have been asked to ensure his personal effects get to his family, such as he had, so if anyone knows of any relatives, we'd be grateful if they'd let us have the names and addresses. This is the second member we've lost over the last few days, and we've already decided that there should be a memorial service to both Nicola and Eddie when we get back to Sanford. We'll let you know where and when once we've made the arrangements. I'm sorry if the news puts a bit of a damper on your day, but we felt that you had a right to know, especially as one or two people were asking about him yesterday."

Joe allowed a few moments for the members to take in the announcements.

Clearing his throat, he went on, "Can I just take this opportunity to remind you all that there's a seventies themed disco in here tonight, and we have to vacate the rooms by ten o'clock tomorrow morning. The bus will be here to pick up the luggage from nine thirty. Beyond that, the bus will be back in Filey bus station from about half past eleven in the morning for a twelve noon departure. Thank you, everyone."

Joe sat down once more and the dining room was filled with the hum of seventy plus patrons dissolving into their own conversational arenas.

"Very professional, Joe," said Sheila, giving him a small, soft round of applause as he sat down again.

"Yeah, well, some of us have it, some don't. We've gotta get a move on. We have to get down to the police station, hand that balaclava in."

Brenda chuckled fatly. "You don't think it'll identify him, do you?"

"He was wearing it, he breathed onto it, they can get DNA from it."

"I hardly think the police will go to such trouble," said Sheila, "but nevertheless, we should report the incident, even though he got away with nothing."

Brenda poured more tea for them. "You don't even know that it was his, Joe. It's just a balaclava you found outside

146

the dunnies."

"It was his. Listen, it was hot as hell out there last night, how many people do you think were wandering up and down the seafront wearing woolly helmets? Only muggers pretending to be joggers. I tell you, it was his." He stirred his tea irritably. "Only he wasn't no mugger, he was pretending to be a mugger pretending to be a jogger."

Sheila sipped her tea delicately while Joe and Brenda slurped theirs. "This key, you still don't know what it's for and you're simply speculating that it's to do with Eddie."

"Because I found it on Eddie's windowsill. It had been discreetly hidden where it could be found only if you knew it was there and you were looking for it."

"You don't know what it fits, either," Brenda pointed out.

"I know what it doesn't fit. It doesn't fit his hotel room or his suitcase. It's not from a left luggage office, either."

"How do you know?" Sheila asked.

"First, it's for a double deadlock, second it's hooked onto a rabbit's foot fob. The Beachside's room keys aren't, and how many left luggage lockers do you know that fit the bill? No, I'm sure it's nothing to do with Filey. I think it's for his Sanford flat, but we won't find the answer to that until we get home."

"Are you going to tell the police about it?"

Joe lapsed into brooding thought for a moment. "No," he declared. "No I'm not. If I did, they'd simply laugh it off, just like you two. So I found a key in a hotel room. People are always losing things in hotel rooms. See, the key on its own doesn't make much sense, and it could literally be nothing. It's only when I add it to someone going through my gear and then someone trying to take Brenda's bag, searching through it and throwing everything away that it begins to look suspicious."

Sheila was dismissive. "Even then, you're still speculating."

"Of course I am, but look at it logically. Suppose, just suppose, that someone knows that the key is for Eddie's flat in Sanford. And all right, so you shot me down on Eddie

147

coming back for it yesterday, but suppose that same someone helped Eddie off the end of the Brigg. They hid the key in the room, knowing that we would have to remove his personal effects. Then when they realised one of us had found and taken the key, they raided my room, couldn't find it and followed us to Scarborough, possibly sat through the show last night and tailed us outta there, ready to snatch Brenda's bag, hoping it might be there. If I'm right, then it means they'll try again today." He smiled grimly. "Only this time, we'll be ready for them."

Sheila laughed pleasantly. "You've been watching too many late night cops and robbers movies, Joe. Logically, if someone murdered Eddie, they would have taken the key with them, not hidden it in the room to collect later. It's much more likely that, if it is his door key, Eddie left it there so that he wouldn't lose it while he was out and about Filey and Scarborough, and he probably hid it behind the curtains to ensure that the chambermaids didn't steal it. Do get a sense of proportion about these things."

Taking out his tobacco tin and rolling a cigarette, Joe disagreed. "Sheila, you do not hide a key on a window sill, even if you are worried about losing it or making sure the chambermaids don't nick it. You do remember how hot it's been? You tend to *open* windows in this weather, and that would run the risk of the key dropping over the windowsill and into the yard out back. All right, all right, so I can see what you're saying and no one who was up to no good would hide it there, but where does that get us? Eddie put it there himself? When he was on his way out to top himself? It doesn't sound likely."

"Except that he was doo-lally."

Brenda's interjection brought the debate to an abrupt halt.

"What?"

"Come again."

"You see," Brenda went on, "if Eddie was going to commit suicide, it's a safe bet that his mind was disturbed. Why would you expect him to behave logically when he was obviously not being logical? He probably put the key

148

there thinking it was a good idea, but we don't know why he thought it was a good idea."

"In that case," demanded Joe, "why has someone tried to get it back twice since Eddie died?"

"But we don't know that they have," Brenda asserted. "You're assuming the two incidents were attempts to get the key back. They could have been completely innocent thefts."

Sheila tittered. "I don't think I've ever heard of an innocent theft."

"I need a smoke." Joe gulped down his tea. "Whatever the score, we have to go to the cop shop and I'd like to get a bit of time for sightseeing and stuff today."

They stepped out onto the terrace where the Staineses were seated enjoying the morning sun.

"Grand night last night, Joe," Alec Staines called out.

"The news about Eddie took the shine off it a bit, though," his wife commented.

"How do you think we feel?" Joe asked. "We knew about it first thing yesterday morning."

"We didn't want to spoil your evening." Brenda said, taking a table several yards from the Staineses.

"Curious coming a few days after Nicola's death, isn't it?" Julia Staines said. "You did know they were having a bit of a fling?"

"Brenda mentioned it," Sheila reported.

"Sounds like a problem for you, Joe," Alec Staines chuckled. "Another mystery to get your dentures into."

"See," Joe said, keeping his voice low as he sat with his two friends. "Even they think there's something iffy about it all."

"The human tendency to draw lines where there are none," Sheila said.

Joe frowned. "What?"

Sheila dug into her bag and took out a paper napkin and a pen on which she drew two circles.

149

"What's that?" she asked.

Brenda shrugged. "Two circles."

Sheila drew a vertical line between them.

"Now what is it?"

Joe frowned again. "Two circles with a line between them. Could be, I dunno, a pair of binoculars."

Sheila took her pen again and drew a curved line under the existing drawing.

Turning it so they could both see, she asked, "Now what is it?"

"A smiley face," Brenda cried with glee.

"Joe?"

"All right," he agreed, "so it's a face."

"No it isn't," Sheila argued. "It's two circles with a line between them and a curve underneath. Your brain makes the connections and draws line that are not there, such as a circle round the whole lot which would turn it into a true smiley face. Well, it's the same with other connections. Nicola died in tragic circumstances a few days ago. Her latest gentleman friend, Eddie, died yesterday. Our minds automatically link the two events, even though there is not the slightest shred of evidence to support such a link."

"In other words, it's all coincidental."

"In other words, Joe," Sheila corrected him, "you've built a fairly convincing case on evidence which is purely circumstantial."

"We'll have to see what John law say about that, eh?"

"You might not have long to wait to find out," Brenda said, nodding at the expanse of road drifting away from the front of the Beachside towards the town centre.

Following her gaze, Joe had a distinct feeling of déjà vu. A police car was cruising along towards the hotel. From this distance Joe could not say whether it was driven by Constable Flowers but there was a passenger in the car, visible thanks to his white shirt and dark tie.

"A detective?" Joe asked.

"Perhaps," Sheila said as the car turned into the drive and crunched to a halt on the gravel.

Mike Flowers climbed out and put his hat on. On the far side of the car, partially blocked by Flowers, the other individual climbed out and reached back in for his jacket. Joe, Sheila and Brenda all exchanged glances.

"That can't be Terry Cummins," Brenda said.

"It could be," Joe replied. "It's a good eight or nine years since he was our community constable, maybe longer. And I remember him telling me he was moving into CID." He frowned. "Mind, I'm sure he said he was going to York, not Scarborough."

Again they watched while the two officers entered the hotel, and still they had not seen the plain clothes man's face.

"I think it is, you know," Sheila said.

Joe disagreed again. "You're the expert on the cops. Why would he be working here when he's based in York?"

Sheila answered vaguely. "I don't know. Perhaps he transferred again. Or maybe..." She gave up the ghost. "Constable Flowers is with him. That means it must be about Eddie."

Several minutes passed before Sarah Pringle ushered Flowers and his colleague out onto the terrace.

From his seated position, Joe looked up into a slim, lugubrious face. Brown eyes gazed from beneath a receding hairline, regarding him with curiosity and the pleasure of recognition. Beneath an aquiline nose, thin, almost cruel lips spread in a smile, which gradually broadened into a grin.

"I couldn't believe it when they said Joe Murray and the Sanford 3rd Age Club were here."

Joe's face split into a broad grin. He stood and shook hands. "Detective Sergeant Terry Cummins, you old scroat."

"Ah," Cummins cautioned. "Detective *Chief Inspector* Cummins, these days."

There followed several minutes of greeting between Cummins and the two women, during which Sarah supplied tea, and Flowers scraped another two chairs to the table.

"What are you doing in Filey, Terry?" Brenda asked.

"I'm on secondment from York. Manpower shortage in Scarborough, and they needed a Chief Inspector to oversee the place while their man is on leave. Mike, here, called me in over this business of your member's death. The minute he told me he'd been talking to Joe Murray, I knew I'd have problems." Cummins laughed good-naturedly. "I'll bet you've already been poking your nose in, haven't you, Joe?"

"Yes. And I've learned quite a lot, too."

"But we're betting most of it will be wrong, Terry," Sheila said.

"First," Joe said before Brenda could sidetrack him, "We wanna report an attempted mugging on the promenade at Scarborough, last night."

Handing over the black balaclava, Joe gave them a rundown of what had happened and Flowers took notes as he went along.

"You really should have handed this into the Scarborough police, sir," the Constable said when Joe was through.

"It was very late and we didn't want to hang around any longer," Sheila explained before Joe could get into the argument. "Mrs Jump was upset, we had all of her belongings back and we just needed to get away from there and back to Filey."

"I understand that, madam. I'll make a report and pass it

on to Scarborough. I shouldn't think anything will come of it, though. You know how it is. It's the busiest time of year; we get a lot of petty crime like this and it will be up to Mr Cummins here if we investigate further."

"Yes, well," said Joe, "I don't think it was just a random, petty crime. I think it's all to do with this Eddie Dobson business, and I also think you're dealing with an insurance fiddle, not a death."

Cummins' eyebrows rose. "Why do you say that?"

Alongside Joe, Sheila and Brenda groaned, but the two policemen were more attentive. Joe was sure that if they had been dogs their ears would have pricked up.

Briefly, Joe explained the things he had learned and the shaky chain of logic with which he had put them together. Cummins listened patiently, but it seemed to Joe that there was a hint of humour in his old friend's face.

When Joe was through, Cummins cleared his throat theatrically. "Well it's an interesting theory, Joe, but I'm sorry to have to tell you you're wrong."

Joe stared. "I am?"

"Eddie Dobson's body was found washed up on the beach in Cayton Bay about ten o'clock last night. Couple of teenagers down on the sands found him there and called our boys out immediately."

Sheila and Brenda were suddenly paying attention, while Joe was too stunned to respond for a moment.

When he did speak, it was with an air of incredulity. "What were a couple of kids doing on the sands at that time of night?" he demanded.

"Teenage hormones don't work shifts, Joe," Brenda pointed out.

"You're probably correct, madam," Flowers agreed. "They were both scared out of their wits when we got to them. We're waiting for the post mortem report, but Mr Dobson had a nasty dent in the back of his head, and it doesn't look as if it was caused by the rocks when he fell. More like the customary blunt instrument."

Sheila and Brenda gawped. "You mean..."

"He means, Sheila, Brenda, Joe," Cummins interrupted, "Eddie Dobson was dead before he went into the sea. He was murdered."

"I knew it, I knew it," Joe gasped.

"I'll tell you something else, too," Cummins went on. "His name wasn't Eddie Dobson."

"It wasn't?" Joe's excited tones spoke for the three of them.

"His real name was Edward Pennig."

"Unusual name," Joe commented.

"Very unusual, sir." Flowers eyed them suspiciously. "Do you not run identity checks on your members?"

"It's a social club, not the Secret Service," Brenda protested. "For people like Eddie, whom we don't know personally, we ask to see a rent book or utility bill, that's all."

Sheila spoke up in support of Brenda. "If Eddie Dobson, er, Pennig, whatever you want to call him, was living in rented accommodation we assume the landlord would have checked his credentials. That was certainly the case with Eddie. He was living in a housing association flat under the name of Dobson."

Joe took out his tobacco tin and cigarette papers. "So we have an oddbod who throws himself off the Brigg, only he didn't, and when it all comes out, he's living under a false handle. And you don't think that's suspicious?" He spread a thin line of tobacco across the paper and began to roll it.

"It's curious, I agree," said Cummins. "As things stand, we have no proof that Dobson was, er, up to no good, and I'd need a damn sight more than your say so before I could link him to Nicola Leach's death, and the fact that he was living under an assumed name has no bearing on the matter, unless someone knows otherwise. Anyone can assume whatever name they want, Joe, provided it's not done for purposes of fraud or deception."

"May I ask, Terry, how did you learn that he was living under a false name?" Sheila inquired.

Cummins nodded to Flowers, who explained, "His

underwear, believe it or not, madam. He had his name inked into the labels. They were also Royal Navy issue. We got in touch with HMS Raleigh and they faxed us a full résumé and an ID picture, which matches the photograph on his membership card for your club."

"Gosh," Brenda said. "He inked the name of his ship into his underwear, too, did he?"

Sheila giggled, Joe scowled, Cummins and Flowers gave her the kind of look usually reserved for those whose sanity was questionable.

"HMS Raleigh is a training base, Brenda," Joe told her. "All ratings pass through there." He turned to the policemen. "We knew he was a navy man. He told us. Was he a frogman?"

"No, sir. A cook."

Joe was crestfallen again.

Brenda beamed. "You see, Joe, you had something in common with Eddie. You're both cooks."

"Yes, well, we have something not in common now, don't we? He's dead and I'm not."

"He also came from Filey originally," Flowers reported. "Well, a village called Hunmanby, about three miles out of town. But he'd been in the navy for twenty-two years."

"Which is why no one here would know him?" Joe asked. "And also why he knew he could cook up his little scheme."

"What little scheme was that, Joe?" Sheila asked. "His plan to get himself murdered?"

Joe lit his cigarette and turned his Zippo lighter end over end on the table top while he considered his response. Eventually, he dropped the lighter in his pocket, and said, "Eddie didn't come here to be murdered. He came here to disappear. Probably so he could reappear under his real name, but considerably richer thanks to an insurance policy on Eddie Dobson. In order to do that, he needed at least one accomplice. Something went wrong. They argued, the accomplice killed him. The accomplice then dumped the body in the sea at Cayton Bay, probably during the night.

Flowers, you told us that other anglers described Eddie to you. Do you have your notes?"

The constable thumbed his notebook. "Here we are. They described him as a tall gentleman dressed in baggy jeans and an overlarge T-shirt, carrying a wax jacket."

"Baggy jeans and a T-Shirt that was too large for him," Joe said. "That's not the Eddie Dobson I spoke to here or back home in Sanford. He had a paunch. What those people described was someone dressed as Eddie Dobson. Someone a lot slimmer. Someone who knew the waters round these parts like the back of his hand. A fisherman, perhaps one of the coble operators." Joe smiled. "There's only one candidate. Ivan Irwin."

"Oh, Joe, you have that man on the brain," Sheila protested. "Just because you got into a spat with him over his Land Rover."

"No, no," Joe argued. "It all fits. We're told that Nicola Leach was run down by a Land Rover, and Irwin owns one that's just had some fresh paint applied to the front end. I saw Eddie go into Irwin's brother's tackle shop. Irwin is tall, but a lot slimmer and fitter than Eddie. On Irwin, Eddie's clothes would hang loose. I think Eddie knew Ivan or Jonny Irwin. Maybe from his young days here in the Filey area. When he came back with this idea of cashing in on Eddie Dobson's life insurance, it was Irwin he turned to. Then there was a fall out. Irwin takes the body out in his coble and dumps it, then goes out onto the Brigg as Eddie, jumps in, picks up the scuba tanks he'd hidden under the rocks, and swims to shore. You guys chalk it down as a suicide, but unfortunately for them, Eddie's body turns up."

Cummins finished his cup of tea. "All you have is a theory, Joe, but I can't just dismiss it out of hand. Why don't you and I take a walk to Jonny Irwin's tackle shop, see what he has to say, and then we'll see if we can find Ivan Irwin at Coble Landing?"

Joe took another drag on his cigarette, drained his cup and got to his feet. "Okay, but I have to tell you, neither of these guys would make my Christmas card list."

Chapter Thirteen

"Detective Chief Inspector now?" Joe's voice was filled with admiration as he and Cummins walked along the streets behind the Beachside, making for the town centre.

Ten o'clock Sunday morning was quieter than the previous days. Joe guessed that most people would still be in bed, sleeping off the previous night's drink, and those that were not would already be on the beach.

Cummins took a pack of Benson & Hedges from his pocket and offered it to Joe who shook his head.

"I'll stick to my roll ups, thanks."

The Chief Inspector lit his cigarette. "Some of my progress must be down to you. All those years when I was a beat bobby in Sanford, and the times I came into your café and read your casebooks. If you remember, even when I was at school, I never wanted to be anything but a copper."

"Ah, get out of it. That was nothing to do with me. Besides, the police don't teach you the tricks I use. It's all forensics and interrogation techniques these days."

Taking a deep drag on his smoke, Cummins disagreed. "We have to use logical deduction, Joe. All right, so most of us don't have your weird mind, but we have to be able to string together a logical case or we'd be torn apart in court. That's why I have to take it seriously when I listen to you. I know how clever you are, and your theory makes a sort of sense. I've got to follow it through, even if it leads nowhere."

"You know me, Terry. I never give in while there are questions unanswered."

"How's the third age club doing, Joe?" Cummins asked as they turned into the narrow street where Irwin's tackle

157

shop was located.

"Going well," Joe replied, relieved to be out of the sun and in the shade of the houses and businesses lining the street. "Over three hundred members and we get around an awful lot. Jaunts like this one every three months, and they're even getting me on a plane to Tenerife in the New Year."

"Tenerife? Isn't that where Alison went after you split up?"

Joe nodded. "It's a busy island, Terry. Chances of me bumping into my ex-wife while I'm over there are pretty slim."

"Who'll run Joe's Caff while you're there?"

"Joe's Caff? You're a bit behind the times aren't you? It's the Lazy Luncheonette these days."

Cummins laughed. "The Lazy Luncheonette? Who came up with that one?"

"Sheila and Brenda." Recalling that Cummins had left for York almost a decade back, Joe explained, "Course, you don't know, do you? Sheila and Brenda both came to work for me about five, six years back. You must know Sheila's husband, Peter."

"I did, yes. A sergeant when I was a probationer. He died, didn't he?"

"Heart attack," Joe confirmed. "Sheila insists it was the pressure of his job. He made inspector, probably not long after you moved to York. Put in maybe five years at that rank, then had a wobbler. He was on sick leave recovering from it when he had a second, and you know what they say about heart attacks. You can survive the first if you get help quickly enough, which Peter did, but the second following on so quickly is usually fatal."

They turned into the entrance, and sheltered under the portico, relieved to be out of the weather, and Joe took up his tale again. "Anyway, Brenda lost her husband, Colin, soon after, and within six months, both of them came to work for me. They're founder members of STAC, Sheila acts as secretary, Brenda as treasurer, and it was them who

158

persuaded me to change the name from Joe's Caff to the Lazy Luncheonette."

Pausing outside Irwin's place to finish his cigarette, Cummins laughed again. "Bit upmarket for Sanford, isn't it?"

Joe puffed at his own smoke. "I s'ppose so, but it works. We get plenya business from the industrial estate and the brewery, same as we always did, but with the name change, we also pull in punters from the retail park behind us. Shoppers dropping in when they've had enough of overpriced, plastic food served by robots who say, 'how may I help you', because the company trained them to say that, instead of 'whaddya want', which is what they really mean."

Cummins chuckled once more. "You always did have a silver tongue, Joe."

"Say what you like, but it works at the Lazy Luncheonette. The place is a gold mine."

"And who will you leave it to, Joe? Lee and his missus."

Joe sniffed disdainfully. "No one else, is there? And Lee's a good cook, you know. He should be. I sent him to that fancy catering college and what they didn't teach him, I did."

"Meat pie and chips."

Cummins stubbed out his cigarette, Joe followed suit and they stepped into the shop.

On the cue of the doorbell, Jonny Irwin appeared, his face beaming a broad smile. It faded to a scowl on seeing Joe.

"You again. I told you yesterday..."

"I'm here at this officer's behest," Joe interrupted.

Cummins dug into his jacket and pulled out his warrant card. "Detective Chief Inspector Cummins, sir. North Yorkshire Police. You are Mr Jonathan Irwin?"

"I am, and I told shortarse here, yesterday, I dain't care if you come with the Chief Constable, I've nowt to say to you."

If Joe had been singularly unimpressed by Irwin's bluster

the previous day, Cummins was even less so.

"Mr Irwin, we have reason to believe that Edward Pennig, also known as Eddie Dobson, bought a large amount of fishing tackle from you two days ago."

"And if he did…"

"Mr Irwin," Cummins interrupted, "Edward Pennig's body was washed up in Cayton Bay last night, but we know that he was dead before he went into the sea. This is a murder investigation, sir, and if you refuse to co-operate, you will leave me with no choice but to apply for a warrant to search these premises and audit your accounts to ascertain whatever information we can regarding Mr Pennig. If, during the course of that audit and search, we come across anything that may be of interest to Customs and Revenue, we will be obliged to pass the information on." Cummins paused to ensure his threat had sunk in. "Now, did Pennig come into this shop on Friday and purchase a large amount of tackle?"

Irwin let out his breath as a hiss. "He told me his name was Dobson."

"And how did he pay for his purchases?" Cummins pressed.

"Cash. I do take credit cards, but he had the cash in his wallet."

"The value of the order?"

Irwin remained silent.

"The value of the order, Mr Irwin," Cummins insisted.

"Four hundred and fifty-five pounds." Irwin sounded as though he did not wish to part with the breath he used to deliver the words.

Cummins made a note of it. "Did you know Mr Dobson, Pennig, whatever he called himself?"

Irwin shook his head. "Any reason I should?"

"Did your brother know him?"

"You'd have to ask Ivan about that."

"We will," Cummins assured him. "Did you see Dobson/ Pennig again after he left the shop?"

"Once," Irwin replied. "Late Friday afternoon when he

came back to collect it."

"And this was definitely Mr Dobson?"

Again Irwin nodded.

"And what time was that?"

"I told you. Late. Getting on for six. Before I closed up." He gestured at Joe. "A good fourteen hours before he came snooping round."

Cummins closed his notebook and put it away. "Thank you, Mr Irwin. It's too early to say whether we will need to speak to you again, but if we do, we'll be in touch." He glanced at Joe. "You ready?"

"Sure." Joe turned to follow Cummins out of the shop. At the door, he paused and looked back at Irwin. "Just one last thing. You're absolutely sure about the amount Dobson spent?"

"You're a Yorkshireman, too, aren't you? Do you ever get money wrong?"

Joe gave him a lopsided grin. "No. Course I don't."

He followed Cummins out into the street, where the Chief Inspector lit a fresh cigarette and they strolled on.

Taking out his tobacco tin and rolling a smoke, Joe said, "He's lying."

Cummins raised his eyebrows.

"Eddie owed me fifteen pounds. I asked him for it when we got here on Friday morning. He didn't have it. He showed me his empty wallet. All he had was what looked like a debit card. He also told me he was a bit strapped for cash."

"Yes? And?"

"He's in a strange town with no money. How does he get some?"

"Hole in the wall," Cummins replied.

"But a hole in the wall will only give you £350 a day. And you need cash in the bank before it will give you some. I just said, he told me he was a bit strapped. It's possible that he could have had some money in his pockets, but if so was he deliberately trying to welch on the fifteen that he owed me? That doesn't make a lot of sense. Irwin lying

161

would make more."

"So you're saying that Eddie could have used a credit card, which you just told me he didn't have?"

They emerged once more into the sunshine of Murray Street and turned down Cargate Hill towards the beach.

"No," Joe said, answering Cummins' last question. "I'm saying Eddie never paid for that gear at all. If I'm even half right, Terry, and Ivan Irwin is mixed up in this business, then what price his brother is in it with him? They're expecting a large payoff when the insurance settlement comes in, and it would be worth it to Jonny Irwin to drop a few pounds on the stock he gave to Eddie, stock he knew would never be used, which he could take back and sell it as shop soiled."

"Except that it came to you," Cummins pointed out.

"Sure, but what would we do with it? Take it back to Sanford, and at some point, a long lost relative would show up to claim Eddie's possessions. No. Irwin would get it back somewhere along the line, and if he didn't, so he dropped a few hundred quid. I've no doubt Eddie would have made it worth his while."

At the bottom of the hill, they turned left along the promenade.

While the streets had appeared quieter, it seemed to Joe that the sea front was even busier today. Day trippers, he guessed, crowding the esplanade and the safe sands. There were several sailboats out on the flat waters, and in the distance, more anglers on the Brigg. At the sea's edge, children and young adults played, splashing in the water, impromptu games of cricket and football had sprung up here and there and further away from the concentrated area, towards Carr Naze, he could see dog owners playing with their pets, throwing balls or Frisbees for them.

"It's all speculation, Joe," Cummins said. "Even if you're right and Irwin is lying, it doesn't link him to Pennig's death. Maybe they were old friends, maybe Irwin is just hiding the money from the taxman. Illegal, sure, but not murder. Tell me something; was Dobson with you people all night on Friday?"

Joe shrugged. "Ask me another. The disco was busy, Terry, and I was running it. I spoke to him at the bar, I saw him pay Sarah Pringle for his packed lunch, and I only noticed that because it looked, er, what's the word? Furtive. Underhanded. Sneaky. After that, I never noticed him and I forgot all about him until Saturday morning when Brenda told me she'd given him his ticket for the show. A minute or two after that, your boy, Flowers, showed up and told us Eddie was dead..." Joe frowned. "Now there's a thing."

"What?"

"What happened to his ticket for the theatre? It wasn't in his wallet. I know. I was there when Flowers pulled the wallet out of Eddie's jacket. It wasn't amongst his personal effects, either. We three packed them all away. Where the hell did it get to?"

"It could be anywhere, Joe. If it was on him, his killer could have taken it, or even left it where it was and it could have been turned to pulp in the sea. The same," Cummins went on, "could apply to any money Eddie had used to pay Jonny Irwin."

"I'm thinking something else, Terry." Joe stopped and looked his old friend earnestly in the eye. "Try and follow me on this one." He dug into his pockets and came out with the key. "I found this key in Eddie's room. Soon after, my room was ransacked. Nothing stolen. I guessed the burglar was looking for this. Now you heard me tell your man, Flowers, that Brenda was mugged on the front in Scarborough last night. Again, the thief took nothing. Again, I think he was looking for this. Now, let's suppose Eddie's killer is staying at the hotel. The Sanford 3rd Age Club are not the only people staying there, remember. Maybe, whatever deal Eddie had cooking, his accomplice is with him at the Beachside and they're deliberately keeping their distance. After Eddie's death, the accomplice ransacked my room, and didn't find the key. But he had Eddie's ticket for the Abba show, so he made his way there, sat through the show with us and then came for Brenda afterwards."

"What's the key for?"

"We don't know," Joe admitted, "but we're speculating that it's for Eddie's place in Sanford."

Cummins scratched his head. "What you suggest is possible, I suppose, but it doesn't get us much further for'ard. The theatre would have the ticket stubs and if you have the number, we can find out whether it was used, but that won't tell us who it is."

"No but it will narrow down the field," Joe pointed out. "And either Sheila or Brenda will have a list of the ticket numbers. If not here, then back in Sanford. I don't know which ticket Brenda gave to Eddie, but it was block booking and I'm sure the tickets were sequential."

"All right," Cummins agreed. "We'll check on it when we get back to the Beachside. In the meantime, let's see what this Ivan Irwin has to say for himself."

When they first arrived on Coble Landing, Irwin was nowhere to be seen, but his Land Rover was parked opposite the amusement arcade. With a glance around and through the crowds to ensure Ivan was not watching, Joe checked the front grille more closely than he had done the day before.

"It's had a new headlamp fitted," Joe said, "and a fresh dab of paint around it. The bumper's been straightened, and look here." He pointed higher up at two lines of screw holes across the upper grille area. "It looks like it had bull bars fitted, but they've been dumped." He stood upright. "Terry, I wouldn't be surprised to find that this is the Land Rover which knocked Nicola Leach down."

"Are you here again? What is it about mah truck that interests you?"

Joe turned and looked into Ivan Irwin's steely eyes. "Terry," he said, "meet Ivan Irwin, the owner of this Land Rover."

"Good morning, sir," Cummins greeted Irwin.

"And who are you? His lawyer?"

"No, sir. I'm Detective Chief Inspector Cummins of the North Yorkshire police, and I need to ask you a few

164

questions."

Ivan remained as unimpressed as his brother had been. "And I might not choose to answer 'em."

"In which case, I shall call for a team of constables and have you arrested on suspicion of causing death by dangerous driving, leaving the scene of an accident, and failing to report an accident." Cummins maintained eye contact. "Now do you want to do this the friendly way, or would you prefer to call *your* lawyer while I have you run into the station in Scarborough?"

Ivan chewed spit. "I only bought the car on Thursday. If it's been involved in an accident, it's nought to do wi' me."

"Can you prove that, Mr Irwin?" Cummins asked.

"Aye. I still have the registration doc. I haven't sent it off yet."

"I'll need to see that."

Irwin huffed out his breath. "Well, it's not here, is it? It's at home."

Cummins offered his notebook and pen. "Write down your name and address and I'll have the local constable call round to see it."

"Who fixed the headlamp and who removed the bull bars?" Joe asked while Ivan was writing down his address.

"You mind your own business," Ivan snapped.

"Mr Murray is assisting us in this investigation, Mr Irwin, and if you don't answer him, I'll ask the same questions and you will answer me."

"I bought it as seen, and there were nay bull bars fitted and nowt wrong with the headlights."

"Who did you buy it from?" Cummins asked.

"Ex navy lad," Irwin replied. "Comes from these parts, but he's been overseas a long time."

"Eddie Pennig," Joe said.

"Might be," Irwin replied. "He took the counterfoil off the registration doc."

"His name will still be printed on the document," Joe said, "and even if it wasn't, Terry, you could get Swansea to track the vehicle's history."

165

"Stop trying to teach your grandma how to suck eggs, Joe," Cummins rebuked him. Of Irwin, he asked, "did you buy this car from Edward Pennig?"

"Yes. I did. Is there owt else you need to know?"

"Plenty," Joe said. "Did you stay overnight in Sanford on Wednesday?"

"I've never been to Sanford. At least not in the last twenty years, I haven't. I bought it off him here in Filey, on Thursday morning."

"Not possible," Joe said. "He was at my place on Thursday."

"He must be a right clever feller, then," Irwin sneered. "In two places at the same time. I told you, I bought it off him right here, and I can bring you witnesses to that." He waved a hand at the landing around him where fishermen and coble attendants mingled with the crowds.

"I wouldn't trust any of these not to back you up," Joe commented. An image came to his mind; a memory of Sarah Pringle and Ivan coming out of the Star Inn. "How well do you know Sarah Pringle?"

"You're a nosy little bugger, aren't you?"

"Yes, I am," Joe agreed. "Especially when two of my members are dead, both in suspicious circumstances."

"I know Sarah, full stop, but she wasn't here when I bought the car off Eddie. Right?"

Joe shrugged. "If you say so." While Cummins asked a few supplementary questions, Joe looked around seeking inspiration. With typical police thoroughness, Cummins was discussing the sale of the vehicle, but Joe knew that the answers did not lie with straightforward questions. Men like Irwin could dodge for weeks or months by spinning their answers in the right direction, and Cummins was hogtied by procedure.

A rust-pitted tractor hauled a coble up the slipway, its engine protesting under the strain. Joe guessed that the old hands here had been doing it so long that, like Cummins and his questioning, the procedure would be automatic. He watched the tractor driver and fisherman manhandle the boat into its parking position, and uncouple the chains that bound the tractor to it. The engine chugged away while the two men passed a moment chatting, and then the tractor driver climbed back on his vehicle, and pulled it away from the boat to park it up.

An idea stuck him. He turned back to the conversation between Cummins and the fisherman.

"Irwin, do me a favour and run the engine."

Even Cummins was puzzled, but Joe dismissed his frown with a miniscule shake of the head.

"Why should I?"

"Because essentially, you're a thoroughly decent chap and you'd like to help Chief Inspector Cummins clear up these two deaths?" Joe suggested. "Listen to me. I've no doubt that you can prove you bought this car off Eddie Pennig on Thursday morning, so that means you're not involved in Nicola Leach's death, but Eddie may have been. It may be the very reason he wanted rid of the Land Rover. But in order to help you, I need to hear the engine running. Now, please, just run it for me."

Puffing out his breath again, Irwin dug the keys out, climbed into the Land Rover and fired the engine.

Listening to it, Joe commented, "I could do with Harry Needham here." He took out his mobile, called up the recording of the 999 call and passed it to the Chief Inspector. "Have a listen at that, and compare the sound."

Cummins did so, holding the phone to his ear, then pulling it away to listen to the Land Rover, then putting it back again.

"Not the same," he said, handing the phone back. "Thank you, Mr Irwin." Cummins concentrated on Joe. "So what was that all about?"

"Tell you later," Joe said. "One last thing, Irwin. How much did you pay for the Land Rover?"

"Mind your own business." Under a menacing stare from Cummins, the fisherman backed down. "Four hundred pounds."

Chapter Fourteen

During the slow walk back along the promenade, the heat rising as the sun climbed higher, Joe told Cummins of the audio tape's findings.

Taking the information in, the Chief Inspector responded, "If Irwin's Land Rover was the one used to run Nicola Leach down, it means that this Cora Harrison woman wasn't in it at the time, so it looks like your niece was right, Joe. She was passing by, saw it, reported it and wanted to remain anonymous." Cummins shrugged. "It happens. More than you may imagine, too."

Joe did not believe it, but now was not the time to say so. "Well, the ball's in your court, Terry. What's your next move?"

"I'll get young Flowers to take official statements from the Irwin brothers, and we'll have the repair work on the Land Rover checked with Scientific Support in Sanford, and see where we go from there. For now I need to build up a picture of Eddie Pennig's movements last night, and I'm waiting for the coroner's report on the cause of death."

Joe chuckled. "I'd have thought having his head caved in would be enough to shuffle him off."

Cummins frowned at the levity. "Yes, Joe, but I need to know what caved his head in. It's all right saying it was a blunt instrument, but what size and shape? We know the damage was not from the rocks off the Brigg. The cuts would have been more randomly distributed, there would have been traces on his face. There weren't. It means he never went off the Brigg. He was dumped in the sea either from the sands or from a boat. The master at Coble Landing has a record of the boats that went out last night and Friday night, and according to him, there was nothing odd about them. No one seen carrying a large bundle, for example. Chances are then, if he was thrown from a boat, it was from Cayton Bay or further down Filey Bay, Reighton Sands, for instance."

They passed the bottom of Cargate Hill, where droves of people were heading down to the beach.

Joe gazed out over the crowded sands. "They'll be lucky to find any room on the beach... Just the same as Eddie was lucky, or unlucky, to find room on our bus."

"You keep going on about that."

"Because it all fits together," Joe argued. "Eddie was here on Thursday according to Irwin, and back in Sanford by the afternoon. Now if he was already in Filey why did he need to be on the bus with us, Friday morning?"

"I don't know, Joe."

"Neither do I, but it must be important, or he would have stayed in Filey and just gone home with us on Monday." Joe tossed the information in his head. "And another thing. If it was Eddie's Land Rover that hit and killed Nicola, why wait until Thursday to turn up here? The accident was Tuesday. Why didn't he drive straight here Wednesday and get rid of it?"

"We only have Irwin's word that he didn't," Cummins said.

Joe shook his head. "He was in my place first thing Wednesday morning and he was in the Miner's Arms on Wednesday evening."

"He could have had the Land Rover repaired on Wednesday," Cummins suggested.

"In Sanford? I think our Gemma would have cottoned on to that by now, but it may be worth ringing her to find out. I'll bell her from the hotel."

"And keep me posted, Joe," Cummins said as they tackled the steep climb up to The Crescent.

Halfway up, they paused to catch their breath.

"If anybody had told me that getting old was gonna be like this," Joe complained, "I'd have gone out in a blaze of glory ten years ago."

Cummins grinned. "You're not old. You've years left in you yet." He yawned. "What will you do with the rest of the day?"

"Bridlington, I think," Joe said. "Or maybe Scarborough again. It depends on Sheila and Brenda."

They set off again up the steep path.

"You never went down on your knees and proposed to either of them, Joe?"

Joe snorted. "No fear. Ten years with Alison was enough to put me off marriage for life. I'm quite happy on my own, living above the café."

Cummins smiled at the cynicism. "It's all about finding the right woman, Joe. I've been wed twenty-four years. Not all joy, but I wouldn't have it any other way."

"Yeah? Well, good on you. For me the right woman is no woman."

"So it's definitely Lee who gets the café when you turn your toes up."

Joe nodded as they passed into the Beachside's drive. "I said earlier, I know he's a gormless sod, but he's a good cook and Cheryl, his wife, has enough brains to run the place." Joe waved at the hotel. "A bit like this place."

"Hmm?" Cummins asked distractedly.

Joe paused in the entrance, and pointed to the licensee notice above the door. "Billy Pringle holds the liquor licence, but Sarah Pringle is the real brains behind this outfit. Her brother and son couldn't run the proverbial in a brewery." A distant look came to Joe's eyes. "Now if I ever did decide to settle down again, it would be with a woman like Sarah Pringle."

"This business of Pennig's key, Joe," Cummins said, dragging him from the realms of his imagination. "Whoever Pennig was working with must be in this hotel somewhere."

"I thought that, too, if you remember, but I've had time to think about it since, and the answer is, not necessarily."

Joe shushed Cummins while they passed through the bar and out onto the terrace.

Sheila and Brenda had been joined by Les Tanner and Sylvia Goodson, other club members and other hotel guests had taken other tables. Joe pulled Cummins to one side where they lit cigarettes and looked out over the bay.

"I'm speculating here, Terry," Joe said, keeping his voice down, "but I saw Sarah Pringle with Ivan Irwin in Filey yesterday. I'm not saying there's anything going down there, but just suppose there is. Would Irwin take advantage of that while he was working with Pennig?"

"I don't know," the Chief Inspector admitted. "Would he?"

"You've met him. I wouldn't trust either of the Irwin brothers further than I could throw Brenda."

Cummins blew out a cloud of smoke and watched the breeze carry it off. "Go on then, Joe. How d you see it?"

"Eddie has turned up dead; murdered. All right, so you shouted me down on the insurance fiddle, but I think that's how it all started. I think Eddie came home to Filey from the navy and fell in with old friends, Jonny and Ivan. And I think they cooked up this little scam that would see Eddie Pennig fall off the Brigg and someone claim on his life insurance. Jonny or Ivan, take your pick. The three of them split the proceeds and everyone's happy. Ivan the terrible is having it off with Sarah and he knows the Sanford 3rd Age Club are coming here, and it was him who came up with the idea in the first place. Eddie moves to Sanford, can't get on the outing, so he mows Nicola down, has his Land Rover repaired, then brings it here where Ivan takes it off him. No money changes hands. Instead, Eddie is supplied with fishing gear from Jonny's shop. Then they fall out. They kill Eddie, dump him in the sea, but they need his flat keys because they don't know what evidence he may have left lying around in Sanford. Ivan talks to Sarah, she tells him I've cleared out Eddie's effects. He raids my room, then comes for Brenda on the front in Scarborough."

Smoking his cigarette, Cummins thought about it, then shook his head. "Sorry, Joe, but I don't buy it, and I'll tell you why. The insurance thing. Eddie Pennig was a jack tar.

A sailor. He wouldn't have any insurance worth mentioning, and what's more important, in order to claim the insurance, Eddie Pennig would have to 'die', which means he'd lose his pension. He's done twenty-two years, so he's coming out on full pension, and he has years to live yet. Is it worth throwing that away for the sake of an insurance policy worth, say twenty or thirty thousand?"

Joe shrugged. "All right, all right, so maybe the insurance thing is wrong, but I'll bet I'm right on the rest of it."

"We'll see." Cummins took out his mobile. "I'll get Flowers to pick up the investigation here and leave you to your weekend."

The Chief Inspector left the terrace and Joe crossed to the table, and joined his companions.

"Still playing Sherlock, Murray?" Tanner antagonised him.

"The investigation I'm really looking forward to, Les, is your murder. Mind you, it won't take much solving. I'll be the guilty party."

"What are you three planning for the day?" Sylvia asked, with the obvious intention of pouring oil on troubled waters.

"It's up to the two ladies," Joe replied.

A former administrator at Broadbent Auto Repairs, she lacked Tanner's autocracy, as a consequence of which, Joe found her much easier to deal with. He watched her click a couple of saccharin pills into a cup of black tea. Diabetic, she was also lactose intolerant, although Joe suspected that the problem was more psychosomatic than physical.

As if to confirm his suspicion, Sylvia pointed at Sheila's bruised leg. "You really should cover that, Sheila."

"It's nothing," Sheila assured her. "I caught it on a fire extinguisher bracket yesterday. Just a scratch."

"Well you should cover it," Sylvia said. "And look at your arms. They're burning in this sun. Are you using a strong lotion?"

"I haven't used any lotion at all." Sheila replied.

With a fussy tut, Sylvia dipped into her voluminous handbag and came out with a bottle of Coral sun lotion.

"Put some of that over your arms. It'll help protect you from the ultra-violet."

She passed the bottle to Sheila who flipped open the cap and sniffed at it. "Smells quite nice," she said. "Are you sure Sylvia? It must be very expensive."

Sylvia nodded. "I have another bottle, and no it's not expensive... well, not as expensive as some of the big names. You can get it at any chemist, but I buy mine at the supermarket."

Sheila smeared the lotion on her arm and began to rub it in.

Brenda took the bottle and sniffed at it. "Coconut oil," she said.

"Aren't they all?" Joe asked crushing out his cigarette. "So Les, what are you and Sylvia gonna do? Lounge around on the beach while you explain what happened at Anzio?"

"Scarborough, as a matter of fact," Tanner replied. "There's a dance at the Spa complex. You should try it, Murray. Quite relaxing."

"It's all right for you oldies, I suppose," Joe said, "but us young'uns prefer something livelier. Don't we Brenda?"

"Oh definitely," Brenda agreed. "We're taking Joe to a rave on Flamborough Head. We'll get him stoned on ginger beer and then clean his wallet out."

Billy Pringle came out and began to clear cups, saucers and glasses from the tables. Sylvia put away her sun lotion, and she and Tanner left, prompting Joe, Sheila and Brenda to depart too.

From Filey they took the bus to Bridlington where their first port of call was the nearest bar for a lunchtime drink.

Over a beer in the Harbour Tavern, while Sheila and Brenda chattered excited as any child on a day trip to the seaside, Joe sank into his thoughts, seeking that elusive something which would put everything together.

Coming out of the pub, the two women wandered into the town, while Joe took himself to the shoreline, north of the harbour, and took pictures of Flamborough Head. The white cliffs jutted out into the North Sea, like some kind of barrier to the land beyond, in the same way that his inability to string together a coherent theory created a barrier to account for the two deaths.

If Flamborough marked the northern boundary of Bridlington Bay, there was nothing to the south. The beach spread out as far as he could see, well beyond the town, with no particular landmark to say, 'This is where the Bridlington Bay finishes', and again it reminded Joe of his departed members. There was no 'end' in sight to the problem of the two murders.

Staring out to sea, north to Flamborough, south to the horizon, Joe rolled and smoked cigarette after cigarette, and when his two companions returned after an hour or more, he was still sitting, smoking, contemplating.

"What is the matter with you, Joe?" Sheila asked as they sat in a restaurant for a light lunch. "You're as quiet as the grave."

"Nicola is what's wrong with me. Nicola and Eddie. Something is not quite right. Something is just too pat about it all."

"Judging by what you told us, the Irwin brothers are up to their eyes in it," Brenda pointed out.

A waitress delivered three tuna salads and they tucked in.

"That is what I mean about it all being too pat," Joe grumbled. "You met Ivan at Coble Landing. He's no fool. Do you think he would be running round in a Land Rover he got from Eddie Pennig if he'd just killed him? And even if he was, do you think he'd have admitted it to Cummins so quickly? And what about the price he paid for it? Exactly the same amount as Eddie spent in Jonny's shop? Do you think Ivan wouldn't have played it up or down if he and his brother were guilty of the killings?"

"You seem to have made your mind up that Eddie ran Nicola down," Sheila said.

"Yes I have," Joe agreed, chewing on a soggy lettuce leaf. "He wanted to be with us in Filey, so he created a seat on the bus. I'm sure of it. But why did Ivan or Jonny kill him?"

"Thieves fall out, Joe," Brenda pointed out. "If you're also right about a possible insurance swindle, then something went wrong, they argued, they fought and Eddie was killed. Now stop brooding on it and eat your salad."

Swallowing a forkful of grated red cheese, Joe pushed his plate away. "I've had enough. Bloody rabbit food. Gimme a steak and kidney pie any time." He leaned back. "All right, you put it all together."

"I can't," Sheila admitted, "but then I wouldn't, would I?" She too pushed her plate away and sat back. "You're linking the two deaths without a shred of concrete evidence to link them. Everything is circumstantial. Nicola is run down, allegedly by a Land Rover, Eddie sells a Land Rover, but even if it is in curious circumstances, there's nothing to suggest it was the same vehicle that killed Nicola, and until you have such evidence, you shouldn't put the two events together."

"And although it's obvious that Eddie was up to something, it still doesn't make him guilty of killing Nicola," Brenda said. "They're two separate events, Joe, and maybe if you cut the one from the other, you might be able to stop worrying about it."

"So who's worried?" Joe asked and picked up the bill. "I don't like to be beaten, is all." He dug out his wallet.

"We'll get this, Joe," Sheila insisted.

He waved her objection away and left a twenty and a ten on the table.

They came out onto the street, shaded from the hot afternoon, and Sheila dug into her bag. "I bought a bottle of that sun lotion Sylvia uses," she said, and poured a little onto her hands before handing it to Brenda. "It really is mild and the bottle says it offers maximum protection."

Joe sneered. "My meat pies claim to be home made, but the Lazy Luncheonette isn't my home."

"Yes it is," Brenda argued taking a little of Sheila's lotion and rubbing it on her arms. "You live in the flat upstairs."

"Don't get technical. You know what I mean" Joe countered. He took the bottle from Brenda while the two

175

women fussed over spreading the lotion. "Coral," he said sniffing at the bottle. "I've never heard of them."

"Budget range of skin and beauty products," Brenda explained. "It's aimed at those who are underpaid and overworked."

"You two are overpaid and underworked," Joe declared, "so why are you buying it?"

They walked on through the town, and cut into the Promenade Shopping Centre. Although it was comparatively small, it still took the better part of an hour to get to the far end, and when they emerged opposite the bus station, the women were once again laden with carrier bags.

"What the hell are you going to do with all this clothing?" Joe asked.

"Wear it," Sheila replied. "That's what clothing is for, Joe."

Brenda held up her carriers bearing famous, High Street names. "We may only be a couple of humble kitchen slaves from Sanford, but when we get dolled up, we could be high society. No one would know the difference."

Brenda's words struck a chord with Joe, but once more, his mind would not make the necessary connection. Throughout the bus ride back to Filey, he nagged at it, and his brain, much like his ex-wife, refused to back down.

When the bus swept down the steep hill and through the roundabout at the turn offs for Reighton on the right and Hunmanby on the left, Sheila's excitement manifested itself. Pointing to a scrub of land on the right, she said, "That was the old Butlins Holiday Camp. We took the children there for a week in the seventies."

Joe was more interested in the view to the left and the village of Hunmanby. Eddie Pennig came from there. His parents had had a house there. What would happen to the house now that Eddie was no more?

The bus continued on its way, turning off for Filey, bumping over the level crossing and turning into the bus station, where they climbed off, and found George Robson idling on a bench by the flowerbeds.

"Busman's holiday, George?" Brenda asked.

He frowned, squeezing sweat through the creases in his brow. "How do you mean?"

Brenda swept a hand around, gesturing at the flowerbeds, a riot of colour in the summer sun. "You're a gardener by trade. I thought you were admiring Filey's display of violets."

George looked them over as if seeing the well-tended gardens for the first time. "Polyanthus, most of 'em, not violets. And no, I wasn't checking them out. I'm waiting for Owen."

Joe sat alongside George and rolled a cigarette. "Where is he?"

"Chemist." George waved at the pharmacy across the street, next door to Harrison's Carpet Centre. "Wasp bite."

Brenda chuckled. "Sure it was a wasp and not one of your tarts."

George pulled his tongue out at her. "We don't mix with tarts, Brenda. Only class, me and Owen. And talking of tarts, have the plod sorted out that business with Nicola Leach yet?"

Joe shook his head, put the freshly rolled cigarette in his mouth and lit it. "No further forward, mate."

"I'd have thought you'd have cracked it by now, Joe."

"They won't listen to me," Joe replied as he dropped his Zippo in his gilet. He stood up. "Don't forget, George. Disco at eight in the Beachside's lounge."

"Might make it, Joe, or we might hit the town again."

Joe and the two women moved on. As they crossed the street outside the bus station, Joe paused and stared again at the carpet centre and adjacent pharmacy.

"What's up, Joe?" Brenda demanded. "Thinking of laying a new floor in the café, or do you need something for the weekend?"

Sheila tittered. Joe ignored the ribaldry. "No. I just get the feeling I'm missing something." He turned and followed them along Murray Street.

In any other town, this late on a Sunday afternoon, the

shops would be closed, but the traders took full advantage of the seaside allowance for extended hours, and many souvenir shops were still open, providing the women with more opportunities for retail therapy, and Joe with a greater feeling of irritation as they made slow progress through the streets in the direction of the Beachside.

Turning towards the hotel, Joe spotted several police cars outside Jonny Irwin's shop. He picked up his pace, hurrying towards Constable Flowers on duty at the entrance to the shop.

"What's going on?" he asked.

"Not sure I'm supposed to tell you, sir," Flowers replied.

"If you don't tell me, Terry Cummins will," Joe assured him. "Have you found something?"

The constable continued to hedge. "No, sir. We're looking for something."

Joe tutted. "You're hard work this afternoon, Flowers."

"Yes, sir, I am, because I'm not sure what I'm allowed to say to you." Flowers pushed back his cap and scratched his forehead. "Look, don't spread it about, but Mr Cummins has arrested both Irwin brothers."

Chapter Fifteen

"It's simple enough, Joe. When we pushed Ivan, he admitted he'd handed over no money, but given Pennig a credit note which he could take to Jonny's shop and exchange for goods."

Joe kept a wary eye on the clock. It was almost six and he was due back at the Beachside to run the disco at eight.

Cummins's office was as small, cramped and busy as Gemma's back in Sanford, but at least the Chief Inspector had a window through which he could look out on the main streets of Scarborough below. Outside, even though the shops had closed, the streets were still packed with holidaymakers and day trippers eager to wring every ounce of pleasure from their visit to the coast.

After speaking with Flowers, he had hurried back to the Beachside, dropped off his purchases and then called a taxi to take him straight to Scarborough, but he need not have hurried. When he arrived, Cummins was still interviewing the Irwin brothers, and he had to wait a considerable time before his old pal escorted him through to the office.

"You suspect, then, that the Land Rover was used to run down Nicola Leach?"

Cummins shrugged. "I don't know. Scientific support will give the front end a good going over tomorrow. It doesn't matter how much work has been done on the vehicle, if it was the one, there will be traces of Nicola on it somewhere. In the meantime, I've arrested the Irwins in connection with Eddie Pennig's death, not Nicola's."

"You believe something was going on between the three?" Joe asked.

"Don't you?" Cummins asked. "Joe, you put me on this

trail, and all you did was ask more questions than I could answer. The vehicle, is a 1975 ex-military soft top, and it's worth anything up to £15,000. Why would Pennig let it go for such a low price? Why would he let it go in exchange for goods rather than cash? Ivan Irwin says he doesn't know why he got it so cheap, and he won't explain why the deal became a barter rather than a sale. Jonny Irwin says it's nothing at all to do with him. Pennig turned up with a credit note to the value of £400 and he honoured it. They're lying, and until I get to the truth, I'll keep them here." Cummins drummed his fingers on the blotter. "And get this. Neither of them has asked for a lawyer."

"Any form?" Joe asked.

"Trivia," Cummins replied. "Jonny was done for a VAT fiddle a few years back. Fined, ordered to pay the tax and interest and that was that. Ivan was done for a fuel fiddle some years back. He had an arrangement with a tanker driver. Most of the coble fishermen use red diesel for their boats. Ivan had the driver dropping diesel into forty gallon drums at his house, but it was blue, regular diesel. The kind you buy at the pumps. And that's how the customs men rumbled it. Ivan was fined and given a suspended sentence. The tanker driver had been pulling the same stunt with other small businesses, and he was jailed for eighteen months. Aside from that, both men have reputations as scrappers and they've been done a few times for brawling. Usually drunk. Ivan is currently bound over after a barney in a pub about nine months ago."

Joe stroked his chin. "It's not up to me to tell you how to do your job, Terry, but I don't like the smell of this. I said to Sheila and Brenda this afternoon, these men are not fools. If they were pulling some stunt with Eddie, Ivan would have likely got rid of the Land Rover after Eddie was killed."

"So you don't think there's anything to all this?" Cummins sounded angry. "Joe, you put me onto it."

Joe shook his head and stroked his chin. "I know that, and something was going on, for sure. But I get the feeling the finger has been pointed at Ivan and Jonny Irwin to direct us away from the real culprits, and I don't want to see you wasting your time and effort."

Joe fell silent, running his mind over all that had happened since his arrival in Filey. It was like a jigsaw, but there was a piece missing, and that annoyed him.

A memory echoed in his head. Following the impulse, he asked, "Are either of them married?"

"According to Flowers, Ivan was, but it fell apart about twenty years ago. His wife walked out on him and she's never been seen in Filey since. Flowers reckons she moved to York."

A light lit in Joe's mind. "Any danger I could speak to Ivan?"

"I don't know, Joe. I appreciate what you're doing, but I don't want to risk upsetting any case we may have against them by involving you."

"It's off the record, Terry. They're playing some game and I have a few games of my own I can play. I promise you will be no worse off."

Cummins drummed his fingers again. Then, as if making up his mind, he snatched up the phone. "It's Cummins. Get Ivan Irwin to interview room two." Putting down the receiver, he stood up. "Come on."

Joe had never liked the interior of police stations, and Scarborough was no exception. Situated on Northway, west of the shopping centres, it was a modern and well-appointed building, its offices smart, airy and comfortable, but the interview rooms were as bad as Joe anticipated; small, pokey, smelling of floor cleanser and old socks.

In deference to Ivan's huge size, Cummins ordered two constables to stay in the room with them. Ivan, already in a surly mood, became even more irritated when confronted with Joe. "What's he doing here?"

Cummins opened his mouth to explain, but Joe beat him to it. "I'm here to help you, believe it or not. Course, I can just walk, if you'd prefer, and leave you facing a murder charge."

"I haven't killed no one," Ivan retorted. "But if I was

gonna, you'd probably be top of my list."

"Mr Murray is an experienced investigator, Irwin, and he has an eye for detail which some of us envy. You don't have to talk to him, but it might help you if you do. The interview won't be recorded and we won't bring anything you say into evidence unless it's repeated in the presence of a solicitor."

"I've a living to earn," Irwin protested, "and you've no right to keep me here. I haven't done anything wrong."

"Then talk to Joe," the Chief Inspector insisted.

Ivan glared at them. He appeared as if talking to Joe was the last thing he would like to do, and for a moment Joe had an insight into the fear of a wounded zebra confronting a hungry lion.

At last, Ivan capitulated. "What do you want?"

"I run my own business, just like you," Joe said. "I know about the stresses and strains of trying to make a profit, and my wife walked out on me ten years ago. Disappeared, just like that." He snapped his fingers. "The difference is, Alison cleared off to the Canary Islands. I didn't kill her and dump her in the sea after finding her fooling around with Eddie Pennig."

The colour rose in Ivan's already tanned face. He threw himself across the table, his fingers stretching for Joe's throat. Joe forced his chair back, scraping it across the floor to keep clear of those huge hands. Cummins half rose, and the two constables restrained Ivan.

"I'll kill you. I swear I will."

"Touched a nerve, did I?" Joe asked.

"Sit down and behave," Cummins ordered. "You two stay where you are," he barked at the uniformed officers. "If he moves again, cuff him."

The two constables ranged themselves either side of the suspect, who fumed at Joe.

"My ex-wife is alive," Ivan hissed. "She lives somewhere outside York. I told you, I didn't kill no one."

"I'll need an address so I can confirm that," Cummins told him.

"I don't think you'll need it, Terry," Joe said. "He's

probably telling the truth. That's not what annoyed him, is it, Ivan?" The big fisherman did not answer. "It was talking about Eddie Pennig and his wife that hit the spot. Am I right?"

Ivan looked away, glowering at the wall.

"See, Terry," Joe went on, "when we spoke to him earlier today, he told us in a roundabout way that he knew Pennig. He didn't actually say so, but when you pressed him to admit that he bought the Land Rover off Edward Pennig, he agreed that he did. Sellers and buyers don't go into such close details. If you'd asked him did he buy it from someone called Pennig, he'd have said the same, but you were specific. Edward Pennig. That told me he knew Pennig. Then, when you said the Land Rover was worth anything up to fifteen grand, the penny dropped. Why would any man let a car go for four hundred notes when it was worth fifteen thousand? Because he needed rid of it urgently. And Ivan, here, knew that, didn't you, Ivan? So you screwed him to the ground on the price, and you didn't even hand over cash. Instead, you let him have a credit note for four hundred pounds so he could do some shopping at Jonny's place. Four hundred was the *retail* value of the stuff Eddie bought. It probably cost Jonny less than two hundred."

"What about it?" Ivan demanded.

Joe gloated in his superior logic. "There are two reasons why someone would do that. One: because he can. In other words, Eddie was in a fix, and he needed a way out of it. Two: revenge. You knew Eddie Pennig from years ago. You actually told us he was from these parts but he'd been away in the navy for years. You caught him screwing around with your wife, but before you could get at him, he was gone, away with the navy, and he never came back until last Thursday, did he?"

For a long moment, Ivan continued to glare at the bare, plaster walls and did not speak. When he finally faced Joe, his face beamed pure hatred. "I'm bound over for eighteen months, see. I was dragged in court for a scrap last year.

183

Another offence, and I go down. When I saw him last Thursday, I felt like ripping his heart out and ramming it down his throat, but I couldn't. Life's tough for us fishermen. If I go down, I lose my business. So I had to keep me hands to meself. Then he told me he needed shot of the car. He'd been in an accident with it. Some old bird got killed. Not here. He didn't say where it was, but he promised us the local plod wouldn't be looking for it. He asked me for ten grand in cash. Dirt cheap, he said. I told him right where he could stick it. He was practically on his knees, begging. So I offered him two hundred notes. We did a bit of haggling and eventually we came to the deal. Four hundred, but not in cash. He'd take a credit note for our Jonny's shop, or nothing at all. There was a bit more arguing and eventually he caved in." Ivan grinned. "And do you know how much I enjoyed shafting him like that? It's the best party I've had for years. And when we were done, I told him to clear off and if I ever saw him again, I'd lamp him good and proper."

"And it didn't bother you when he turned up dead forty-eight hours later?" Cummins asked.

Ivan shrugged. "Until you dragged me in here and told me, I didn't even know it was him. All I knew was they'd pulled some dead angler from the water." He jabbed a hard finger into the table top. "But I'll tell you this, again. I didn't kill him, and neither did our Jonny. We had nowt to do with killing him."

"Lamp him good and proper," Cummins repeated Ivan's words. "That sounds to me like you would have killed him."

"Aye, happen I would, but I didn't because I never saw him again. Our Jonny did when he went to the shop to order and collect on his credit note, but shortarse here saw him after that." Ivan pointed at Joe. "We had nowt to do with killing him, me and our Jonny."

Cummins pushed a pen and paper across to Ivan. "Your ex-wife's name and address."

"I dain't knah where she lives, man. Only that it's Copmanthorpe near York."

"Write her name down. I'll get the community officers to check it out."

Ivan scribbled down the information and Cummins spoke to the uniformed men. "Take him back to the cells."

"I've told all I know," Ivan protested. "I have to be out to catch the tides."

"You've put me to a great deal of trouble, Irwin. You could have told me all of this earlier today. You'll stay put until I have some confirmation of your story," Cummins nodded to the two officers, who took Ivan by the armpits.

"Hang on, Terry," Joe said.

Everyone paused.

"Irwin, what did you do for a vehicle before you bought the Land Rover?"

"I have an old van. It's at my place."

Joe felt his anticipation growing. "Bit of engine trouble? Piston slap?"

"Aye, it's getting on a bit."

"Did you lend that van out last Tuesday night?"

Ivan shook his head. "Nope. It was on the dock while I was out fishing."

Joe's heart sank again. Another image leapt into his mind. "Do you own a set of ladders?"

Ivan's eyes widened in surprise. "What? You think I hook ladders to the boat and dive in to catch the fish by hand? My boat's a coble, not a bloody pirate ship."

Joe fumed. "Do you own a set of ladders?"

"Yes, I do. They're at home."

"Are they usually on your van?" Joe pressed.

"So now you think I'm moonlighting as a window cleaner, do you? No, they're not on my van. I don't even have a roof rack. All right?"

Joe nodded and the constables led Ivan from the room.

"Well?" Cummins asked.

"We're no further forward," Joe admitted.

"Irwin could be lying."

"He could be, but I don't think so." Joe took out his tobacco tin and rolled a cigarette. "It's all too easy to check.

185

What we do know is that Eddie killed Nicola Leach. He was panicked into letting the Land Rover go for a fraction of its value. Beyond that, we're no nearer learning why he wanted to be in Filey, or why he was murdered." Dropping his tobacco tin back in his pocket, he held up the cigarette. "Where do we go for a smoke?"

"Car park at the rear," Cummins said, and led the way from the interview room.

Joe followed him along the gloomy, ground floor corridor, to a rear entrance, where the Chief Inspector pushed open the door, and let them out into the warm, evening air.

Lighting his cigarette while Cummins fished out his own pack, Joe said, "I'm trying to string this together. Eddie hit Nicola. I believe it was intentional to create a seat on the Filey outing. After he'd hit her, he either panicked or, more likely, he deliberately approached the Irwin brothers. All that begging and haggling was so much bull. He was willing to take a serious loss on the car. Why?"

Cummins lit up and blew smoke into the sunshine. "Because he had something cooking worth so much that it made the fifteen grand for his car look like pocket money."

"Correct," Joe agreed. He took another deep drag on his smoke. "Tell you what I was thinking on the way back from Bridlington, this afternoon. His parents' house in Hunmanby. Are his parents still alive?"

"I don't know," Cummins replied. "We haven't got that far into his life story yet. Or, at least, I haven't. Young Mike Flowers might know." He took out his mobile and punched in the numbers.

While Cummins spoke to the Filey policeman, Joe looked around the car park with envy. There were many police vehicles, but just as many private cars, too, most of them late model compacts, with one or two larger cars here and there. He mentally compared them with his ageing Vauxhall and asked himself how it was that a businessman like himself could not afford anything on the scale that these police officers could. The truth was, he could afford it, if he wanted. It was the luxury, he could not afford. What use would a flash and fancy people carrier like the one parked under the high walls of the police station car park, be to him? It would sit in his back yard most of the week, going out only to deliver sandwich orders on a morning. It would be a waste of money.

"Well that answers that," Cummins said, putting his phone away. "The Pennigs died several years ago, within months of each other. The old man went first, the wife a while later. Flowers remembers the inquest into the old man. To his knowledge, the house was sold off by the family solicitor after the wife passed on, presumably on orders from Eddie who, as far as Flowers can recall, never even came home for the funerals, and was probably still overseas with the navy."

"I think if I knew Ivan Irwin was waiting for me, I wouldn't have come home, either." Joe chewed his lip and drew on his cigarette again. "I'm trying to string this together, Terry, and I can't. Eddie has served his twenty-two, he must have had a decent pension, and he'd soon find somewhere to rent. What the hell was he playing at that would be worth throwing all that away?"

Cummins stubbed out his cigarette and took his car keys from his pocket. "I'm sure the answers will show up, Joe. Come on, I'll run you back to Filey."

They climbed into Cummins' Ford Mondeo and drove out of the car park, mingling with the light, evening traffic.

"You're in service, Terry, just like Eddie," Joe said, as they followed the Filey signs through and out of town. "How much would you need to make you chuck up your pension?"

Cummins braked for a set of traffic lights. "It would have to be something like a lottery win. A couple million. A large amount of money I could bank anywhere in the world and spend my time doing nothing."

"And where would Eddie get that amount of money?" Joe demanded. "Drugs? Weapons? Illegal immigrants?"

"All possible, Joe, but why would he need to kill himself

off to become involved with that kind of business? Why the fishing gear? Why the need to come back to Filey with your club?" The lights changed and Cummins pulled away. "None of it makes sense, Joe."

"Unless you consider an insurance fraud," Joe said, "but why would any company insure Eddie's life for that kind of money? He was a nobody. A jack tar and a cook. What was so special about him that he should be insured for millions?"

"When I find out, I'll let you know," Cummins said.

The road opened out and the sun blazed in across the farmlands off to their right. Cummins lowered his sun visor. "Tell me, Joe, how did you rumble this business of Eddie and Ivan's wife?"

"I didn't," Joe admitted, "but I saw Ivan yesterday, coming out of some pub with Sarah Pringle, and it occurred to me that there was something between them. I don't know for sure, mind, and Sarah was coming onto me last night. Again, I figured 'not likely'. Not if she's fooling around with Ivan the Terrible. While we were in your office, I suddenly thought about it, and I wondered why Ivan was still single. He's no youngster, is he? Then I remembered that Eddie had wasted no time hooking up with Nicola Leach, and I took a shot in the dark."

Cummins laughed. "That brain of yours. It's wired up differently."

Joe chuckled, too. "Not wired up well enough to get me through all this, though."

Chapter Sixteen

With the disco in full swing, the Sanford 3rd Age Club jiggling around the floor to the Bee Gees' *Night Fever*, Joe left instructions for Sheila and Brenda to run *You're the One That I Want* next, and stepped off the podium out into the gathering dusk.

The sun had disappeared, setting somewhere behind the hotel. Out here, the sky was a pale pearl, the Moon, waxing past first quarter, hung in the sky over Flamborough Head and in the far Northeast, the approaching night could be seen casting its shadow over the sea.

It felt cooler out here, but Joe knew that it was comparative. The day had been another scorcher, and in the Beachside's lounge, the energy of all those bodies combined with the heat of the disco lights to raise the temperature. Out here it was probably still in the high fifties, but it was cooler and the onshore breeze helped chill the sweat on his forehead.

To his left, Tanner and Sylvia sat with drinks, looking out over the bay. To his right, Billy Pringle was smoking a cigarette. Joe lit his own and drew the smoke deeply, gratefully into his lungs.

He had returned from Scarborough too late for dinner, but Sarah Pringle had managed to scrounge a meal for him, and he ate alone in a corner of the dining room. It suited him. If he was to crack the problem of these two deaths, he needed to machinate the gears of his agile mind, and that was always difficult when he had his friends around him. Loyal, faithful and trustworthy though they were, they could be a proper pain when he needed to think.

There was nothing at stake but his pride. Puzzles and

mysteries had been a joy to him since his childhood when he had thrilled to the writings of Conan Doyle, Christie, Simenon and Creasey. Not for him the hard-edged, American detectives Mickey Spillane or Raymond Chandler. Give him a good, old-fashioned line of logical deduction and he was in his element. When he reached his teens, he was determined to join the police and become a great detective, but family matters had put the blocks on that.

His father, who always addressed him by his full name, had told him, "Our Arthur won't work in the café, and one of you has to, so it's you, Joseph."

Arthur, his older brother and Lee's father, had cut away from the family, and gone to work for the Gas Board as a fitter. His skills proved useful in later years, whenever any of the gas appliances needed servicing or repair, but Arthur's determination in the face of Alf Murray's demands had set him apart as the black sheep of the family. Much later, he had isolated his position further by emigrating to Australia, one of the last of the 'ten pound poms'.

Older and wiser, Joe no longer resented his brother's decision, but at the time, he had been livid. Arthur's obstinacy had put paid to whatever career Joe wanted for himself, leaving him to run the café, like it or not. Maturity had brought a new perspective on the matter. Aside from anything else, at the time, there were minimum height requirements for the police force, and Joe was a couple of inches too short. He could hardly hold his brother responsible for that.

Instead, he settled into the routine of catering for truck drivers and factory workers, and he remained convinced that he did a better job than his father ever had, but while he busied himself in the kitchen or at the counter, he nevertheless honed his deductive skills.

At first, his observations were the easiest. A regular customer calling in when clad in a suit, collar and tie, where he usually wore overalls, was obviously not working. Likewise a young woman turning up in a frock instead of a wraparound overall. As his skills developed, he tackled deeper deductions. The man with a shaving cut had either been clumsy or in a hurry that morning, and usually the speed with which he ate his meal would tell Joe which it was. The woman constantly checking her appearance in a compact mirror was likely on a date, the man and woman glancing furtively round while they ate were on some kind of clandestine meeting.

And it was not just mannerisms or in-depth knowledge of people. Even if they were complete strangers, Joe could usually tell something about them, and a little light, friendly chatter as he delivered meals would soon elicit whether he was right or wrong. The stranger who sat facing the windows, and kept an eye on the industrial estate opposite was either waiting for his car to be returned from Broadbent's or was watching for someone.

His skills grew, so did his reputation, and before he was thirty, people from all over Sanford began to talk about this whizz-kid detective. Individuals and companies called him in to clear up mysteries and puzzles, and over the following decade, he established a reputation for the accuracy of his deductions. Even the police, albeit usually in the shape of his niece, called on him now and then.

He did not solve every problem, however, and as he watched the lights on ships begin to appear in the growing darkness, he concluded that the killing of Eddie Pennig would be one of his failures. He would have to be satisfied with having solved Nicola Leach's death.

"Whisper is the cops have arrested the Irwin brothers for killing that mate of yours."

Billy Pringle's questions snapped Joe out of his irritated reverie.

"What? Oh, hiya, Billy. Yeah. Terry Cummins has them both on ice in Scarborough."

Billy, who had been on his way back into the bar, sat with Joe, took out another cigarette and lit it.

"On a break?" Joe asked.

Billy nodded. "Another five minutes and I'm back on the

horse. You know how it is."

This time, Joe nodded. "I do. No rest for the wicked when you run your own joint. No Kieran to help tonight?"

Billy laughed. "Slight managerial cock-up, Joe. He asked for the night off. This was a couple weeks back, and like a right pair of idiots, we said yes. Completely forgot about you and your disco."

Joe grinned. "Kids eh? Big date, has he?"

"Must be," Billy said. "He's borrowed my van for it."

Silence fell. Joe was glad of it. He needed to concentrate on every aspect of the two deaths.

"Good call, I'd say," Billy commented, breaking into Joe's abstract thoughts again.

His words puzzled Joe. "Hmm?"

"The Irwin brothers. Right pair of tearaways, those two. Always have been."

"You know them? " Joe asked.

"Small town, Filey. Everyone knows everyone." Billy fingered his crooked nose. "I have Ivan to thank for this. Bar fight years ago. Tunnel bloody vision that man when he gets into a scrap. Hits out at everyone and everything. If anyone was going to smash your mate's head in, it's Ivan Irwin."

Joe slotted the information into place. "Trouble is, Billy, Ivan denies it, and I think he's telling the truth for once. He knew Eddie years ago, and he admits he'd loved to have taken him apart, but he couldn't, because he's already under a court order."

Billy laughed. "Court order? Never stopped Ivan in the past. I'm telling you, mate, the police have it right. When they dig deep enough, they'll find out the truth." Billy crushed out his smoke. "I'd better get back inside. Thirsty lot, your mob."

Billy disappeared inside. Joe pulled on his cigarette one last time, then rang Cummins. After a brief conversation, he put the phone away and smiled to himself. Imbued with fresh energy he made his way back into the lounge and onto the podium.

"We thought you'd never get back, Joe," Sheila said. "*Grease* is nearly finished."

He grinned. "Never despair. Joe is always here."

As the song faded out, Joe took the microphone. "That was John Travolta and Olivia Neutron-Bomb from about 1978. Before we go on, can I just remind you all that we have to vacate the rooms by ten in the morning. Keith will be here at half past nine so you can load your luggage onto the coach. You'll have a couple of hours to yourselves, and he'll pick us all up at Filey bus station at twelve noon." He paused to ensure his message had sunk in, and ran his finger down the list of tracks on the laptop screen. "All right. We saw the Abba tribute show last night, now here's the real thing with *The Winner Takes It All*." He smiled over at the bar where Billy was serving George Robson and Owen Frickley. "Thank you, Billy," he muttered under his breath.

***

A combination of heat and habit had Joe out of bed at five thirty on Monday morning. But as he yawned his way to the window, he realised it was not simply those two factors. The noise of an engine chugging away outside had helped disturb his sleep.

Parting the curtains, he looked out onto another glorious morning and at the rear gates saw Billy Pringle with his head under the bonnet of his Transit van.

With another gaping yawn, Joe let the curtains shut and went back to bed.

He was up again by seven, and after a shower and shave, he wandered out through the front entrance, onto the street and around the back of the hotel where he found Billy still working under the hood of his van.

"Morning, Billy," he said.

Billy looked up in some surprise. "Morning, Joe. Bit early to be up and about, isn't it?"

"This is late for me," Joe replied. "I'm like you, mate. Up with the larks every day. Thought I'd take a walk, see if the paper shop's open yet." He indicated the van with a nod. "Having trouble?"

"Touchy starting her up on a morning. Getting past her best, you know. Have to keep on top of it." Billy frowned. "Lending Kieran the bloody thing doesn't help. He thraips the hell out of it. You know how kids are."

"Out to impress his girlfriend, huh?" Joe laughed. "I remember those days. Never thought of buying a new one?"

Billy shrugged. "Why? It never goes further than the cash and carry or the wholesale markets. Lashing out ten grand or more on a new van would be a waste of money."

Joe understood immediately. Hadn't he thought the same himself the previous night when admiring the shiny cars on the police car park?

"I know where you're coming from, buddy. Well, catch you at breakfast."

"Yeah. Try the newsagent on Murray Street. It should be open by the time you get there."

Joe wandered off and turned the corner towards the town with the noise of Billy's van chugging away in the background.

He was back thirty minutes later, sat on the front terrace enjoying a smoke and working on the *Daily Express* crossword, when Sarah stepped from the dining room.

"Good morning, Joe. Sleep well?"

He shrugged and put down his pen. "So, so. You know."

Sarah sat opposite and looked out over the bay. "Back to Sanford and the reality of earning a living later today."

"It's been a nice change," he said, memories of Saturday night flooding back to him.

It appeared that memories of Saturday night were also on Sarah's mind. "It could have been a lot nicer."

Joe smiled thinly. "It was a non-starter, Sarah. I don't like disappointing any woman, but…" he trailed off, and left her to draw her own conclusions.

"That's not the only thing to spoil your weekend, though, is it?" Sarah suggested and when Joe's eyebrows rose, she explained, "The death of your friend."

"Oh. Eddie?" Joe lit a cigarette. "Like I said before, he wasn't really a friend. Truth is, I didn't know him at all. Sheila persuaded him to join the club, and he did his own groundwork to get him on the Filey trip."

"So I understand. Why on earth did he want to come here?"

Joe shrugged. "That's the question everyone is asking themselves, Sarah. Did you know he was a local man?"

"I've been told," she admitted. "In fact, I think you told me. Hunmanby, I believe. Is it true that the Irwin brothers have been arrested for his death?"

"They have," Joe said. "There's some doubt, though. Right now, it's difficult to see what they stood to gain from killing Eddie."

"Perhaps," Sarah suggested, "it was accidental."

"It's possible," Joe agreed, "but that doesn't explain why Eddie came here in the first place. The police will need to do some serious digging into our Mr Pennig to find out what the hell he was up to."

Sarah shook her head. "What a strange tale."

"Bizarre," Joe agreed. "Still, Terry Cummins is on the case and I'm sure he'll get to the bottom of it." He smiled at her. "And what about you, Sarah? What does the rest of your life look like?"

She laughed softly. "My life is what it always is, Joe. The hotel. The season ends in mid-September and I'll take a holiday in October. Probably Cyprus. By the time I get back, we'll be getting ready for Christmas and the New Year. We're very much alike, you and me. We live to run the business and run the business to live. It's a non-stop merry-go-round, with no way off." She stood up. "If you'll excuse me, I must drag Billy away from that damned van and get on with supervising breakfast."

"Sure. See you later."

Joe made his way back to his room, took down his suitcase and packed away his clothing. Last in the bag was the netbook. He hesitated a moment before putting it in the case. All his notes on the Eddie Pennig case were on it. In the end, deciding that he would make no more progress on the matter, he tucked the computer between a couple of shirts, closed the suitcase and zipped it up.

He joined Sheila and Brenda for breakfast just after eight.

"Did you have another secret rendezvous last night, Joe?" Sheila asked.

He maintained a silent air of aplomb.

Alongside him, Brenda seethed. "I've been trying to get you into my bed for years. Two nights at the seaside and you're jumping Filey's answer to Knickers-off Leach."

"I hope you're both packed," Joe said, blatantly ignoring her. "Keith will be here for the cases in an hour."

Sheila nudged her best friend. "This must be serious. He's telling us absolutely nothing."

"I will tell you this," Joe retorted. "The Eddie Pennig business has me beat, and you know I don't like to be beaten."

Brenda became more serious. "The police will get there, Joe, and I'm sure you've done your fair share to lead them in the right direction."

"Yes, Joe," Sheila insisted, "you should look on the bright side. Without you nagging them, they would have written Nicola's death off as a hit and run and got no further with it. It's only because you pushed it that they narrowed it down to Eddie, and I'm sure they'll find his killer and uncover all the motives for it at some point."

Joe ate the last of his scrambled egg and put down his knife and fork. "Maybe you're right." He drank a swallow of tea, and took a piece of toast from the rack. "It's galling, all the same. I don't need much to wrap it all up. Just that final little hint." He shrugged. "It just won't come."

"Still," Sheila said, "all the problems aside, it's been a lovely weekend."

After breakfast, they strolled out onto the terrace to bask in the morning sun.

Joe took out his tin flipped the lid and looked in dismay at the thin dusting of dried tobacco. "I knew there was something I wanted while we were out yesterday." He scraped enough together to roll, and put the lid back on the tin. "I'll get Keith to drop me in Filey and buy some."

"Now be careful, Joe," Brenda cautioned him. "We don't want you spending all your money in one mad rush."

Joe was about to snipe back, when the roar of a van distracted him. He glanced at the gates in time to see one of Scarborough Gases flash past and up the side of the hotel. "Delivering the bar gases again," he muttered.

Brenda stretched and yawned, thrusting her ample bosom out. Glancing at her wristwatch, she said, "Well, we'd better get a move on. We've the last of the packing to do and the beds to strip."

"I thought you said you'd packed," Joe said. "And who strips the bedding before..." His eyes glazed. "Oh, my God, I never thought of that."

Brenda laughed lasciviously. "Joe, if your bedding has any evidence of naughty business, you'd better get up there and..."

"No," he cut her off. "Don't you see? Eddie's bed was made."

The woman frowned and glanced at each other.

"So?" Sheila asked.

"What kind of man makes the bed when he's on his way out to commit suicide?" he hurried on to answer the question. "One who never slept in it."

They were still puzzled.

"Eddie was never in his bed the night he was killed. Does that mean he wasn't even in the hotel? And if he wasn't in the hotel, how could the hotel serve seventy-one breakfasts? And if the hotel did serve seventy-one breakfasts, does that mean the killer took Eddie's place, instead?"

Sheila considered the matter, chewing her lip to find fault with the argument.

In the end it was Brenda who got there first. "He was ex-navy, Joe. They do make their beds."

"Ready for the Sergeant Major's inspection," Sheila concurred. "Or the Chief Petty Officer's in the case of the Royal Navy. Nice try, Joe."

He was crestfallen. "I thought I was onto something there. If there was a stranger at breakfast, one of our crew would have noticed him."

"Our crew, as you call them, haven't been interviewed," Sheila pointed out. She, too, looked at her watch. "Come on, Brenda. Let's get upstairs and finish off."

Joe nodded in the direction of the promenade, where the Sanford Coach Services bus could be seen making its slow way to the Beachside. "Keith's here now. I'd better get my case, too."

Joe and his two companions spent the next hour supervising the loading of luggage onto the bus, reminding every member that they would depart Filey bus station at 12 noon, sharp.

"Joe," Sheila said when the final piece of baggage had been loaded, "Brenda and I are going down onto the beach for an hour."

"I'll catch you there when I've picked up my tobacco," he promised climbing on the bus.

Negotiating the narrow streets as the holidaymakers began to turn out, Keith, complained, "Why couldn't you just walk into town, Joe?"

"Do you know how far I've walked over the last few days?" Joe retorted. "My bloody feet are killing me."

At the junction of West Avenue, Station Road and Murray Street, Keith stopped and opened the door. "If your feet hurt, get to the chemist and buy summat to ease 'em," he pointed across the street at the pharmacy. "See you later, Joe."

Joe stood on the kerb until Keith had gone. "Smartarse," he grumbled, and looked across at the pharmacy. "As if they could help me walking in this weather." He stared again at the shop, next door to Harrison's Carpet Centre. A large advertising banner above the pharmacy's double windows advertised Coral Beauty products, but the 'L' on the end of Coral had been faded, weathered away, so that it read more like 'Cora!' than Coral.

Joe frowned. Was it trying to tell him something? A

driver waiting for him to cross tooted his car horn. Joe shook himself out of his stupor, stepped back from the kerb and waved the car on. He stared again at the sign. *Cora! Beauty Products, on sale here*, and right next to it *Harrison Carpet Centre.*

The penny dropped. His heart beating faster, he dug feverishly into his pockets, pulled out his mobile phone and dialled Gemma's number.

"I'm glad you've rung, Uncle Joe," she said when he got through. "I'm at Eddie Dobson, Pennig, call him what you will, I'm at his flat."

"Never mind Eddie," Joe interrupted. "The 999 call on Nicola Leach. I don't suppose you got a GPS track on it?"

"No, Joe, we didn't. It's not the kind of thing we do by routine."

"It was made here, in Filey."

The announcement was greeted with silence for a moment. "What? How do you know?"

"It's the… well I've… never mind how I know. Can you get the original recording and email it to Terry Cummins at Scarborough police station?"

"Uncle Joe, you already have it. I sent…"

"That was the engine recording you sent to me," Joe interrupted. "I need to hear the original, with the caller's voice on it."

"All right," Gemma agreed. "I'll bell the station and get it done for you."

"Good. This thing is beginning to make a bit of sense at last. Now, you were saying you're at Eddie Pennig's place. Why?"

"Someone broke in last night. Place looks like it's been hit by a tornado."

Joe beamed. "And I know who."

Chapter Seventeen

Armed with fresh tobacco, Joe sat on the terrace rolling a cigarette when Sheila and Brenda returned from the beach after he had called them.

Les Tanner and Sylvia Goodson were sitting with George Robson and Owen Frickley a few tables away. Sarah Pringle was watering flowers in the planters at the bottom end of the drive, and from the lounge bar came the sound of Billy and Kieran stocking up the bottles.

Joe had had a busy time after calling his niece. First he rang Cummins and told him the information he needed, and then he took a taxi to Filey Country Park, where he found Keith putting his feet up on the bus. Joe badgered him into digging out his suitcase, from which he took his netbook, and then climbed in the taxi for the journey back to the Beachside. Once there, he sat with the computer, running it on battery while he made more notes. Then, plugging it into an outlet in the lounge bar to charge up the battery, he rang Sheila and asked her and Brenda to come back from the beach.

"What's happened, Joe?" Sheila asked when they arrived. Her face was etched with lines of worry.

With a furtive glance round and back into the bar to ensure no one was listening, Joe said, "I know almost everything and I'm waiting for Terry Cummins to turn up with the final evidence. The only thing I don't know is why, but Terry may be able to tell me."

"Almost everything about what?" Brenda asked so loudly that their members on the nearby table turned their attention on her.

Joe shushed Brenda. "Keep your voice down, for God's

sake. I don't want to panic anyone. I know everything about Eddie Pennig's murder except the motive, but I can even guess at that. If I'm right, we'll have it all wrapped up when Terry gets here." He glanced along the promenade and a police car making its way towards them. "And I think this may be him, now."

The car wove its way through the morning traffic and the crowds of people making for the beach or Coble Landing, disappeared for a moment, hidden by the white, stone walls of the Beachside, the reappeared, turning into the drive.

Flowers cranked the handbrake on, and he and Cummins got out. The constable greeted Sarah cheerily, Cummins ignored her, and both men passed into the hotel, to emerge a few moments later from the bar, out onto the terrace, where they joined Joe and his companions.

"Well?" Joe asked.

Cummins nodded grimly. "You were right about everything, Joe. But we still have no proof."

"Let's see if we can get it, eh?" he looked down the drive and raised his voice. "Sarah? Would you join us, please?"

Slightly surprised, she put down her watering can and strode up the drive to them.

"What can I do for you, Mr Murray?" she asked.

"You can tell us why you murdered Eddie Pennig," Joe said.

Her initial reaction was stunned shock, quickly recovering to anger. "Forgive me, but have you taken leave of your senses?"

"No. I came to them this morning when our coach driver dropped me off on the corner of West Avenue and Murray Street. That's where you were when you dialled 999 about the death of Nicola Leach."

Sarah opened her mouth to protest, but Joe talked right on, suppressing her words before they could get out.

"You were using an unregistered phone, but the emergency operator would need a name, so you had to think of one quickly: Coral Beauty Products advertised right next door to Harrison's Carpet Centre. But the 'L' on the end of

Coral is faded. To me it looked like an exclamation mark, but in the dark it would be near invisible and the word would look like the name Cora. Add that to Harrison and you have the name of the mystery woman who rang 999 to report Nicola's death. And if Chief Inspector Cummins compares the recording I have of the vehicle engine to the sound of your Billy's van, they'll sound the same."

Sarah sat down heavily and clutched her forehead. "What is this madness?"

Joe ignored the dramatics. "What I can't work out is why you bothered to ring 999 at all. Why didn't Eddie just drive away and forget it? Someone would have found Nicola."

"I, er, I don't know what you're talking about."

Joe shook his head and lit his cigarette. "Still denying it. Y'see, Sarah, between you, you and Billy made too many mistakes." Joe switched the focus of his attention. "Constable Flowers, would you pass me my netbook from in there." He pointed into the lounge bar.

While Flowers went to collect it, Joe pressed on. "I'm sure we'll find out that money is behind all this, as I suspected all along. A large amount of money. An amount of money equal to the value of the Beachside Hotel. One of the things I noticed when we first arrived was the age of the fixtures and fittings in my room. This place looks very grand on the outside, but it needs some refurbishment on the inside. That costs. At a thousand pounds a room, Sarah is looking at fifty thousand. A lot of money."

Flowers returned with the netbook, Joe switched it on and while he waited for it to go through its boot routine, he continued with his tale. "What you'll hear is a story of deception, and if it hadn't been for Sheila and Brenda's well intentioned tearing apart of my theory, I may have got there twenty-four hours earlier."

"Thank you, Joe," said Brenda. "That's the kind of support we enjoy."

"It's not a criticism, really," he said to her. "I might have got there yesterday, but I'd have been coming at it from the wrong angle, and it would probably have fallen apart." With the computer now working, Joe opened up the file on Nicola and Eddie. "Wherever we go, whenever we get involved in any puzzle like this, I make lots of notes, and amongst those notes are two things that lead me straight to you, Sarah. A woman with black hair and a delivery driver who talks too much."

Puzzlement crossed the faces of those around him.

"One of the earliest notes I made on this case happened back in Sanford, when a woman with extraordinary black hair and a pasty white face came into my café."

"I remember her," Sheila said.

"It was one of her black hairs that you got on your T-Shirt that morning," Joe told her, and briefly explained to the others how both Sheila and Brenda had complained about the state of his car. "That woman had black hair, a face lathered in white makeup, and large sunglasses for a reason," he went on. "To prevent me recognising her when we got to Filey." Now he fired an accusing glance at Sarah. "It was you."

"I deny it," she said. "I have never been to Sanford."

Joe remained equally defiant. "Eddie Pennig was in the café early that morning. You were there a couple of hours later. Why? Because Eddie ran Nicola Leach down the night before. He wanted a seat on the Filey bus. That was the *only* reason Nicola was killed." Joe jabbed his forefinger into the table top to emphasise his point. "Eddie was in my place pestering Sheila at half past seven. What he really wanted to know was whether we'd heard of Nicola's death. He couldn't nag me for her seat until we knew about her, because to do so before would implicate him. I gave Sheila short shrift, and Eddie cleared off, but they still needed to know, so you, Sarah, came back and sat in the Lazy Luncheonette until my niece, Detective Sergeant Craddock turned up. The moment she told us of Nicola's death, you left and told Eddie that the coast was clear, that he could get his seat on the bus."

"This is utter drivel," Sarah protested.

"We'll see," Joe countered. "Let's bring us to Filey, and

see what we can learn. You introduced yourself as the joint owner of the Beachside, along with your brother, Billy, and Kieran as your son, Billy's nephew. But I was speaking to the driver from Scarborough Gases before we left for the Abba show on Saturday night. We were talking about scuba diving gases, and he said, and I quote, 'Billy and his lad, Kieran are members of the local club'. Billy and his lad? You and Billy made a mistake, Sarah. You forgot that I'm in catering, too. The delivery drivers who come to my place are all regulars. They know me, they know Sheila and Brenda, and they know my nephew, Lee. None of them would describe Lee as 'my lad'. They might say, 'your Lee', but not 'your lad, Lee'. The gas driver had to be a regular or he wouldn't have been able to reel off your names so easily. That means he knows you well. Kieran is not Billy's nephew, he's his son, and Billy is not your brother. He's your husband. Your second husband. And before you deny it, Chief Inspector Cummins has already checked on this. You divorced your first husband, *Edward Pennig* twenty-three years ago, just before Kieran's birth."

Sheila and Brenda both gasped. Billy stepped from the lounge, carrying a cup of tea. He placed it in front of Sarah.

"We're not going to deny it, Murray," Billy said. His overt, friendly approach was gone. He was now the fierce protector of his wife. "We've been man and wife these last twenty-two years."

"We know," Cummins said.

Sarah picked up her cup with shaking hands and drank from it. "All right, so Billy and I are man and wife. So I was married to Eddie. It was a long time ago. What does this prove?"

"Nothing," Joe agreed, "but Chief Inspector Cummins has a voice recording of the 999 call made by Cora Harrison. I haven't heard it, but I know it's you, Sarah. And if there's any doubt about it, Cummins will run a voice pattern check. But you didn't make the call from Sanford. You made it right here in Filey using an unregistered mobile, and the police never had a GPS track on it because they don't. Now to make that call from Filey means you were in contact with Eddie. He told you everything, described the area so you could tell the police."

Joe studied the trembling woman opposite and gained in confidence.

"And there's one more point," he pressed on. "Last night, your husband said to me, and again I quote, 'If anyone was going to smash your mate's head in, it's Ivan Irwin'. Who told him that Eddie's head had been caved in? Neither constable Flowers nor Chief Inspector Cummins mentioned it while you were within earshot yesterday, none of us has spoken about it, so how did Billy know?" With great satisfaction, Joe answered his own question. "Because he was there when it happened."

Tears formed in Sarah's eyes. Brenda offered her a tissue. She took it and dabbed her eyes. Looking straight at Joe, she said, "I swear this was not how it was supposed to turn out."

Cummins nudged Flowers who took out his pocketbook and began to make notes.

"You're a clever man, Joe Murray," Sarah said, "but your reputation goes before you. None of us had ever heard of you but when Eddie moved to Sanford, your name was everywhere. A brilliant private detective. Eddie became worried. He was frightened that you'd ask too many questions, so we decided to keep a close eye on you while you were here."

"And to do that you pretended Billy was your brother. That way you could offer to take your knickers off for me and I wouldn't be any the wiser."

Brenda stared. "You jumped her, Joe? You randy old sod."

"Shut up, Brenda," Joe ordered. "Sarah?"

Sarah nodded dumbly. "I will do anything to protect my hotel, even if that means prostituting myself with men like you."

"Because while you're taking them to heaven, men will talk," Joe suggested, and Sarah nodded again. "It would have been the most natural thing in the world for me to tell you all about my cases, including the progress I was, or wasn't making on Eddie's murder. That way you could either sleep easy, or, if I was getting too close, arrange for me to have an accident like Nicola."

Again she nodded. "I didn't bank on you being gay," she said.

Brenda laughed raucously. "Joe? Gay? He's not gay."

"He turned me down," Sarah insisted.

"That doesn't make him gay," Sheila said. "Merely cautious, and we know Joe well enough to know how cautious, don't we, Brenda?"

"Especially when he's looking after his wallet," Brenda agreed.

Diverting the levity, Cummins suggested, "Please go on with your story, Mrs Pringle."

Standing behind Sarah, a comforting hand on her shoulder, Billy said, "None of this was her doing."

"Shut up," Sarah snapped. "Do you really believe that they'll think you have the gumption to carry this off?" Her hands shaking she sipped some tea, and put the cup down. "Eddie Pennig was my husband, yes. We were married for less than five years. The hotel belonged to my parents, but it was losing money, so Eddie borrowed from his father and we bought it out and invested heavily in it. That was twenty-seven years ago." She glared at Joe. "You've been clever to learn the things you have, but what did you learn about Eddie? Nothing. You don't know that he was a drinker. When we took over the Beachside, it was perfect for him. His very own bar where he could drink himself into a total stupor every night. And when he was sober, his hangover made him violent. I lost count of the times I had to wear pancake makeup and dark glasses to hide the bruises. That was why it was so easy for me to disguise myself in your café." Sarah raised a hand to her shoulder and clasped Billy's. "Billy was our barman and he was more than a match for Eddie. He helped me over the worst of it and naturally, we had an affair. Kieran was the result. Eddie threatened all sorts of retaliation, but before he could make any moves, I learned of his affair with Ivan Irwin's wife."

"Stalemate," Joe said.

"Not quite," Sarah disagreed. "Difficult but not impossible. Ivan was after his blood and he needed to get out of Filey, so we came to an arrangement. He would divorce me, I would keep the hotel, but he would become a sleeping partner. He left and the next thing I heard, he had joined the navy. That was perfect for me. Peace, at last. I married the man I loved, and I kept the hotel I loved. I paid Eddie's share of the spoils into the bank every quarter, and he hid them away in an offshore account or something. It was an ideal world."

"So what went wrong?" Brenda asked.

"Eddie came out of the navy," Sarah replied. "Worse than that, the tax man caught up with him. He had never declared the money I paid to him over the years and he owed a fortune in back taxes. Since he'd spent the money, probably on drink, the taxman took his pension lump sum and all he had was his monthly payout. He was broke when he came back to Filey earlier this year. He asked me for money, I told him to go to hell, he demanded to be reinstated as a full partner, and I told him where he could go. He threatened legal action, so we had to find a compromise again."

"He was heavily insured, wasn't he?" Joe asked.

She nodded. "He'd arranged the early mortgages on the hotel, and I had him insured to cover them. Two hundred and fifty thousand pounds; the value of the Beachside when we took the insurances out. Of course, the mortgages on the Beachside were paid off some years ago, but the insurances were not a part of the loan deals. They were separate and still in place. Due to administrative lethargy, I'd been paying the premiums on them."

"You mean you should have cancelled them but never got around to it?" Cummins asked.

"Correct," Sarah said. "By the time I realised we should be no longer paying them, I'd already handed over a fortune to the insurance companies, so I thought it best to leave them there. Eddie would die one day and I would reap the benefit of those policies. When we were trying to come to an agreement on the hotel, I saw a way we could all come out of it as winners. If Eddie were to 'die' – inverted commas – the insurances would pay out and I would give him half."

"Fraud," Cummins said flatly.

"A difficult one to pin down, Chief Inspector, if Eddie really disappeared," Sarah argued. "And doesn't everyone defraud their insurers?"

"Not to the tune of £250,000 they don't," Cummins retorted.

"You should spend less time in your office and more time reading the newspapers, Terry," Joe suggested. "There have been any number of cases over recent years. Go on, Sarah."

"Putting the details together was troublesome," Sarah admitted, "but when your booking came in, it was a godsend and we were able to put it all together. Eddie would move to Sanford as Eddie Dobson, his mother's maiden name, join your silly little club and come back to Filey where he would then fall into the sea off the Brigg and drown. Kieran and Billy are both experienced scuba divers. They would be waiting for him under the water and they'd get him back to shore." Sarah glared at Joe. "But he couldn't get on your outing, could he? It was full."

"So he ran Nicola down," Brenda gasped. "The rotten –"

"He was supposed to hurt her, not kill her," Sarah interrupted. "As usual, he got it all wrong. He'd been sleeping with her, so he knew her habits. He knew she would come out of some pub, drunk out of her mind."

"The Foundry Inn," Sheila commented.

"That's the one" Sarah agreed. "He would drive at her, clip her and break a few bones. Enough to stop her joining you on the outing. But he didn't, did he? He'd been drinking, too, and he hit her full on and killed her, the bloody fool. He rang me from Sanford in a panic. I told him to calm down. He said he'd have to go to the police, hand himself in. I wasn't having that, so I told him I would deal with it."

"And that's when you dialled 999?"

Sarah nodded. "Eddie gave me a good description of the pub and the hotel nearby. I got the name, as you suggested, from the carpet centre here in Filey, and the pharmacy next door, dialled 999 and gave them the gist of what had happened before ringing off."

"Then you made your way to Sanford on Tuesday night to calm him down again?" Joe said.

Sarah nodded. "Billy and I got there about two in the morning. Billy and Eddie worked on the Land Rover during Wednesday to repair it. I, as you know, came to your place to listen for you learning of Nicola's death, and Billy and I came away again at lunchtime. But I left Eddie some instructions."

"He was to see me, get himself on the Filey trip, then come to Filey to get rid of the Land Rover," Joe guessed. "Not necessarily in that order."

Again Sarah nodded. "Billy took him back to Sanford, which is why he was so late getting to you on Thursday."

Silence fell for a moment.

"I'll tell you what I don't understand," Sheila said. "Why describe the vehicle that hit Nicola so perfectly. You told the police it was a Land Rover. Why not lie about it? Tell them it was a van or it was too dark to see?"

"I think I can answer that," Joe said. "It was all about having a go at Ivan and Jonny Irwin, wasn't it?" He did not wait for Sarah to confirm, but went on, "Terry, you told me Jonny Irwin got done for VAT fraud, and that Ivan had been prosecuted for a fuel fiddle. I know the tax people. When they go to town, they don't pull punches, unless there's something in it for them. I guess the only way they stayed out of jail was by shopping Eddie and his secret income."

Sarah agreed again. "In many ways, Jonny and Ivan were responsible for the position we found ourselves in. Brutal, arrogant men, both of them, who think they own the town. When Eddie rang me after knocking your friend down, I saw a way I could get Eddie out of a spot and give the Irwin brothers a metaphorical kick between the legs. I had a word with Ivan on Wednesday, the day after the accident, and told him Eddie was back and needed to be rid of a Land Rover that had been involved in a hit and run. He would get it for next to nothing if he played his cards right. He hated Eddie and he jumped at the chance."

"So Eddie drove over on the Thursday as instructed," Joe said, "concluded his business with Ivan and then Billy took him back to Sanford."

"All according to plan," Sarah admitted. "With your reputation in mind, if the Land Rover was traced, the death of Nicola Leach would be dropped at Ivan's feet." She glared defiance once more. "And it couldn't happen to a nicer pair of brothers."

"How did Ivan and Jonny know about your payments to Eddie?" Cummins asked.

Sarah laid accusing eyes on her husband. "Men talk. And not only when they're in bed, but certainly when they're drunk."

Joe nodded his understanding. "How come I saw you and Ivan coming out of the Star Inn the other day looking like best friends?"

Sarah stared sourly at him. "How come I offered to sleep with you the other night?"

Joe understood at once. "Throwing him off guard. Pretending that old wounds were healed. Sarah, you would have been great working for the Allies during the war."

"We were enjoying a little joke at Eddie's expense," Sarah agreed. "How we had managed to stitch him up between us. Got him to sell his pride and joy, the Land Rover, for next to nothing."

"If all this had come off, what would Eddie have done?" Cummins asked, bringing the discussion back on track. "He might have been a hundred and twenty-five thousand pounds richer, but he'd have lost his navy pension, and he couldn't live anywhere under his real name."

Sarah sighed. "He may have been a drunk, but he was no fool, Chief Inspector. He knew he was on borrowed time.

210

Cirrhosis of the liver. At best, he probably had three or four years to live. He would have moved somewhere where no one knew him, and drunk himself to death. I don't know, and I didn't care, as long as he was away from me and my hotel."

"And that's where it all went wrong, isn't it?" Joe asked. "He changed his mind when he got here, didn't he?"

The barest incline of her head told them Joe had hit the mark again.

"Everything was going according to plan," she said. "He went to Jonny Irwin's shop, picked up the fishing gear and brought it back here. Then on Friday night, after we closed up, he came to our room. He'd seen a better solution, one that was not illegal. He would stay here, we would employ him as a cook, and everything would be rosy. He was a trained chef, you know." Bitterness crept into her voice. "He was drunk, of course. We told him, no. He wouldn't have it. An argument developed. It got out of hand, and I hit him with a bedside lamp. He fell, hit his head on the wall and he was dead."

Cummins shook his head. "I'm sorry, Mrs Pringle, but that doesn't tally with the coroner's report. There were traces of red paint around the wound."

"From a fire extinguisher? Joe asked.

The Chief Inspector agreed with a surprised nod. "How did you know?"

"Saturday morning I was woken in the very early hours by a terrible argument on the floor below. That argument came to an end with a loud clang, as if someone had dropped a metallic, er, something. But it was the noise of a fire extinguisher hitting the back of Eddie Pennig's head." Joe gave Sarah a half-sympathetic smile. "You don't lie very well, lady. You told me that the engineer had probably left the fire extinguisher in the back yard, yet you forgot again that I'm in the catering business too, and I know about these people. They never leave premises without cover. If your extinguisher was taken for service, they would leave a replacement. If they don't, they leave themselves as well as

211

you wide open to prosecution. The extinguisher was a replacement, but it was probably Billy or Kieran who left it there and forgot to bring it in."

Kieran stepped from the bar doorway. "Tell him the truth, Mum."

"Kieran…"

"They know it all," Kieran argued. He rounded on Cummins and Joe. "I hit him, not Mum. We were all together in Mum's room, the argument got out of hand. He stormed out of Mum's room swearing he'd force her into selling the hotel, if he couldn't have his way. I followed him, tried to talk him round, but he turned on me and pushed me away. He called dad and me some really vicious names and he cursed Mum even worse. I tried to stop him again and he hit me. I fell and bumped my head against the fire extinguisher. I just saw red, snatched the extinguisher from the wall, ran after him and hit him with it."

Sarah sighed. "When we realised he was dead, we knew we couldn't just carry the body out through the front door. Ivan and Kieran carried Eddie out through the window of room 102."

"Eddie's room," Joe commented. "Hence the need for the ladders. But that doesn't make sense. Eddie left his flat key on the windowsill. You'd have knocked it off."

"I left the flat key there, Mr Murray, not Eddie," said Kieran. "Mum said you'd want to clear his room when you learned of his death. I realised we'd need the key and I found it on his dresser. I didn't want to take it with me because I might lose it while we were disposing of Eddie, so I left it on the windowsill thinking it wouldn't be found."

"And you forgot all about it when you got back." Joe said, and Kieran nodded. "I was right about you. You're like my nephew. Thick as a brick. Why did you need the key in the first place? Oh, I know, you needed to dig out the insurance policy."

"Wrong, Mr Murray," Sarah declared. "I have the insurance policies. We needed to check Eddie's flat over to ensure that the damn fool hadn't left any incriminating evidence in Sanford. That's all."

"And that was you dressed as Eddie throwing yourself in the sea off the Brigg, and you who tried mugging Brenda in Scarborough, wasn't it, Kieran?" Joe demanded and the young man agreed. "So when you couldn't get the key, you went to Sanford last night to burgle Eddie's place, didn't you?"

Again Kieran nodded.

Silence fell over the table. Cummins cleared his throat, but before he could speak, Joe got there first.

"Just one thing, Mrs Pringle. Friday night in the disco. I saw Eddie pass something to you. You told me it was the money for his packed lunch, but I'm not stupid. People don't behave like that. People pass keys to each other under the table, like Les Tanner and Sylvia Goodson did the other day, and that's what I think Eddie was passing to you: the key to his flat. So why –"

Sarah cut Joe off. "As detectives go, Mr Murray, you're probably better off running a café. You notice everything, misinterpret too much and still come to the right conclusion, but for all the wrong reasons. Eddie didn't pass me anything on Friday night. He was broke, so I passed him something: twenty pounds to pay for a few beers."

Chapter Eighteen

Keith eased up and slipped into the nearside lane, ready to leave the motorway at the Sanford intersection. Over to the right, the dormant floodlights of the moribund Sanford Main Colliery struck into the cloudless, afternoon sky. To Joe it was a welcome home sign.

Sat behind him, Sheila skimmed the pages of a magazine while beside her, Brenda dozed. From behind him came the hum of low chatter, punctuated occasionally by raucous laughter. The Sanford 3rd Age Club winding down after another successful weekend outing.

Sheila looked up from her magazine as the bus braked. "Hadn't you better whip round with the hat, Joe?"

He pointed to a basket on the driver's console, to the left of the dashboard, where a small, wicker basket sat. "What century are you living in, Sheila? People drop coins in as they get off these days."

"Then remind them, Joe. And they should be dropping paper in, not coins. These drivers serve us well all weekend."

"Ask 'em to put paper in, and that's just what they'll do," Joe grumbled as he took the microphone from her. "Old raffle tickets, till receipts, anything." He switched the microphone on and blew into it to ensure it was working. "Okay, folks, about five minutes now, and we're back at the Miner's Arms. Can I just remind everybody that the weekly disco will be on Thursday this week instead of Wednesday. It gives you all an extra day to get over the excitement of Filey."

His announcement was greeted by a few laughs.

"I'm sure you all want to show your appreciation for

Keith as you get off the bus, and there's a basket where you can drop him a few quid. We all know our driver. He's a bit choosy. He can't spend old menu cards or cardboard library tickets. Coins and notes only. And no foreign coins, either. Hope you all enjoyed your weekend and we'll post notices on the website when we have the next one arranged. Thanks everyone."

He received a smattering of applause, some of it sarcastic for his announcement.

"Well done, Joe," Sheila said as Brenda stirred beside her. "We'll make a human being of you yet."

"Not if I have anything to do with it."

Gazing beyond Keith, Joe watched as Sanford town centre grew large in the windscreen.

"Been a funny old weekend."

"It's been absolutely crazy," Brenda said with a yawn. "And you, Joe, scoring with Sarah Pringle."

He sneered. "I did not 'score' with her, as you put it. In fact, it was her interest in me that made me suspicious in the first place. I'm not totally gormless. I know I'm no catch for any woman; especially one so vain she'll wear a wig to cover the grey hair. I told her, James Bond, I'm not. I'm 55 years old and I stand five feet six, not six feet five."

"You'd make some woman a good husband, Joe," Sheila said.

"If you ever learned to open your wallet," Brenda agreed.

Sheila, too, stared sadly through the windows. "That poor woman." She looked from Joe to Brenda and back again. "Sarah Pringle, I mean."

Joe spluttered. "What? What about Knickers-off? What about Eddie Dobson?"

"Eddie Pennig." Sheila corrected him. "Yes, Joe, it's tragic, particularly for Nicola. Eddie was to be pitied, but so too was Sarah Pringle, and her husband and son. They never set out kill Eddie and he never set out kill Nicola. They were simply trying to protect their interests. It just goes to show you how sour things can turn when relationships go wrong."

"It may have escaped your attention," Joe said as the coach turned right onto the broad, dual carriageway of Doncaster Road, "but they all set out to fiddle Eddie's insurance company out of hundreds of thousands of pounds. That cost Nicola her life. Eddie too. And if they'd got away with it, who pays? Honest businessmen like me. My insurance rates go through the roof when people like them take the companies to the cleaners."

Brenda pointed through the right hand window. "Right now, Joe, I think it's your nephew who's putting up your insurance rates."

Joe's head snapped to the right. Across the road, the door of the Lazy Luncheonette was still open, and he could see his nephew, Lee, clearly visible through the large windows, shovelling broken crockery into a black bin bag.

"Stop, stop," Joe urged Keith. "Let me off here."

The bus came to a halt and Joe hurried down the steps, onto the pavement. "I'll catch you all later," he shouted and hurried towards the rear of the coach and out of sight.

"What about his bags?" Sheila asked as Keith closed the door and pulled away again.

"We can take them in tomorrow morning," Brenda said with a grin. "If Lee's smashed that many plates, Joe won't even notice his suitcase is missing."

THE END

Thanks for reading this Sanford Third Age Collection title.

Why not read the next? **STAC #2: The I-Spy Murders**

Fantastic Books
Great Authors

darkstroke is
an imprint of
Crooked Cat Books

- Gripping Thrillers
- Cosy Mysteries
- Romantic Chick-Lit
- Fascinating Historicals
- Exciting Fantasy
- Young Adult and Children's Adventures
- Non-Fiction

Discover us online
www.darkstroke.com

Find us on instagram:
www.instagram.com/darkstrokebooks

Printed in Great Britain
by Amazon